STARSTRUCK

What Reviewers Say About Lesley Davis's Work

"*Playing Passion's Game* is a delightful read with lots of twists, turns, and good laughs. Davis has provided a varied and interesting supportive cast. Those who enjoy computer games will recognize some familiar scenes, and those new to the topic get to learn about a whole new world."—*Just About Write*

"*Pale Wings Protecting* is a provocative paranormal mystery; it's an otherworldly thriller couched inside a tale of budding romance. The novel contains an absorbing narrative, full of thrilling revelations, that skillfully leads the reader into the uncanny dimensions of the supernatural."—*Lambda Literary*

"[*Dark Wings Descending*] is an intriguing story that presents a vision of life after death many will find challenging. It also gives the reader some wonderful sex scenes, humor, and a great read!" —Reviewer RLynne

"[*Pale Wings Protecting*] was just a delicious delight with so many levels of intrigue on the case level and the personal level. Plus, the celestial and diabolical beings were incredibly intriguing. ...I was riveted from beginning to end and I certainly will look forward to additional books by Lesley Davis. By all means, give this story a total once-over!"—*Rainbow Book Reviews*

By the Author

STARSTRUCK

by
Lesley Davis

2016

STARSTRUCK

ISBN 13: 978-1-62639-523-7

This Trade Paperback Original Is Published By
Bold Strokes Books, Inc.
P.O. Box 249
Valley Falls, NY 12185

First Edition: January 2016

Credits
Editor: Cindy Cresap
Production Design: Susan Ramundo
Cover Design By Sheri (graphicartist2020@hotmail.com)

Acknowledgments

Many thanks to Radclyffe for making Bold Strokes such an amazing place to write for and be a part of.

Thank you, Cindy Cresap, for stretching my tiny brain cells as far as they will go in order to make my stories so much more than even I imagined. Your patience and humor is a constant blessing to me.

To Sandy Lowe and all the hardworking people at Bold Strokes Books, thank you all so much for everything you do behind the scenes that I may never see but will always appreciate.

Thank you, Sheri, for a marvelously menacing cover! I love it!

Thank you to my fantastic friends and unwavering supporters: Jane Morrison and Jacky Morrison Hart, Pam Goodwin and Gina Paroline, and Annie Ellis and Julia Lowndes.

A big thank you to my amazing readers all over the world who always make me want to write more because of their enthusiasm and encouragement. Thank you! I'm working on the next book for you!

And thank you, Cindy Pfannenstiel, for listening as the ideas form, for reading when the words are written, and for being my best friend in all things else. xx

Dedication

To all the marvelous actresses out there
who add fuel to the fantasy fire

Prologue

With her trademark hair tucked up under a wide brimmed hat, Cassidy Hayes was almost unrecognizable from her TV persona: C.J. Hayes. Dressed in a simple sun dress and a pair of strappy sandals, she slipped through the busy crowd to hail a taxi. She gave the driver a destination a block away from where she lived. Cassidy settled back in her seat to enjoy the ride. The driver tried to engage her in a conversation. Cassidy was mindful to use a perfected American accent to answer him so as not to reveal her native tongue. The British accent always drew attention, and today she didn't want to be noticed. She just wanted to go home, pour a large glass of wine, and relax. Cassidy was riding high on the excitement of her successful TV show *The Alchemidens* being renewed for another season. Everything she'd worked so hard for was finally falling into place and was bringing her the roles she'd dreamed of playing. Life was good.

It wasn't long before the taxi pulled to a stop, and Cassidy got out to pay her fare. She turned her face to the sky to enjoy the warmth from the sun. All this sunshine was such a marked contrast from the changeable weather she had grown up with in London.

Cassidy walked up the street a little way and popped into her local Mexican restaurant. Her apartment building was just a few doors down from it, which meant Cassidy was treated like a member of the family from the second she walked in. She had been a permanent fixture in there since first sampling their food. Its formidable elderly owner Maria was already waiting for her with a bag of her regular takeout. She also had a burrito for her to sample that she wouldn't take no for an answer until Cassidy had a taste. Cassidy made suitably appreciative noises over its rich filling.

"Maria, you are a goddess." Cassidy licked her lips as she finished off the spicy treat.

Maria ran her hands over her hips. "I know that pretty girl you play on TV, all action and fighting. I've put you a little extra something in your bag for you to eat tonight. You're too skinny. You need more meat on your bones to be beautiful like me."

Cassidy laughed. By Hollywood's standards, Cassidy was considered positively curvy. Though to her mother's critical eye, she was constantly wasting away. "I'll need all my costumes refitted if you keep slipping me extra food, Maria." Cassidy had dropped the false accent the minute she'd stepped through the door. In here she was able to be herself. "You know I have very little will power when it comes to what you make."

"You're good for my restaurant." Maria leaned over the counter and patted Cassidy's cheek.

"And my gym membership loves you too," Cassidy teased back. She hugged her bag to her chest and blew Maria a kiss as she left.

Cassidy greeted the doorman at her building with a cheery smile. She loved where she lived. The old building was full of character and had been mercifully affordable while still being situated in a relatively safe area of Burbank, California. Her neighbors were all friendly but not intrusive. It was the perfect place to live. Somewhere she could escape the falseness and craziness that came packaged along with all the glitz and glamour of Hollywood. It was her safe place.

❖

The elevator doors opened on the third floor letting Cassidy out. She dug in her purse for her keys and walked the last few steps up the corridor to her front door. She juggled her food in her arms while pushing her key into the lock. There was a knack to opening the door since it had the unfortunate habit of sticking. This time the key went in smoothly and the door opened with ease. Cassidy just stared at it.

"What the hell?" She couldn't remember the last time she hadn't had to push her shoulder against the door to get it free. "That is just bizarre." She nudged the door closed with her hip and walked into her living room to deposit her food on the table. Cassidy tossed her hat aside and began freeing her hair from the pins that held it in place. While fluffing her hair out she just...stopped. There hadn't been a noise that had made her pause, but she strained her ears to hear something, *anything*, that had caused her feeling of disquiet. All she could hear was her own breathing.

Her gaze fell to the table in the center of the room. She kept all her mail on it, her scripts, and anything else that needed to be dealt with in a timely manner. It was *never* tidy. Cassidy wasn't known for being a perfect housekeeper. The table was usually inches deep in old mail and catalogues. It had been in its usual disorganized mess when she'd left that morning.

The table was now tidy, fastidiously so.

Her heart began to pound in her chest. Cassidy looked around the living room for any signs of an intruder. There was nothing. She walked toward her kitchen area and eased the largest knife she had out of the cutting block. Its presence in her hand didn't make her feel any less scared. She knew she should just get out now and phone the police. Cassidy really didn't want to call them just because she was frightened because her living room table's chaos had been tidied up. Cassidy knew the straightening up of her mail was not of her doing.

But she had the dreadful feeling she knew exactly *who* might have been to blame.

Her apartment wasn't exactly large, but the slow, measured walk down the hallway toward her bedroom seemed to take Cassidy forever. The knife in her hand shook as she inched along hugging the wall. She tried to keep her footsteps as soft and soundless as possible on the polished wooden floor. She listened for anything that meant someone was still in her apartment. There was nothing she could pick out but the familiar sounds of the neighborhood outside.

Cassidy made herself call upon her acting talent to channel Karadine Kourt, the superhuman character she played on TV. She wished she could actually do all the aggressive fighting that character lived by. Having the fight moves mapped out for her by a stunt choreographer didn't help her much in this reality. Cassidy stopped for a moment. She had to wipe her hand free of the sweat that was threatening to make the knife slip from her grasp. A part of her brain wondered just what she thought to accomplish brandishing a knife when she barely knew one end from the other when it came to even using one for cooking.

The bathroom door was open. Cassidy looked inside; it was empty. She couldn't see anything that looked like it had been moved in there so she continued to her bedroom. The door was ajar, just like she'd left it. Her hand trembling, Cassidy pushed it open further.

Red rose petals were scattered on the floor. They led a decorative path to her bed. The white framed headboard had long stemmed roses threaded through the ornate spirals. It all looked very pretty.

It brought bile up into Cassidy's throat.

Her closets were door-less so she could see no one was hiding among her dresses and coats. The large framed mirror in the room was positioned just right to let her see that no one was hiding behind the door she had been so hesitant to open wider. She knew there were suitcases under her bed so the only thing there was room for under it was a dust bunny. She took a cautious step inside, moving toward the bed. The knife slipped from her fingers. It clattered loudly on the floor. Cassidy's hands flew to her mouth to stifle the scream that ripped from her chest.

Splashed across her clean white bedspread, in a blood red paint, was a message left for her.

You're mine.

❖

Adam Bernett sat in the window seat of a small coffee shop. He sipped from his cup, savoring the rich drink and enjoying the frothy milk that stuck to his newly cultivated moustache. He let his tongue run across his top lip, feeling the bristles tickling him as he removed the foam. He scratched at his beard. It was taking some getting used to after being clean-shaven most of his life. Adam caught sight of his reflection in the window. He barely recognized himself anymore. Both he and his reflection smiled at that.

His eyes were fixed on the apartment building opposite. He was waiting for his girlfriend to get home. He hoped to surprise her today. He'd been working away from home for longer than he'd cared. Now he just wanted to show her how much he'd missed her while he'd been absent and she'd been all alone. It had killed him being away from her. Every day apart had felt like a slow death to him. Being able to see her again was his only reason for living. He *needed* her. He loved her and he knew she felt the same. He understood her need for privacy though. She was a famous actress and he…well, he moved around a lot in jobs lately. But he was here for her now. Just like always. He just needed to remind her he was there for her, just like old times. How they used to be, before he had to leave.

Adam caught the distinct whine of sirens in the distance and glanced down at his watch, timing how long it would take for them to arrive. A police car pulled up opposite his window, closely followed by an unmarked vehicle. Adam made sure to take a photograph of the license plate and one of the detective that got out of it. He hadn't missed the flash of a badge attached to the man's belt. He took another sip from his drink while he watched the officers run inside the building. He imagined their journey inside, how long the elevator trip would take, and raised his eyes to a specific window on the third floor.

How he'd missed his love. It wasn't the same just watching her every week on TV or searching for clips on the Internet just to see that beautiful smile he loved directed his way.

It wasn't long before a van pulled up alongside the others. The crime scene techs had arrived. As they walked in, arms full of equipment, Adam saw the detective walk out, shielding a woman who was cowering in his arms. They both got in the unmarked car and left at speed.

Adam smiled and raised his cup to them as the car drove right past him.

"Hi, honey. I'm home."

Chapter One

Aiden Darrow absently stirred the simmering pot of chili she had cooking on the stove. She had one eye on her laptop as she reread the paragraph she was working on. She made a slight adjustment to a sentence then made a more concerted effort on her stirring. Aiden checked the time on the kitchen clock, lowered the heat under the pan, then covered it with a lid. She settled herself back down at the table to begin typing again. The world she was weaving swirled in her head, and she described it vividly in the words she spun. The kitchen disappeared, and Aiden was transported to a time of Victorian England, complete with the cloying fog for effect.

A high-pitched scream brought Aiden's attention out of her writing abruptly. Her head shot up as the screaming didn't abate. Her chair screeched against the floor as Aiden stood up. She hurried to her front door to get outside. The screams were even louder there. She pinpointed where the noise was coming from and peered cautiously over the dividing fence into her neighbor's yard.

There was a woman caught on the lush grassy lawn, soaked to the skin by the sprinkler system furiously spurting out its timed watering. She was running around like a child playing in the spray, but she wasn't having fun. The woman was so drenched she couldn't see to escape the water. Her long hair clung to her face, obscuring her view.

Aiden bit back a laugh at the poor woman's plight. Taking pity on her, Aiden jumped the fence and skirted around the lawn to go turn the sprinklers off. Her neighbor, Lori Alan, had left Aiden with a set of spare keys. Aiden had them on her own keychain that she had scooped up automatically as she'd run from the house. Lori had warned her she was having a permanent house sitter while she took an extended honeymoon with her latest husband. Aiden had a feeling she hadn't warned the squealing woman about some of the extra features of the house she would be sitting.

Aiden opened up the garage door and turned the sprinklers off. The screaming stopped as soon as the water did. A very grateful and all too noticeable British accented, "Oh, thank God!" drifted over to Aiden's ears. Aiden locked the garage back up and went to check on the drowned visitor.

"Please tell me someone is there," the woman said. Her long hair, the deepest, darkest brunette Aiden had seen, was heavily plastered all over her face as she stood shivering on the lawn.

"Hi, I'm Aiden. I live next door." Aiden ventured closer. The poor woman was soaked to the skin. Aiden tried not to notice how her summer dress was now clinging to her body and leaving little to the imagination.

"I'm Cassidy, your new neighbor for the duration, and this is so not how I wanted to introduce myself." She lifted a heavy swath of her hair from one side of her face and wiped at the water in her eyes.

"Let me guess. You wandered onto the lawn to check out the view and Lori hadn't warned you of the specific times the sprinklers are set for to keep her grass looking so green."

"The view is amazing from this vantage point, but I didn't need to be nearly drowned for it." She shivered again. The force of the chill shook her slender frame.

Aiden rushed to her side. She gently touched a hand to Cassidy's arm. "How about I get you inside and straight into the shower?" Aiden nearly tripped over her own feet as she guided Cassidy across the lawn and back to the driveway. "What I mean is, let me use my keys to get you inside Lori's place, and I'll point you in the direction of her bathroom. Unless you feel you've had one shower too many already today?"

Cassidy laughed at Aiden's rambling as she tried to wring out her hair. "Be honest with me. On a scale of one to ten, how bad a first impression was this?"

Aiden pretended to consider. "Well, I did come in on the scene as you were running around in a very girly fashion shrieking like a banshee...." She chuckled as Cassidy lifted up her hair to fix her with a piercing eye. "But I'm getting you inside quickly before you draw any more attention to yourself in what is now a rather revealing ensemble."

"Oh, for God's sake. Just kill me now! I haven't even moved in and I'm going to be held to account for lewd and lascivious behavior." Cassidy groaned dramatically as she let herself be guided to the front door and waited while Aiden opened it. Once inside, Aiden quickly keyed in the code to stop the alarm from going off and gestured for Cassidy to enter. Cassidy looked at the floor where she was leaving puddles and began apologizing even though it wasn't Aiden's home.

"Don't worry about the water. That's easy to clean up. If you'll trust me with your car keys, I can go get your bags from the car and bring them in to you." Aiden pointed her up the stairs. "The bathroom is the first room on the right. I'll drop your bags by the door so you can change. When you're done, I'm right next door at number twenty-six. Lori left some instructions for you there."

Aiden took the keys from Cassidy's fingers and watched as she carefully picked her way up the wooden staircase to the second floor. Aiden wished she could see more of what Cassidy looked like beneath the long hair that had hidden most of her face. The clingy material of her dress had hidden nothing so Aiden was all too aware how Cassidy had curves in all the right places. Yet she was slender and almost delicate to look at. And apparently had a penchant for lacy under garments in a delightful shade of baby blue, Aiden recalled all too vividly.

"Obviously a high maintenance femme," Aiden muttered as she trotted to Cassidy's rental car and lifted out two suitcases. "And probably straighter than an arrow." She sighed. "Pity. I'm sure that gorgeous British voice would sound amazing screaming in a much more pleasurable context." She shook her head at her inappropriate thoughts and hurried back inside to bring Cassidy her clothing and tried not to think of what was going on in the bathroom beneath the sound of running water.

❖

Aiden cleaned up the wet footmarks, not wanting Cassidy to slip on any damp patches. Before she left, she made sure to reprogram the sprinkler system to cause less havoc. Then she hastened around to her own home to gather up her laptop to take it back into her office. She saved her work then powered it down at her desk. While waiting, she looked around the room. Here was where she created her stories. Her writing room had a desk, a comfortable chair, and a series of framed artworks and photographs all around the walls. Shelving housed her collections, and Aiden's eyes fell on her favorite poster.

Positioned right above her desk, so Aiden could receive inspiration from it, hung a framed picture of a character from her favorite TV series. Karadine Kourt, the mind manipulator for *The Alchemidens*. It was a fantasy series where people with magical and mystical superpowers helped to save a stylized New York from the evils it housed. The poster displayed Kara's usual pose, hands on hips, challenging all to take her on. Ornate guns hung on her hips and a katana sword was strapped on her back. A large silver belt buckle drew Aiden's eyes to the narrow hips, but it was her face that always caught Aiden's attention. She knew enough about the actress, C.J. Hayes, and her body of work that this was just one of the characters she could bring to life. But it was this one that Aiden was drawn to the most. Karadine Kourt, the woman with the ability to fell foes with her fighting skills and manipulate their minds to make them do her bidding. Dark brown hair, so dark to be almost black, escaped from under the tilted fedora she wore that kept her face in shadow. Even darker brown eyes stared out from an angular face. A face that was softened only by the wry smile that lent a small curve to her full lips. Aiden wished she'd created this character. She was by far her favorite to watch for many reasons. She's beautiful, Aiden thought, and everything a hero should be. She knew that, being thirty-five years old, she should be long past the need for a hero or heroine in her life. She even wrote of them herself. But sometimes, a fictional character just took a hold of her heart, and for Aiden, this one was her ideal.

Aiden heard the sound of the alarm being set again next door. She pulled her office door to, hiding the treasure she kept in there that only she could appreciate. Aiden left her front door ajar and then hurried back to the kitchen to check on her food. She was giving it a stir when she heard the soft tread of footsteps behind her.

"Would you like to stay for lunch?" Aiden was busy preparing the rice to accompany the meal. "I make enough for at least four people so you'd be doing me a favor stopping me from living off this for a week." She turned to greet her and got to see Cassidy properly for the first time.

Aiden's breath caught in her chest.

Oh my God. Cassidy is C.J. Hayes. Karadine Kourt is in my kitchen, in little more than shorts and a T-shirt where the neck is ripped right down to her... Aiden prayed her face hadn't given her away and hastily turned back to the rice. The sound of her spoon clattering against the saucepan was jarring even to her ears. Aiden cursed her suddenly shaking hands.

"You're very kind. I'd love to, thank you."

Aiden heard a chair pull back from the table. *C.J. Hayes is sitting at my kitchen table wearing something conjured up out of one of my wet dreams. Be calm! You can do this. She's just like any other actress you've met. It's no big deal. Do not freak out and become a fan-girling asshole!*

Aiden forced herself to turn around to face Cassidy properly and smiled warmly. "So, what do you say to some of the best damn chili you've ever tasted?"

❖

Cassidy felt much better after the warm shower had banished the chills from the icy drenching she had received courtesy of the sprinklers. Surprised by the sudden invitation she'd been offered, but never one to turn down food, Cassidy soon found herself warmed by Aiden's cheerful charm too. She sat at the kitchen table with a large plate of chili and rice before her. While Aiden was busy preparing her own plate, Cassidy was able to observe her unnoticed.

Aiden was definitely broader than Cassidy, but it appeared to be all muscle. Cassidy noticed how well Aiden's shirt fit her, tucked into a pair of jeans that molded to a lean pair of legs and a tight butt. Aiden was also quite tall. Cassidy was certain she was at least three inches taller than her own five foot five. Cassidy brushed her hair back from her face, flicking it back over her shoulder out of her way. Aiden's hair was ash brown, cut short in a casually unkempt style. She was handsome in an understated way.

"Do you run to the rescue of many stray women, Aiden?" Aiden's gentle grin made Cassidy pause for a second in her eating. Oh, that's a heartbreaker if ever I saw one, Cassidy thought.

"You'll be relieved to hear that I have reset the sprinkler system so that it only comes on at night. So, unless you're a night owl with a penchant for running around the front yard in your nightwear worshipping the moon, you should escape its clutches."

Cassidy liked the humorous twinkle that lit Aiden's eyes. She appeared older now that Cassidy could see her close up. She recalled Lori's comment when they had spoken briefly on the phone before Lori had left for her third honeymoon and to live in Aspen for a while. "She's one of those strong, silent types you never go near, Cass, so she'll be safe from your feminine wiles." Cassidy had been riled by Lori's flippant remark. She wasn't a predatory lesbian; she was mindful of who she hooked up with because Hollywood was notoriously loose lipped. Cassidy was out and proud, but she didn't want to be written about salaciously in the tabloid columns. She did, however, have a habit of falling for women who were as commitment phobic as she was. And bad girls usually fell in that category.

Aiden was not a bad girl. Cassidy eyed her from under her lashes. She *was* handsome though, with her jaw just a little too strong and square for her to be ever considered pretty. Her eyes were a stormy blue that shone out from behind a pair of dark framed spectacles. No, Aiden wasn't a bad girl, but she did look kind of geeky in those glasses. Cassidy's eyes drifted lower. Aiden wasn't flat chested either. In fact, she looked like she had ample—Cassidy felt the brakes slam on in her musings. *Whoa! Where is this coming from?* She ran a hand over her cheek, feeling how hot she had gotten from the direction her unbidden thoughts had taken.

"Can I offer you that drink now?"

Cassidy nodded dumbly, enjoying the deep tone of Aiden's voice.

"I've got soda or water, if you prefer something cold with the meal."

"Water's fine." Cassidy was a wine drinker, and she craved a glass now to try to calm her all too over-active senses where this woman was concerned. She busied herself with her meal and moaned at her first bite. She savored the explosion of tastes that burst on her tongue. She wasn't too far gone in her wanton moans not to see a blush color Aiden's cheeks. "Oh my God! This is wonderful." Cassidy took another mouthful. The appreciative noises she made over the food only made Aiden's face even redder. "I'm going to be purposely running around the yard under those damn sprinklers all the time if this is what I get treated to."

"How about I save you the laundry and the pneumonia and just offer you an open invitation instead?" She sat down opposite Cassidy and began to eat. "Good food should always be complemented by excellent company." She held out her glass in a toast. "Welcome to the neighborhood."

Cassidy clinked their glasses. "And thank you for the warmest welcome I have ever received."

Chapter Two

C assidy's appetite was legendary among her friends and associates. She could pack away a substantial amount of food and never appear to gain a pound. Cassidy knew she burned it off as nervous energy and on her regular gym visits. Playing a kind of superhero also meant she had to keep her figure perfect for the screen. She was proud of her defined abs but hated the fact she had to work to keep them around her love for food.

Satiated from her unexpected lunch, Cassidy was now back next-door and wandering around her new home alone. The décor screamed Lori's idea of good taste and eccentric money wasting. The walls were lined with artwork that looked like it would be more at home on a fridge and done by a five-year-old. Otherwise, it was bright and garish and signed by names Cassidy knew but wouldn't choose for herself. She preferred landscapes to the random splashes of color called modern art. She also steered clear of the rather unattractive fertility goddess that stood on a shelf.

"Lori's on her third husband in ten years. She has no time for children while she's still test-driving marriage mates. You, my dear, are merely decoration." Cassidy stepped away from the carving. "And don't think I'm touching you either. No matter how happy it would make my mother for me to settle down with a nice girl and raise babies."

She wandered into the kitchen. "Not really much point in me being in here," she muttered. For someone who appreciated the culinary arts, Cassidy's own cooking skills were nonexistent. Pop Tarts or some form of sandwiches were as far as her talents lay. She looked outside the big picture window and could see straight into Aiden's yard. Now there was a woman who could cook.

"I wonder if I could pay her to cook for me while I'm living here." She racked her brain trying to remember what Lori had said Aiden did for a living. She couldn't recall, probably because she'd still been fuming at Lori's scathing comments about Cassidy's dating habits.

She wandered around the rest of the house, checking behind every door to see what lay inside. She picked out a bedroom and then set to bringing upstairs all that she had brought with her that Aiden had kindly carried in from the car. The rest of her belongings would be sent on to her by her assistant. She sat down with a tired thump on the bed she had chosen. She'd been happy at her last apartment. It had been perfectly situated for the studio. It had plenty of restaurants within walking distance for her to frequent. Her neighbors had been friendly but had also left her in peace. It had been perfect. Cassidy hated that she'd had to leave so abruptly.

"The price of fame, dear girl," she grumbled with a heartfelt sigh as she tried to push the morose thoughts aside. "Someone always ends up paying."

He was so tired of waiting. Adam had all but burned holes into the walls of the apartment building's brickwork staring at it so hard. He was waiting for C.J. to come home. He had been haunting the coffee shop day and night since she'd left with the detective. In the daytime, he watched for her familiar form to walk through the main doors. At night, he sat until the coffee shop closed, then he moved outside under the cover of a nearby shop awning. He was just waiting for a sign from her. He was watching for the telltale light to go on in her bedroom window, showing him she had returned.

But she hadn't come home.

Adam knew she wasn't at the studio yet. Social media was such a gift to those who liked to keep a watchful eye on their favorite stars. The studio posted messages about the show and their cast daily when the show was in production. It built up the excitement for the new season. All he had to do was keep his phone on hand and just scroll through Twitter, Instagram, and Facebook. Locations for filming were usually leaked by over exuberant fans or the cast themselves. It had made his life so much easier when C.J. was filming *The Alchemidens* while he was away. Privacy was a thing of the past thanks to TV and films bombarding their audience with behind the scenes photos and spoilers.

Unfortunately, C.J. didn't post her whereabouts anymore. But the studio included her when she was on set. They had to because, in Adam's opinion, she was carrying the show.

He was surprised her detective hasn't put a stop to that too. He remembered C.J. being manhandled from her building by the burly man. *If I find he's the one behind the restraining order I was slapped with....* He tightened his grip on his coffee cup and stared down at the pattern designed in the milk. He took a large mouthful to spoil it. The scalding brew burned his mouth, but he purposely didn't swallow. He deliberately let it burn. The pain would only serve to make him stronger. He finally let the coffee wash down his throat. The restraining order had seared his flesh a lot more than simple hot coffee could. The consequences had been laid out to him loud and clear as to what would happen to him if he dared to violate any of the rules and regulations that saw to keep him away from C.J. Hayes.

"They didn't understand," he muttered to himself, ignoring the startled look from the woman at the table next to his. "None of them do."

She was meant to be mine from the very first moment I laid eyes on her. And I am hers. We are destined to be together, in this life and the next. And no fucking restraining order is going to keep me away from her. Wherever she is, I'll track her down and find her. I always do.

He smiled at the memory of following her home one evening. She'd never realized he was just a hand's breath away. He'd been so close he'd smelled her sweet perfume on the air. She'd been so near all he had needed to do was just reach out and he could have touched her.

Then he'd been forced to leave. He'd been sloppy. He wouldn't make that mistake again. He'd been traced by one of the letters he'd sent her. To add insult to injury he'd then been fired from his job at the studios because the police were labeling him a stalker.

Adam took another drink and let the white-hot pain fuse with his anger. He had to find where she was now because it didn't look like she was coming back to her apartment any time soon. He slammed the cup down hard on the table. It smashed into the saucer beneath it, shattering them both to pieces. The noise brought the whole café to a halt. Everyone's eyes turned on him.

Adam looked up at the woman behind the counter. "Don't worry. I'll pay for it." He reached for his wallet and pulled out some bills. He tossed the money on the table among the broken crockery then walked out. "Your coffee sucks anyway," he tossed over his shoulder before shutting the door behind him.

Once outside, in the early evening light, he took one last look up at the third floor window that he had fixated on for so long.

"I'll find you, C.J., and when I do? You'll pay for all you've put me through."

❖

Aiden might only have had soft drinks on offer, but Lori's home was well stocked with the very best wine ex-husband number two had hoarded. He'd also lost the whole lot in the settlement the very best lawyers had brokered for Lori. Cassidy sat in the living room with a large glass of red wine that boasted both an excellent vintage and a very expensive price tag. Lori had told her to take whatever she wanted, being strictly a vodka drinker herself. Cassidy smiled as she savored the rich taste of fruit on her tongue. She held her glass aloft.

"Here's to Clint. The guy who couldn't keep it in his pants but had an amazing taste in wine. I appreciate your skills, Clint, even if

Lori didn't appreciate you screwing her niece at your first wedding anniversary party."

She slipped off her Louis Vuitton shoes and propped her feet up on the small table adorned with fruit and nibbles. Lori had made sure the house was well stocked with food for Cassidy to come in to. A grocery delivery every week had been set up for Cassidy from the local store. Lori had threatened her that she'd better make use of the fresh fruit and vegetables that had been included on the list. Cassidy just hoped for a jar of peanut butter and a loaf of bread too, as that was pushing the limits of her culinary talents. She was just grateful that once she returned to the studio, her meals would be catered on set.

Cassidy wiggled her well-manicured toes as she stretched lazily. The hiatus between filming had seemed never ending. The upheaval of having to leave her apartment and finding new accommodation had taken up most of her time between filming. She was due in tomorrow for a meeting while some previously finished scenes tied to the finale were reshot because of a continuity error that the fans would have run rough shod over had it aired. Cassidy was glad it wasn't any of her work she had to redo. Her scenes were usually physical, and she'd been out of that mindset for long enough that the thought of having to start training again made her groan. Tomorrow, she would go pick up her new script and then start shooting the day after. She'd be pleased to get back to familiar territory. The shadowy world of Divinestra that *The Alchemidens* inhabited was a re-imagined version of New York City bedecked with steam punk architecture and gothic spires. It was more a home to her than where she was currently living.

Cassidy sighed and took a large sip from her wine glass. "There's no place like home," she said as she reached for her cell phone to call her best friend. Mischa Ballantyne played alongside Cassidy in *The Alchemidens*, and they had forged a very strong friendship right from the start. Cassidy knew she needed to call her to put Mischa's mind at rest that she was safe. She grimaced at her own thoughts. Safe and sound in a new home, miles from her comfort zone, having to start over again.

Determined not to wallow, Cassidy deliberately put on a cheerful voice as her call was answered. "Mischa, I'm all tucked in for the night in my new digs. You wouldn't believe what happened to me today."

"You haven't been in that house twenty-four hours yet. What priceless heirloom have you shattered to pieces already?" Mischa let out a deliberately dramatic sigh, and Cassidy could picture the exasperated look on her face.

"No, nothing like that. I was a damsel in distress." She laughed at the inelegant snort of derision from Mischa. "Well, darling, we all know how well I play that role to perfection." She launched into the tale of the sprinklers and her geeky bespectacled knight who had come to her rescue.

By the end of the call, Cassidy felt much better, but she wouldn't truly feel comfortable until she was back on Soundstage One with the cast and crew who were more family to her than her own flesh and blood.

CHAPTER THREE

A iden let out a noisy yawn while scrubbing at her eyes. She'd stayed up until the early hours working on a chapter for her new book, and before she knew it she had been greeting the dawn chorus. She'd managed just a few hours of sleep before she'd woken up again ready to start the new day. She was pleased with what she had accomplished so she wasn't going to complain. Aiden gathered up a piece of toast that was serving as her breakfast and padded out her front door to see where the paperboy had tossed her newspaper today. She spotted it halfway up her path in a flowerbed.

She'd taken only a few steps toward it when she heard the unmistakable tone of Cassidy's voice raised in indignation. That was followed by a stream of colorful British swear words, the sound of a car door being flung open as Cassidy apparently got out of the car, and then the same door being slammed shut with a muffled scream of frustration. Aiden went to investigate and was in time to witness Cassidy slapping ineffectually at the roof of her vehicle. Aiden couldn't help herself; she laughed out loud at how flustered Cassidy appeared. She really was beautiful, even with her lips drawn into the biggest pout Aiden had ever seen on that familiar face.

"I warn you, Aiden, I've been trained in many a martial art." Cassidy's voice broke through Aiden's chuckles. "I could incapacitate you with just one blow and will be tempted to demonstrate if you don't quit laughing at my apparent misfortune!" She slapped at the car again. "My damn rental car won't start. I thought it was making strange noises yesterday, but I was so busy moving I put it out of my mind. But now it won't even switch on without sounding like a damned walrus in heat!"

Aiden drew closer to look through the driver's window of the top of the line Toyota Camry. "Hmmm, I'm guessing if I tried to hotwire it for you it might screw with your rental agreement with them."

"You can hotwire cars?" Cassidy looked scandalized.

"Yes, I can. I admit it isn't something I learned in order to benefit society. I was taught by a foster brother who had me hotwire cars for him because I was smaller and couldn't be seen over the dashboard while he kept a lookout nearby. He was stealing cars, with my help, while he was supposed to be walking me home from school. However, he did pay me handsomely in comic books and candy."

"He sounds like a real charmer."

"He was one of the good ones, oddly enough. Still landed himself in prison though."

"And yet here you are, willing to carry the tradition on, still remaining at large."

Aiden grinned at Cassidy's dry tone and decided to come to her rescue once more. "My dodgy past aside, do you need a ride somewhere?"

Cassidy's relief was almost comical. "Oh God, yes! Yes, I do. I don't want to be late on my first day back at the studio. I'd never hear the end of it. My timekeeping isn't the best even when I have a car that *does* work."

Aiden finished her last mouthful of toast and brushed her hands off on her jeans. "Let me go get my car keys and I'm at your disposal."

"You're a great neighbor, Aiden."

"I'm just a sucker for a pretty girl," Aiden said, enjoying the smile that lit up Cassidy's face at the compliment.

"I'm going to wear out my welcome with you at this rate." Cassidy slung her purse over her shoulder and followed swiftly after Aiden.

"You'll never do that," Aiden said, heading back inside and scooping up her keys from a hook in the kitchen. She walked back to where Cassidy was waiting at her front door. "I warn you now, my car isn't half as fancy as your rental." She added slyly, "But it runs."

"Then it's a king among cars. For your kindness, you'll have to come in and see where I work. We never did talk about our jobs last night. I'm an actress."

Aiden didn't dare look in Cassidy's direction. "I'd love to see what you do. But last night was wonderful just getting to know you." She startled a little when Cassidy slipped her arm through hers and gave her a gentle squeeze.

"This move of mine might not have been as bad after all."

Aiden had to agree as she breathed in the gentle scent that Cassidy wore. It tantalized her senses and made her giddy. "Come on, Thelma. Let's get on the road."

Cassidy laughed. "You're equating us to Thelma and Louise? They had a very sad ending."

"Well, I'm a writer and I can bring about happy endings if I choose to. Let me show you my car and you can tell me where you're heading today, Ms. Thelma. Burbank or Mexico."

Aiden locked up her home and raised the garage door. Her car was her prized possession. She furtively looked over her shoulder to watch Cassidy's face. Cassidy's squeal made Aiden laugh. Cassidy brushed past her to run her fingertips reverently along the fins of the car.

"You have a Thunderbird."

"A 1966 Thunderbird convertible, with a blue/green paint job and resplendent sparkling chrome," Aiden boasted. She gallantly opened the passenger door for Cassidy and then hurried around to get behind the wheel.

Cassidy was now running her fingertips over the interior. Aiden wondered if she was as tactile in all things.

"You have a bona fide Thelma and Louise car."

Aiden couldn't help her grin. "It was nearly impossible to get the exact model, but I did it. Then I got her all sprayed up and fitted out to be the beautiful ride you are now seated in."

"You couldn't sound prouder if this was your first born child." Cassidy leaned back in her seat as Aiden backed out of the garage. The garage door shut automatically as Aiden pulled onto the driveway.

Aiden then caught Cassidy's appraising look. "You're staring at me."

"I'm wondering if you acquired this car via your foster brother's tutelage or is it best I don't inquire?"

Aiden chuckled. "I gave up my Grand Theft Auto days long ago. This baby is all mine, legally. Bought and paid for with hard-earned cash." She idled the car to the edge of the road. "Where to, my lady?"

"Burbank Studios, please." Cassidy took the sunglasses she'd had perched on her head and put them on. She gave Aiden a bright smile.

"Say it. You know you're dying to." Aiden revved the engine, playing along.

"*Hit it!*"

Aiden laughed at Cassidy's dramatic flair and pulled out onto the street.

❖

The ride to the studios was the most entertaining drive Aiden had shared in years. Cassidy turned out to have an amazing talent for mimicry and had provided a hilarious running commentary all along their route. Aiden couldn't remember laughing so much as she listened to Cassidy talking about people, their clothing, and their cars, all the time switching back and forth between the lazy Southern drawls of Susan Sarandon's Louise and Geena Davis's Thelma.

Aiden pulled up at the studio's guard station. Cassidy greeted the man by name in a sultry Sarandon voice. "Hi, Felix. Did you miss me?"

"Nice to have you back, Ms. Hayes." He grinned, flushing a little at her teasing tone. He glanced over at Aiden. "Ms. Darrow? I don't think I have you…" He flicked through his clipboard sheets.

Aiden caught Cassidy's sharp look directed her way.

"You won't. I'm merely driving Ms. Hayes today."

"Nice work if you can get it." Felix's grin grew bigger as he waved them through.

"They know you here?" Cassidy shifted in her seat to face Aiden.

"I did say I was a writer." Aiden drove directly to the sound stage Cassidy was due at. She parked and got out to hurry around the car to help Cassidy out. Cassidy kept hold of Aiden's hand.

"What kind of writer exactly?"

"A bit of this, a bit of that," Aiden said with a shrug. "I've assisted on the odd screenplay, which is why I'm known at the gate."

"Why didn't you tell me?"

"Like you said, we were too busy talking about other things last night to have occupations get in the way." Aiden noticed Cassidy still hadn't loosened her grip. The softness of her skin made Aiden want to run her own fingers along the long length of Cassidy's. She'd seen these same hands grab assailants and handle weapons. Having one of those hands in her grasp, Aiden was surprised to feel how fragile it felt. Just another reason why Cassidy wasn't like Karadine Kourt. Aiden was starting to appreciate the differences.

"A woman of mystery. How intriguing." Cassidy tugged at Aiden's hand. "Come, let me show you where I work so you can see I can do something other than just get myself into trouble."

Aiden followed after her dutifully. Excitement was building inside her at what she hoped to see inside. She was also aware of how disappointed she was that Cassidy had to let go of her hand to open the stage door. Her feelings toward Cassidy were confusing and overwhelming. Aiden knew Karadine Kourt, Cassidy's on-screen persona. She had spent many hours watching her and adoring her character. With just a few hours spent in the company of Cassidy Hayes, Aiden was fearful of mixing fact with fiction. But she found herself being drawn to Cassidy like a moth to that ever tempting, flickering flame. A part of her welcomed the burn; she'd been out in the cold for too long.

CHAPTER FOUR

The sound stage was huge and housed a series of sets from *The Alchemidens*. Aiden tried to take in the reality of everything she could see. She knew the places intimately from watching the show. But there was one set Aiden found herself drawn to, and it dominated the biggest part of the stage.

"The Conclavian," Aiden whispered, thankful Cassidy's attention was distracted elsewhere when someone shouted her name.

"Can I leave you a moment while I just go make my presence known?"

Aiden nodded almost eagerly, trying so hard to be nonchalant about where she was. Once left alone, Aiden took a few tentative steps forward, edging closer to where the floor changed into the weathered stone of the ancient church appropriated by the Alchemidens as their base of operation. Inching closer, Aiden's eyes traced the symbols carved out in various patterns on the floor. Each marking was a symbol of the alchemy performed by Meriva, the high priestess, the leader of the Alchemidens.

Aiden was sorely tempted to step foot onto the set and take a closer look at the altar to see how much of the large stone plinth was real and what was CGI wizardry. In the show, Meriva worked her magic while the plinth turned around in a circle of shining symbols. Alchemic imagery always weaved around the priestess and poured forth from the stone in fractured light. Aiden bit back her disappointment. She knew the magic wasn't real, but it was still disheartening to know Meriva's plinth had visible wires when she looked closer. Aiden was a great believer in suspending your imagination for as long as possible. She craned her neck to look up along the heavily bricked walls that befit the old church. The green screen that covered half the wall made Aiden sigh.

"You're disappointed there are no gargoyles, aren't you?"

Startled by the voice that sounded over her left shoulder, Aiden spun around. There stood the high priestess herself, Meriva, bedecked in her elaborate robes and richly patterned headdress.

"I was astounded myself when I watched the show and saw what the special effects crew envisioned to hide that hideous green screen. They gave us vaulted walls, gorgeous carved arches, and butt-ugly gargoyles nesting in every nook and cranny." Mischa Ballantyne pushed a hand through the mass of curly hair that even the constricting headdress couldn't tame. "I like the gargoyles. I just love how they come to life and do my bidding. I'm of the belief that if they were truly real they'd be more manageable than Chris is."

Aiden tried not to grin at Mischa's dig at her costar Chris Garrick who played the man-turned-monster Ragnar Rhodes. He had a reputation for being a practical joker on set. Aiden was much more interested in Mischa though. She was a commanding presence on screen. In the flesh, she was even more striking.

"So, are you a new gopher? Because, no offense intended, but I like to get my own coffee. No one ever makes my coffee how I like it so I figure to save myself the hassle of spitting it out, I'll just make the damn drink myself."

Aiden finally found her voice. "I'm here with Cassidy Hayes. I drove her here this morning."

Mischa rolled her eyes. "Oh God, don't tell me she's wrecked another car? That girl can't go near a vehicle without locking herself out of it or blowing a tire. She's vehicularly challenged."

Aiden was thankful that nothing had happened to *her* precious car if that were true.

"And you are? I mean, you're standing here mourning the loss of gargoyles and haven't even told me your name." Mischa's dark eyes fixed Aiden to the spot expectantly.

Politely, Aiden held out her hand. "I'm Aiden Darrow, and it's a real pleasure to meet you, Ms. Ballantyne."

Mischa shook her hand. "Aiden Darrow?" She kept shaking while she contemplated. Her eyes grew wide and her hand squeezed Aiden's tighter. "Oh my God! Let me look at you." She cupped Aiden's chin and turned her head to the side. "Oh, saints alive! You're *Aiden Darrow! The* Aiden Darrow! I'm with Aiden Darrow and what am I doing? I'm talking about fucking nonexistent gargoyles! I am such an ass!"

Aiden found herself suddenly squeezed tightly to Mischa's chest. It afforded her a closer look at the intricate detailing on the robe but also pressed her too close for comfort into Mischa's cleavage. In her priestess heels, Mischa was an Amazon.

As days went, Aiden considered, trying not to count Mischa's numerous breast freckles, this one was revealing itself to be quite the stand out day.

❖

Cassidy walked back onto the sound stage just in time to hear Mischa's excitement. She stumbled to a halt as Mischa flung her arms around Aiden and pulled her into a bone-crushing hug. Cassidy noted Aiden looked a little stunned by the over friendly body slam.

"Mischa, kindly stop manhandling Aiden and explain yourself." She tried not to laugh at Aiden's flustered face as she was peeled from Mischa's chest. Cassidy shook her head. The priestess's garb was designed to keep Mischa's cleavage front and center and very much on display. Even as a lesbian who could appreciate breasts decoratively, Cassidy was tired of telling Mischa to cover them up for propriety's sake. She swore she saw more of Mischa's breasts than she did her own.

"She's Aiden Darrow!" Mischa squealed, clutching Aiden's shoulders and turning her around to face Cassidy as if they had never met.

"Yes, she's my new neighbor and she's very kindly brought me into work today because the rental place gave me a lemon of a car again." Cassidy couldn't help but stifle the feeling that she needed to pull Aiden out of Mischa's clutches. Irrational jealousy sparked through her, and she was taken aback as to where it had sprung from.

"You never said your neighbor was Aiden Darrow. *The* Aiden Darrow." Mischa's tone was accusing as if Cassidy had purposely kept this from her.

"Darling, I told you who had rescued me from the sprinklers."

Mischa stared at her baldly. "With that accent of yours it sounded like you said *Hayden*. You have no idea who she is, do you? God, sometimes I forget you only read fashion magazines and the gossip rags."

Cassidy bristled. "I do not!"

Mischa cupped her hands on Aiden's cheeks as if she were something precious. "This woman is my favorite author." She turned Aiden's face to look at her and stated, deathly serious, "You're my favorite author."

Aiden laughed softly, apparently much amused by Mischa's enthusiasm and sincerity. "Thank you so much. That's very kind of you to say so."

"I mean, I know I'm straight, and married with too many babies thanks to my husband who is too fertile for his own good." Mischa slung a friendly arm around Aiden's shoulders, which only served to set Cassidy's teeth on edge again. "Believe me, Aiden, after the first kid? Any more you pop out is just too much to deal with."

"I'll take that under advisement," Aiden said dryly.

Cassidy, however, was used to Mischa's ways. She was loud and boisterous and didn't always employ her censorship button when she needed to, but she was the best friend Cassidy had ever known. That didn't stop Cassidy from almost growling with annoyance at the familiarity Mischa was employing with Aiden.

"Anyway, I know I'm not a lesbian, but I love your stories so much. Dammit, girl! You make me cry! I mean the inconsolable 'just bring me some chocolate and then stay the hell away from me for an hour' kind of crying." She batted her eyes at Aiden playfully. "Damn, I wish I'd known you were coming today. I'd have brought my books for you to sign. My sister, Sorcha? She got me hooked on your stuff. She's gay so at least that's one of your target audience covered." Mischa grinned mischievously. "She'll cream herself when I tell her I've actually met you."

Cassidy was impressed with how Aiden reacted to that comment. She just blinked owlishly and moved the conversation right along.

"I have books I'd be more than happy to sign for you and your sister."

Mischa squealed and hugged Aiden again. Then she began rummaging in one of the many folds of her flowing gown. She pulled out her phone. "Cass, be a sweetheart and take a photo of us together. I want to send it to my sister and gloat like a mother!"

Cassidy did as she was told, totally thrown by Mischa's fangirling attitude. She fought against rolling her eyes as Mischa hugged Aiden close and they both smiled for the picture. Cassidy handed her the phone back. Both Mischa and Aiden were happy with the shot as they crowded over the screen with huge smiles.

"That's awesome. Can you send it to me, please?" Aiden gave Mischa her number and Cassidy all but gasped aloud in a fit of pique. She didn't even have Aiden's phone number, and they had shared a meal last night *and* a drive into work that morning! She just barely caught the unheard of whispered tones of Mischa's voice as she conspired with Aiden.

"I'll text you when I'm free for you to drop the books by, and maybe we can take a tour for those gargoyles you're so interested in."

Cassidy was captivated by the look of utter joy that brightened Aiden's face.

"I'd love that."

"It's a date," Mischa said and waved a hand at someone who was coming toward her. "Yeah, yeah, I know. Time to make magic." Her tone was uncharacteristically serious when she turned back to Aiden. "It was lovely meeting you."

"The pleasure was all mine."

Cassidy coughed loud enough for them both to look up at her.

"Oh, are you still here, Cass?" Mischa grinned at her. "I'll leave you to say your farewells to your handsome neighbor. Who, by the way, has credits on at least four blockbuster films due for release this year. So she's a writing genius as well as the savior of your finely toned ass!"

Aiden covered her mouth swiftly with a hand, barely masking her laughter in a cough while Cassidy glared after Mischa and her parting shot.

"She's certainly a force of nature," Aiden finally said when left alone with Cassidy.

"She's a royal pain in my *finely toned ass*!" Cassidy watched Mischa imperialistically shooing people out of her way, very much in character of the priestess. "But she's the best friend I could ever have wished for despite that."

"She's awesome. A little grabbier than I expected, but awesome."

Cassidy didn't want to talk about Mischa anymore. "So, you're a famous author then?"

"I'm someone who has been very fortunate to have an excellent fan base for my writing to reach a certain level of success," Aiden said modestly. "My earlier books caught the attention of a scriptwriter, and I get drawn into the world of screenplay writing on occasion. It pays the bills and got me the car of my dreams."

Cassidy felt the need to explain not knowing who Aiden was. Mischa's unthinking words had stung her. "I don't read a lot. It's not because I'm an airhead or can't, contrary to Mischa's veiled dig. I'm a huge fan of J.K Rowling. I think I've read the print off all of those books. I just always seem to be too busy to find the time to read anything other than a script these days."

"Just because we didn't talk about who we were, Cassidy, doesn't mean I'm not aware of you. Between this show and the films you've been in, I'm surprised you have time to take a breath." Aiden's smile was warm. "I also think you're fascinating whether you have read my books or not. It's not a requirement to get to know me."

The look Aiden favored her with made Cassidy's heart pick up its pace. She felt flustered and uncharacteristically shy all of a sudden.

"Thank you for bringing me inside to see these sets and to inadvertently meet Mischa. I'll go back home now and get some writing done on my latest book so she doesn't take me to task for wasting precious time away from my laptop."

"She's incredibly pushy. Don't be surprised if she starts texting you for spoilers."

"I've dealt with pushier, believe me, and I don't ever cave in to their pleading."

Cassidy didn't want to say good-bye but saw someone waving to capture her attention. "I have to go. Thank you for coming to my rescue for the second time. And for letting me ride in that magnificent car of yours."

"Just so you know, I'm never letting you drive it. Mischa warned me of your lousy luck with cars."

"It's not my fault. It just happens." Cassidy grimaced. "Story of my life, that."

"If you need a ride home, just call me."

Cassidy gave her a pointed look. "Unlike *some* people you've only just met, I don't happen to have your number. Mischa, your *greatest* fan, has it. I, however, do not."

Aiden chuckled at Cassidy's grumpy tone and the purposely pronounced pout. "Then let me fix that right this second." She gave out her number for the second time. "You know where I am if you need me. Just whistle." Slyly, Aiden peered down at Cassidy. "You do know how to whistle, don't you?"

Teasingly, Cassidy raised her fingers to her lips. Horrified, Aiden stopped her.

"Lauren Bacall is resplendent on her heavenly cloud tutting at you, Ms. Hayes." Aiden hesitated for a moment and then reached out to squeeze Cassidy's hand. "If you want me, I'm just over the fence. Don't forget."

"I'll remember." Cassidy watched her leave. *You're kind of hard to forget.*

❖

Cassidy loved the catering service that was employed by the studio to feed the cast and crew. She made certain to fully avail herself of all the food that was on offer. It would be rude not to. Mischa gave her plate a disparaging eye when they finally had a chance to sit down and catch up.

"I don't know how you manage to keep looking so sexy when you eat like a damn trucker." She picked at a plate covered in salad. "Must be something in your British heritage because you should seriously be the size of a duplex with the amount of food you can pack away."

"Don't forget, I do exercise." Cassidy sampled a spoonful of the chili she had in a bowl. It wasn't a patch on Aiden's so she put it back down.

"I'll give you that. I've seen you hot and sweaty on a treadmill." Mischa picked up the bowl Cassidy had cast aside and began tucking in. "But you're thirty-one now. Surely it's about time something on you started drooping."

Cassidy ate for a moment then tried to be nonchalant about her topic of conversation. "So, you've read all of Aiden's books then?"

"Sorcha got me into them. She was going on and on about how amazing they were. Finally, she brought me a copy of one to read because she refused to let her own copy out of her sight. I'll never forget it. *A Pocket Full of Time*. I loved it so I bought all the rest in that series and had a binge read to catch up. Joe and the kids had to make their own meals those days. Momma was on a mission."

"You said they made you cry?"

"You get so invested in the story. There's this woman, Hollister Graham, who is an inventor and she pieces together an old pocket watch her dying father left to her. When its hands start moving, it causes a shift in time. She triggers it by accident and ends up being taken from her world and her wife. The series is about her desperate search to return to her time and to her beloved Emily."

Cassidy was startled by Mischa visibly tearing up. "What's wrong?"

Mischa wiped at her eyes. "Her stories stay with you. She writes of such yearning to return to her loved one and, gay or straight, anyone can sympathize with that pain. In each book, Hollister visits a different period in time and meets Emily in a previous incarnation. Time after time, she falls for her all over again, only to have to leave when time runs out and the hands on the watch start moving again." She flapped her hands expressively, trying to dry her eyes with her frantic fanning. "It's just sooooo romantic! But how your heart bleeds for Hollister, always finding her love but having to leave her behind. Forever drawn to that one woman, no matter what the time or place." Mischa took a shaky breath. "It makes you wonder what kind of anguished life poor Aiden has suffered to write it so desperately on each page."

"She's a writer. It's their job to create worlds and situations from their imagination. Just because she writes heartbreak doesn't have to mean she's writing from experience. I'm pretty certain Tolkien never met a real Hobbit in order to write his books."

Mischa sighed. "I guess. But, honey? Did you see those soulful eyes of hers behind those lenses? I'm telling you, if I wasn't married, I'd be sorely tempted to toss my hat into her ring."

Cassidy couldn't hide her surprise. "Are you serious?"

"Cass"—Mischa laid on the dramatics—"I've read her words. She has a beautiful soul that speaks of a love everlasting. Also, her sex scenes are as hot as fuck, so hell yes, I could get mighty serious if she writes those from experience!"

Snorting, Cassidy shook her head at her. "You're wicked."

"And I'm married to the man of my dreams, but that doesn't stop me from being happy to get down with some hot and heavy lesbian loving in my favorite choice of literature." Mischa bumped her shoulder against Cassidy's. "And believe me, there are plenty of chapters I have bookmarked and left for Joe to read so he can get some inspiration."

Cassidy slapped her hands over her ears. "You need to stop right this second! God, it's a wonder Joe lets you out of the house."

"He knows I'm all his. But I'm going to tease Sorcha to death with the fact I got to meet her idol and got to cuddle up with her." She tapped her phone that lay on the table beside her. "And I have the picture to back up my claim."

"I think you startled Aiden with how hands-on you are."

"Probably, but she was the perfect gentlewoman. She didn't make a grab for my ass once."

Cassidy had to smile at Mischa's disappointed tone. Deliberately, she let slip, "Aiden's got a Thelma and Louise car." Cassidy knew one of Joe's passions was cars of any shape or size.

"Oh my God, Joe will be pushing me out of the way to get to her now. I can't wait to tell him. Thank you for bringing her into our lives. I wonder if I should throw a party to show her off."

"Mischa!"

"Hush you, and give me your iPad." Mischa all but snatched it from Cassidy's handbag. She began tapping on the screen.

"Tell me again why you know my password?" Cassidy grumbled as she watched Mischa commandeer her tablet.

"Because you forget every password you make up," Mischa said and then handed the tablet back to her. "There you go. You now have Aiden Darrow's first book on your iPad for you to read." She turned her attention back to her salad, pursed her lips at her choice, then stole something else off Cassidy's plate to eat instead. "Read it. If you don't shed a tear you're a heartless bitch."

Cassidy stared at the book cover now dominating her screen. She ran her finger over Aiden's name. "She *was* just a neighbor." She didn't know if she was trying to convince Mischa of that fact or herself.

"Last night you were singing the praises of this woman to me more than I have ever heard you wax lyrical about some woman you are bedding." Mischa snagged a piece of Cassidy's fruit. "Admit it, you like her."

Cassidy nodded. "She's come to my rescue twice and fed me, of course I like her."

Mischa eyed Cassidy furtively. "She watches the show too."

"She told me she was familiar with my work."

"So you're okay if I invite her to tour the sets?"

"Knock yourself out in your search for gargoyles."

Mischa chuckled darkly. "I so knew you were listening to us."

Cassidy leveled her with a hard stare as Mischa began reaching for her dessert. "Aren't you due back on set soon?"

Before Mischa could argue, her name was called out by the director. Cassidy gave her a toothy smile and waved her away. Mischa rose and settled her priestess robes about her.

"It's creepy how you do that. We'll talk more when I drive you home tonight," she said.

"Oh joy," Cassidy muttered, watching as Mischa sauntered away before turning her attention back to the book downloaded on her iPad. The cover showed two women, hands reaching out to try to draw the other back beside her, while an old-fashioned pocket watch kept them apart.

In every life, she'd touch her heart.

Cassidy read the tag line again and let out a sigh. "Aiden Darrow, what are you going to do to me with your words, I wonder? Isn't it bad enough you're way too distracting as it is?"

She pushed the tablet back into her bag, but the temptation to just give in and start reading was almost too much to bear. Cassidy was relieved when she was called back to the set and she could concentrate on her own work and not that of someone else.

Chapter Five

Frustrated on a scene that wasn't going exactly to plan, Aiden spun away from her desk to stare at the pictures on her wall for inspiration. She stretched her neck, grimacing at the loud crack that exploded from her muscles. She checked the time and was startled to see it was nearly three a.m. Time had gotten away from her while she was in the writing groove.

She groaned as she stood, feeling her back complain about her having remained in one position for way too long. She made sure to save her work, closed down her laptop, and padded into the kitchen. The fridge was well stocked, but Aiden picked out a candy bar first and then an apple to at least try to be healthy. She opened the back door and slipped out into her yard.

The night was warm, the air never cooling no matter how dark the sky. Aiden stared at the stars shining brightly above her. She traced the constellations with a knowledgeable eye. For a while, she sat on her deck, eating her snacks and just letting the stars distract her from the words tumbling around in her head.

A voice called out from next door, startling Aiden from her musings.

"I should hate you, you know that?"

Aiden's eyes were drawn to the fence where Cassidy stood peering over. "What are you doing up this late?" Aiden walked over to her so she could keep her voice low. "Aren't you due on set today?"

"I am, in roughly four hours, but you kept me from going to bed."

Intrigued as to where this line of conversation was going, Aiden stepped closer to the fence. She could see Cassidy had been crying. It pained her to see the obvious signs of distress reddening Cassidy's eyes. "Are you okay?" She took a tentative step nearer. Cassidy stood there in her night attire, topped only by a thin pearl gray silk robe that was apparently more for show than actual cover.

"I read your book, *A Pocket Full of Time*." Cassidy's breath caught on a barely restrained sob. "You broke my heart!"

Aiden couldn't help but smile. "I'd apologize, but that *was* kind of the premise of the story."

"Well, you achieved it. I've been bawling like a baby for the last half an hour. I wasn't going to start it tonight, but I couldn't put it down once I'd picked it up. Your story sucked me right in, and then the end?" Cassidy's voice broke. "Damn you, Aiden! I don't cry over books unless it's when Dobby dies!" She dabbed furiously at her eyes with the sleeve of her robe.

"I'm glad you enjoyed it?" Aiden asked hesitantly, watching as Cassidy tried to rein her emotions in.

"I loved it. I've already downloaded the rest of the series on my iPad. If I wasn't expected on set in just a scant few hours, I'd have started in on the second one already."

"Oh, *The Shores of Time*. That was a fun one to write."

"But it will still end up with me crying my heart out because Hollister never gets to be with her true love, right?" Cassidy's heated glare only made Aiden smile.

"Probably. That's the whole idea of the series, after all. Hollister meets her soul mate in a different incarnation in every lifetime she is thrown into."

"God damn you!" Cassidy grumbled, fussing with her robe ties in annoyance.

The robe slipped just enough to give Aiden a glimpse of pale white skin in a shiny lilac negligee. She swallowed hard and quickly averted her eyes.

"You're an excellent writer, and I apologize for not knowing your name straight away." Cassidy leaned closer to the fence. "You deserved my recognition for your writing, both for your books and the films. I've seen all the films you've had a credit on already. You've gotten quite a pedigree."

Aiden felt her cheeks burn under Cassidy's intense gaze. "Thank you. But like I said, you didn't need to know any of it to be a friend."

"At least now Mischa can stop chastising me about my ignorance and tomorrow we can talk about your book." Cassidy let out a heartfelt sigh. "When I'm not falling asleep in the makeup chair and having them bitch about my puffy eyes from *you* making me cry."

Aiden stepped back. "You need to go to bed. Do you have a ride into work?"

Cassidy nodded. "Mischa is coming by to pick me up. Her car isn't as majestic as yours though. I'll have to fight to find a place to put my butt cheeks on that isn't littered with children's toys."

"Thank you for that image before I go to bed myself," Aiden said.

"Don't talk to me about images. I've read your very potent love scenes, Aiden Darrow. There are some paragraphs that are emblazoned in my head tonight."

Laughing, Aiden gave her a quirky bow of gratitude. "Glad to have entertained you in every way this evening."

"Yeah yeah. Like I'm going to be able to sleep now knowing that some of those scenes are what Mischa uses as how-to guides for Joe."

Aiden almost tripped over her own feet. "I did not need to know that!"

"Consider it payback for making me go through a whole box of Kleenex sobbing over your book."

Aiden held Cassidy's gaze, enjoying the spark of mischief that lit her red-lined eyes. "Did you really enjoy it though?" she asked quietly, needing her approval of a story well told.

Cassidy's smile softened. "I loved it. I could only wish to find a lover who'd search for me in every lifetime."

"You'd be worthy of that kind of devotion," Aiden said, meaning every word, both as a fan and as someone slowly getting to see the real woman behind the characters she portrayed.

Cassidy shrugged lightly. "Well, I've not come across it yet."

"Maybe you've been looking in the wrong direction. Maybe the one for you is going to appear out of the blue, as if dropped out of time. They'll search you out and show you how true love works."

Cassidy's laughter was soft and melodious to Aiden's ear. "Are you a hopeless romantic, Aiden?"

"I write romances for a living. What do you think?" Aiden reluctantly took another step back. The warm night air was rustling Cassidy's robe further off her shoulder, and Aiden was getting hard-pressed not to leap the fence and show her just how romantic she could be. She only wished she was half as fearless and confident as the characters she wrote. The moonlight striking Cassidy's pale skin was mesmerizing Aiden in the worst way. She'd seen Cassidy in various stages of nakedness in her work, all artfully done and never explicit. The screen didn't do justice to what Aiden was witnessing in the flesh—literally. She'd been drawn to Karadine Kourt from the start, and knowing the woman that played her was just within her reach was confusing. She felt like she was being made to choose who to desire the most. Karadine was just a character Cassidy portrayed, a heroine Aiden adored. Cassidy was all of that beauty and more.

"I think you need to write a blockbuster film that requires me as its leading lady. I can do most of my own stunts thanks to *The Alchemidens*, within reason of course. I would like it to be a film with more women in the roles than men for a change too."

"I'll see what I can do," Aiden said, knowing she was being teased and thankful for the distraction. "But for now, you need to get some sleep so you don't get fired from the role you already have."

"Crap!" Cassidy hustled back to her home. "Good night, Aiden. Thank you for a very pleasurable evening spent in your company, albeit in print."

Aiden watched her go inside and then turned her attention back to the stars. *She thanks me for keeping her from sleeping and it's my* words *she was wrapped around and not me*. She let out a disgusted sound. Living next door to your ideal woman totally sucked.

❖

"Are my eyes deceiving me? Are you actually reading something between breaks?" Mischa slid into a seat beside Cassidy and peered over her shoulder to see what had Cassidy's rapt attention.

Cassidy spared her a quick glance before her eyes returned to her iPad. "Hush. I just need to read this chapter before I'm called back on set."

Mischa invaded Cassidy's personal space to rest her chin on her shoulder. "You're reading Aiden's book." She squinted at the screen. "Her *second* book?"

"I read the first one last night."

"Which would go a long way to explaining why Charlotte in makeup was complaining about the black smudges under your eyes when we were in there. You pulled an all-nighter."

Sighing at being interrupted, Cassidy made a show of putting aside her pad and turning her full attention to Mischa. "I couldn't put it down so I ended up reading it in one sitting."

Mischa grinned at her. "Addictive, aren't they?"

"I cried my heart out too," Cassidy admitted. "The loss is just so poignant and real."

"I did warn you. Ooh, wait until Aiden hears!" Mischa clapped her hands together like a little child.

"She already knows. She was out in her yard when I finished so I went out to tell her off for making me a blubbering mess."

Mischa laughed. "And what time was this?"

"Late, well, more like way too early, to be honest. I saw her porch light on and her sitting out there so I stormed out preparing to tell her off. Instead I ended up gushing about how much I'd enjoyed it."

"Only you would get it into your head to go confront the author."

"I know. But I just had to talk to her. I at least remembered to put my robe on, as I was only in my nightdress."

Mischa's eyes widened. "You were out in your backyard at night talking to your neighbor while wearing one of those silk handkerchiefs you have the audacity to call sleepwear?"

"They're not that bad!" Cassidy argued, defending her skimpy attire that she knew she brought more for looks than warmth. "I happen to like the feel of silk on my skin."

"You forget, I've shared a room with you at the conventions. You dress to thrill at night, whether you're entertaining a purpose to romp in the sheets or to keep me awake all night telling me about those times."

"Mischa! I never kiss and tell and you know it."

"Face it, Cass. You like pretty things. You're vain enough, and rightly so, to want to look good all the time. And with your body, honey, I understand why."

"I'm not vain." Cassidy flipped her hair in annoyance then fluffed it back into place just so. Mischa laughed at her, and Cassidy felt her defenses rise as she caught herself toying with her hair. "Besides, my wiles were apparently way off target last night if Aiden was anything to go by. She never even stared down my cleavage and I was wearing my racy little gray number. You remember the 'come fuck me' negligee with the saucily positioned lace?" She gestured around her nipples as discreetly as possible.

Mischa tutted softly. "Did you perhaps consider she might have been showing you some respect? Maybe, also, she could actually be shy."

Cassidy gaped. "She writes hot and steamy sex scenes. There can't be anything shy going on there."

"I understand you're used to being adored and fawned over by the adoring public, darling, but your neighbor has a brain. She's a very successful writer, with a string of credits to her name. The last thing she's going to be doing is drooling down your cleavage. She's better than that. Plus, I think she likes you. Not the you we see on the screen but the real Cassidy Hayes. After all, she rescued you from wild sprinklers and fed you. *Then* she drove you to your job when you were stuck. You know the neighborhood you're living in. No one cares who lives next door to them as long as they cut their grass and don't dare park their Mercedes in front of another's driveway."

Cassidy ran her hand nervously through her hair. It was an unconscious action that did little to calm her this time. "The real Cassidy hasn't been seen by many for a long time, Mischa. I'm not sure how to deal with that. Especially now that C.J. Hayes is the one firmly in the spotlight."

Mischa leaned forward and planted a kiss on Cassidy's forehead. "One day at a time, sweetie. You deal with it one day at a time." She leaned back and tapped Cassidy's knee to bring her focus back to her. "Now, let's talk about book one before you're dragged back to that hideous gargoyle they're setting up to dangle you from perilously. So, was I right or was I right?"

Cassidy sighed at Mischa's smug smile. "You are the undisputed queen of 'I Told You So.'"

"Music to my ears. Now, tell me, how fast did you fall for the charms of Hollister Graham?"

The groan Cassidy let out was heartfelt. "From the very first chapter."

"Good, then we're on the same page. Did I ever tell you I named my daughter after this character?"

Cassidy was honestly surprised by that revelation. "No, you didn't. That's incredibly geeky of you."

"It's not like when you finally get a cat you won't do the same. Now, let's talk plot twists."

CHAPTER SIX

A change in the show's shooting had left Cassidy with a rare free morning and a late callback on set. She was used to the rigidity of her schedule directing her day so still found herself getting up at her regular time. She stood in the kitchen drinking coffee, wondering how best to fill her morning. She puttered around the large house aimlessly for a while before giving in to the temptation burning inside her.

She unlocked the front door and cautiously looked out. She checked her front yard and looked up and down the road. Satisfied there wasn't anyone to see her, she fastidiously locked the house up and made her way around to Aiden's home. She knocked briskly on the front door and soon heard the sound of footsteps heading her way. Cassidy was already smiling at how she was going to surprise Aiden with an invitation to breakfast. Admittedly, it was going to be one she just intended paying for at a local restaurant. Cassidy's meager cooking skills didn't even stretch past pouring milk on cereal.

A pretty blonde opened the door and just stared at Cassidy for a long moment.

"Christ, I thought Aiden was delusional when she said who her new neighbor was." She stepped back and waved Cassidy inside. "She wasn't lying when she said the television didn't do you justice either."

Cassidy enjoyed the thrill of hearing Aiden found her attractive. She tried to be nonchalant, but she was genuinely pleased. She followed after the woman who led her into the kitchen.

"Aiden will be down in just a minute. Apparently, I kept her up all night."

Cassidy's steps faltered.

"I've had to drag her out of bed this morning and threaten her to put something decent on before we go out."

Cassidy was aware that her smile was now frozen to her face. She had a moment of sheer panic. She hadn't recalled at their meal Aiden mentioning she had a girlfriend. She cast a curious gaze over the blonde who was looking very sporty in her crop top and three-quarter-length leggings. Her honey colored hair was tied high on her head in a ponytail.

"I'm Karen," she said as she walked around the kitchen getting juice and a glass with an obvious knowledge of where everything was kept. "You're CJ, right?"

"Cassidy outside of work." Cassidy accepted a glass of orange juice but wasn't quite sure what to do with it. Should she stay and see what was obviously going to be a post-coital Aiden interacting with her girlfriend? Or maybe she could leave before Aiden came downstairs and spare herself watching the two of them be love's young dream.

Aiden walked into the kitchen before Cassidy could take a step either way. When she saw what Aiden was wearing, there was a part of Cassidy that was thankful she had procrastinated. Aiden wore a dark T-shirt that showed off her broad shoulders and revealed her toned arms. She had a pair of black tracksuit pants on and brightly colored Nikes on her feet. Cassidy couldn't tear her eyes away from how sexy Aiden looked in her sports gear.

"Cassidy? Good morning." Aiden's smile of welcome was warm. Karen held out a glass of juice for her and Aiden swallowed it down in just a few gulps.

"Slow down. You'll choke yourself, and I'm not extending your deadline," Karen said.

Aiden wiped at her mouth. "You're the reason I'm late this morning. If you hadn't wanted me to work on my story all night then you shouldn't have sent me an e-mail picking out a plot point I'd missed."

"I didn't expect you to work on it so that when I arrived this morning, you were running late for our Zumba class. You know that once those kids of mine are dropped off at school it's strictly mommy time."

Aiden picked up a banana and peeled it. "I'm ready now. We'll be there in plenty of time. Don't worry." She took a big bite from the fruit. Around the mouthful, she spoke to Cassidy. "Our class doesn't start for another hour. Karen is always determined that once she has me in the gym she can drag me through every warm-up session going before we hit our class."

Cassidy's head was reeling. Karen was Aiden's editor. She hadn't been here last night rolling in the sheets with Aiden. Instead, she was here to drag Aiden out for some exercise of a different kind. Cassidy had to admit she was surprised by Aiden's choice.

"You don't strike me as the Zumba type, Aiden."

Karen laughed while Aiden just shrugged.

"No, I didn't think so either, but a writer's job can be very sedentary. I don't need my waistline spreading so when Karen invited me to a class, I agreed. I figured I wouldn't like it and she'd leave me to pound the treadmill like I intended."

Karen interrupted. "But instead she loved it. You should see all those women in the class falling over themselves trying to get her attention."

Cassidy was amused at Aiden's blush.

"Karen, quit it. You know that's not true. I just kind of stick out because I'm not as girly as the rest of you getting your groove on."

"It's a pity you're hidden away with the mommy brigade and the exercise obsessive straight girls. Because, with your moves, sweetie, you'd have the lesbians flocking to your side to see what other moves you can bust out on them."

Aiden scoffed at her, obviously embarrassed. She deliberately turned back to Cassidy. "Why aren't you at work, Cassidy? Do you need a ride? We can drop you off on our way."

"No, I was just…being neighborly. I thought I'd drop by, see how you were, and maybe see if I could take you to breakfast. I didn't realize that in between writing amazing stories you also trip the light fantastic."

Aiden was busy grabbing herself a bottle of water from the fridge. "Thursday is my Zumba morning. It wakes me up."

"Which is more than I could do this morning," Karen said under her breath.

Aiden deliberately ignored her. "And it makes me happy. Everyone should do something that makes them happy for the rest of their day."

Cassidy agreed. Which, she was finally admitting to herself, was why she had sought out Aiden's company. She was disappointed Aiden was already otherwise engaged.

"I'd better leave you to it. I'd hate for you not to be properly warmed up for your class." Cassidy took a step and found Aiden standing right in front of her. She hadn't seen her move. Aiden's closeness stole Cassidy's breath away.

"I'd invite you along, but from what you've shared with me, exercise isn't something you do unless it's expected for the job."

"It's sweaty and energetic. I prefer those situations to arise in a more pleasurable form of exercise that is less public." Cassidy grinned at Karen's burst of laughter. She couldn't help herself; she tugged at the waistband of Aiden's pants. "I'll try to catch you another time." She looked over her shoulder at Karen. "A pleasure to meet you."

Karen looked at her enviously. "I just wish I had your figure, then I wouldn't have to be getting all hot and bothered to keep my shape in shape."

"You look beautiful, my dear," Cassidy said sincerely. "I'm sure your husband...?" Karen nodded and Cassidy felt a strange sense of relief. "I'm sure he thinks you're just perfect as you are."

"What about me?" Aiden made a show of flexing her arm to display her muscle.

Cassidy indulged in the chance to sweep her gaze blatantly all over Aiden's body. "Who knew writers could be so buff?" She stared a little too long into Aiden's eyes until a rising flush colored Aiden's pale cheeks.

"Aiden, we need to go. You're not getting out of at least ten minutes' warm-up on a stationary bike."

Cassidy stepped back reluctantly. "Have a good morning. Be careful not to pull any necessary muscles."

"Do I get a rain check on that breakfast?"

Cassidy turned back from the front door. "Maybe, if you perhaps want to cook it for me?" Cassidy couldn't help but hope.

"Sneaky, very sneaky." Aiden's eyes narrowed at her with humor. "I see how your mind works. I think, if you had your way, I'd be chained to the kitchen just feeding you constantly."

Cassidy prayed her eyes wouldn't give her thoughts away. *It wouldn't be just the kitchen I'd chain you in, Aiden.*

"Well, on that thought to keep in mind all day..." Karen pushed Aiden out of her house after Cassidy. "You, me, Zumba!"

Cassidy waved them off and slinked back to her house. She locked and bolted the door then leaned against it. She envied Aiden's ability to just go where she pleased and do what she wanted. Cassidy wished for that part of her life back again. She shoved away from the door with a sigh. She began singing to herself, dancing a little as she toured her way around the rooms that suddenly seemed too small and enclosing. This wasn't her real home. That was something else she'd had to leave behind along with the life she'd once lived. She sighed as she continued her dance.

I wonder if Denny's delivers.

❖

The rest of Cassidy's working week sped by so indecently fast that she didn't realize it was nearly the weekend until Mischa brought it to her attention.

"I have a date tomorrow." Mischa waved her phone in Cassidy's face as she joined her in the costume department to get changed. "I've palmed the kids off on Joe so I can visit with one fair Aiden Darrow."

Cassidy couldn't stop her head from whipping up at Mischa's announcement. She then tried to appear nonchalant about it, but from Mischa's bright smile directed at her, she knew it was too late. "You're really bringing her for a tour of our sets? Are you sure she's not just being polite and accepted so as not to hurt your feelings?

She worked on the film *Thornmere*, for heaven's sake. Our church walls have to pale in comparison to the grandeur they conjured up for that film's castle. The set designs alone won an Oscar."

"She's a fan of the show, I tell you. Her eyes lit up on our set like my Theo's do when he's in the candy aisle at the grocery store. You should have seen her checking out the seat of my power."

Cassidy snorted. "I hate to burst your bubble, Priestess, but your magic plinth is powered by a battery pack run by George the electrics wiz." She slipped out of her long duster jacket and handed it over to a hovering aide who was trying to be inconspicuous as they talked.

"Do not make fun of my power base. You forget I've seen you trussed up like a Thanksgiving turkey with your harness and your wires as they help you do your mystical ninja stunts."

"That harness chafes too," Cassidy grumbled and shook out her legs gingerly. "It's murder on a new bikini wax."

"You should get your new neighbor to take a look at that for you." Mischa took off her headdress and shook her hair out with a grateful sigh. She missed the dirty look Cassidy shot in her direction.

"You know I've sworn off romantic pursuits for a while."

"Yes, I know, but Aiden's very cute. She wouldn't be like your usual women that you toy with for a while until you get bored with their empty conversation and move on for pastures new."

"I'm not that bad!"

"You haven't been with anyone long enough to ever pick a tableware pattern with."

"Maybe I'm happy enough eating off paper plates and out of Chinese cartons for now." She tugged off her boots with a disgruntled growl. She didn't want to be discussing her love life with Mischa. Mischa was a happily married woman who wanted everyone to have the same hearts and flowers view of life.

"Keep telling yourself that, Cass, but sooner or later, you're going to find a keeper. I just hope you're ready for that day because when the right one comes along you won't know what hit you. I should know. Been there, done that, and chosen the china for the dining room table."

Cassidy looked up from her feet at Mischa who was shimmying out of her priestess gown. "You are so disgustingly smitten with Joe. You make my teeth ache with how sweet you are on each other."

"He's my soul mate. I love him. He loves me. You need someone like that, someone who'll be by your side through everything."

"I don't want anyone having to deal with my 'everything' at the moment."

"But one day you will. Just don't frighten her off now because you think you're not worthy of having someone in your life. For *Cassidy*, not C.J. Hayes the actress, but Cassidy, the woman who should not be putting her life on hold for anything or anyone."

Cassidy nodded but she was distracted by the sound of her phone she had hidden away in her costume. She began shaking as she recognized the number on her screen belonging to Detective Whitmeyer who was in charge of her case.

"What has he done now?" Cassidy asked, dreading whatever Whitmeyer was going to report.

"Ms. Hayes, we were informed an hour ago that Bernett had been leaving threatening messages on *The Alchemidens* Twitter account. We've been in contact with the owner of the account. Apparently, it's one of your bosses?"

"Yes, Claude Saunders. He wanted to keep it in the family so there were no spoilers posted."

"I thought I recognized the name. He's the boss who knows of your situation. He got in touch with us immediately when the posts started appearing. He's been deleting them and stopping Bernett from posting any more. Trouble is, Bernett just keeps making up new names for himself and posting what he pleases."

Cassidy felt Mischa settle down beside her to unashamedly listen in on the conversation. Cassidy switched the phone to speaker so Whitmeyer was loud and clear for her.

"What's he posting this time?" This wasn't the first time Bernett had used social media to menace Cassidy into taking notice of him.

"You really don't need—"

"Detective, please?" She heard Whitmeyer sigh and rustle some paper so she knew he obviously had all the messages printed out for evidence. A ding on her phone signaled she had a text. Cassidy opened it with trepidation. It was a screen shot of one of the postings.

C.J. Hayes the police won't stop me from finding you bitch no matter where you hide away I will find you and you'll learn who you belong to.

Cassidy stared at the screen. "He's impressive. All that anger condensed into one hundred and forty characters." She read the following Tweets where the language got cruder and more explicit in what exactly he intended to do to her. Cassidy didn't need to read any further. She'd lived long enough with his threats hanging over her.

"We've got one of our IT guys overseeing the site to help clear these type of comments off the page before your real fans read them. Something about trigger words that cause the Tweet to be automatically blocked? Anyway, it will save Claude sitting up all night policing the net for you," Whitmeyer said.

Cassidy was thankful for that. She'd tried to keep the fact she had a stalker out of the press so as not to fuel Bernett's obvious desire for recognition of his name alongside hers.

"We'll see if we can trace him through these messages. I hate to say it, Ms. Hayes, but this bastard has quite the talent in stalking you by any means."

Cassidy agreed. Bernett was blatantly violating the restraining order she had placed on him. If the police ever caught up with him, Bernett stood no chance of ever being given parole. She'd be free of him finally. *If* they could just catch him.

"I'll keep you posted on what's happening, Ms. Hayes. Your boss has been doing a great job of clearing him off the second he posts his stuff. You might want to send him a bottle of whatever he favors."

Cassidy had to smile at that. "I'll be sure to do that, Detective. And I'll do all that and more when you and your men stop Bernett for me."

"I'm a single malt man, don't forget. Sorry to have to spoil your evening with this kind of news, but I promised I'd keep you informed."

Cassidy thanked him and they said their good-byes.

"I'd be happier if you just moved in with us," Mischa said, draping an arm around Cassidy's shoulders and pulling her close.

"It's not safe for me to do that. I won't put your family in danger because of him."

"But *you're* part of our family and I hate to think of you going through all this without someone by your side."

Cassidy appreciated Mischa's words and sentiment, but until she felt safe again, Cassidy felt she was best on her own.

❖

With great care, Adam Bernett ran his fingertips over the flowers lying in their pristine white florist's box. The roses were blood red, looking unbelievably bright nestled amid the pale tissue paper. He rearranged a few blooms until everything looked just right. They had to be perfect for C.J. Maybe now she would see what she meant to him when she received these. Red roses meant love, after all. He looked up at the photographs he had tacked to his motel room wall. He mourned the loss of the hundreds he'd lost when the police had raided his home and taken apart his shrine. He'd narrowly missed being caught when they were ransacking his place. Because of them, he'd had to skip town for a while until they forgot about him again. Which they would because he kept his distance from his beloved like a good boy. Never getting too close to the woman he adored and worshipped, though it killed him to be apart from her. And he knew she missed him.

But now he was back. He had tried to stay away, but C.J. Hayes was like a siren call to his blood. Maybe if he'd manned up and approached her earlier in their relationship they'd be together now like he'd dreamed of. Instead he'd sent her fan mail. Then, as he'd fallen more deeply for her, love letters proclaimed his devotion. He knew she felt it too. She was never seen with a man on her arm. She even misdirected the press by insinuating she was a lesbian. Adam knew that was to hide their growing relationship from prying eyes.

He'd tried to see her before, but there was always someone who stopped him from getting near. He'd been escorted off the damned studio lot more times than he cared to remember. It made him furious. As the memories engulfed him, Adam's hand tightened around one of the roses. He squeezed it maliciously as the anger built inside him. The savage sting of a ragged thorn dug into his palm. He watched impassively as his blood dripped onto the roses. Its red mingled amid the petals as if it were one and the same. He liked that analogy. It was true; he'd bleed a thousand times for C.J.

However, while he'd been poring out his heart to her, she'd had him served with that restraining order. Then somehow she'd managed to cost him his job, which was infuriating because that had kept him on or around the lot where she worked. He'd become ostracized from the studios and the entertainment business as a whole while they branded him a stalker. How he hated that label. It belittled all and everything he felt for C.J. Hayes. Adam crushed the already ruined rose further then littered the box with the bloodied petals.

She'd been his from the first moment he had laid eyes on her. He'd followed her every performance and then physically followed her much more closely. After she'd again stated she was single and a lesbian, he just couldn't let her live that lie any more. He'd managed to break into her apartment and left her that message to leave her in no doubt as to who she belonged to. But C.J. leaving her home and disappearing completely hadn't been something he'd bargained for.

So now he played the waiting game. Sooner or later, he'd pick up her scent again and be lead right to her door. Until then, he'd keep sending her proof of his love so she knew he hadn't left her like she'd abandoned him. He'd been deliberately playing with the studio to garner her attention. He believed that had to draw her out from where she was hiding. Besides, she couldn't remain hidden for much longer.

The show needed publicity for its new season, and she was its leading lady after all. He'd been hoping to tease her out with his messages on the sites the show ran. His heartfelt words managed to capture all he was feeling, and he was certain they would be brought to her attention. He felt she'd appreciate the romance of it all because he had left his feelings Tweeted for all to see. But he only needed C.J. to see them. He needed her to see him and him alone now. He'd come back for her. She wasn't alone anymore.

He tucked the carefully composed card in among the flowers. He'd wait until the time was right to deliver these. He'd noticed a new guy at the studio gates being trained. He wouldn't know who Adam was like the rest who ordered him away on sight. Adam didn't resemble the man they had on their watch lists anymore. He'd just wait a few more days and then deliver the flowers when he felt their appearance would say more than he ever could.

Adam pressed his bloody fingertips to his lips and transferred the kiss to the card. He hoped she got his message loud and clear this time. He was through waiting on her. They were meant for each other, and he was coming for her, ready or not. He smiled as he mouthed the words on the card:

Violets are blue, roses are red,

If I can't have you then you're better off dead.

CHAPTER SEVEN

Curiosity plagued Cassidy all day Saturday. She had counted at least four times where she'd almost picked up her phone to text Mischa to ask how her "date" was going. She had chickened out each time before pressing the send button. She knew Mischa would have teased her with something about being a nosy neighbor. Cassidy bristled at the thought. *Neighbor.* That really was all Aiden was, just a neighbor Cassidy had shared a meal with, ridden in her fancy car, and cried all over her stories.

"I'd just be inquiring as to how my best friend's day was going," she reasoned aloud with herself. "A text that says '*Did the kids have fun swimming?*' Or '*Hi, just checking that no one drowned today. And wondering what you two did on an empty set, seeing as there is no filming again until Monday.*'" Cassidy groaned into her hands. "I'm certain she'd buy that as just idle curiosity."

Embarrassed by her pathetically apparent need to know something that wasn't any of her business, Cassidy threw herself onto the sofa to work up a good sulk. Within a minute, she had picked up her phone again. She was used to Mischa texting her on and off all weekend checking she was okay. It was something she had done regularly since Cassidy had moved. It normally drove her insane, but today she missed the intrusion. Cassidy flung herself on her back and stared at the ceiling. *If Aiden had wanted a more detailed tour of the set, she could have just asked me. I'd have been happy to show her around.* Cassidy knew that was what had hurt the most. Aiden hadn't let Cassidy see her interest but had taken Mischa up on her offer instead. Although, Cassidy had to admit, no one really had a chance to say no where Mischa was concerned.

"Especially when she blatantly fawned all over poor Aiden like some cheap hussy in heat." Cassidy snatched up her script for the coming week and begrudgingly reached for her reading glasses. She was vain enough not to want to admit to needing them but smart enough to know she had very little choice about having to wear them. Not if she wanted to read something with writing that couldn't be digitally enlarged.

The sound of a text arriving eventually broke through the silence. Cassidy was distracted enough by what the writers had in store for Karadine in the next episode that she only paid half a mind to her phone as she picked it up. She looked at the photo she'd been sent. It was a shot of Aiden being fed a big piece of pizza by Holli, Mischa's three-year-old daughter. Five-year-old Theo was stuffing his mouth full while sitting on Aiden's lap. The message accompanying it said, *"She's a sucker for kids, so divorcing Joe and moving her right in!"*

Cassidy stared at the image far longer than necessary, but she couldn't seem to tear her eyes from it. Aiden looked like she was having fun with Mischa and Joe's cute offspring hanging off her. Cassidy debated what to text back that wasn't dripping in jealousy. Jealousy she couldn't for the life of her explain right now. She settled on *"Mazel tov!"* before putting her phone aside with a sigh.

Forty minutes later, another text sounded, and Cassidy lurched for her phone. This time it was a photo of Joe posing beside Aiden's car. Cassidy knew that meant just one thing. The Ballantyne clan were right next door. She pushed her script pages aside and stood up slowly, deliberately trying to calm her suddenly racing pulse. Lastly, she removed her glasses. She checked her appearance in the hallway mirror and swept a hand through her hair making sure it was perfect. Then, putting on her game face, she stepped out to face her audience.

❖

Cassidy couldn't miss the sound of Joe's deep voice enthusing over Aiden's car. She purposely draped herself decorously on the fence, just watching them all.

"Mischa, I think Joe is looking to trade you in for a racier model." She was thrilled to witness the smile that lit up Aiden's face when she heard her voice.

"Hey, Cassidy. Joe's just checking out my baby." Aiden brushed her fingertips over a car panel and Cassidy almost shivered in response.

"I know. I've just received a text showing me that. Thank you, Mischa, for keeping me up to speed on your play date today."

Mischa just grinned at her knowingly. Cassidy barely resisted the urge to scowl at her.

"Aunt Cass!" Theo yelled. He and Holli ran toward the fencing. Holli banged into it when she didn't stop in time. They both beamed up at her regardless.

"Theo, Holli, how are you, my darlings? Have you been good for Mommy today?"

"We went swimming, and then we had pizza with Mommy's new friend, and Aiden writes books but not ones that Mommy can read to us." Theo managed to get his news out all in one breath.

"Apparently, my not having written *Green Eggs and Ham* is something of a grave disappointment," Aiden said. She grinned as Holli came racing back over to her and crashed into her knees, gripping onto her jeans and swinging slightly.

Cassidy couldn't help but smile at Aiden's obvious enjoyment of the crazy family surrounding her. She noticed the light in Aiden's eyes dim a fraction and her shoulders dip when Joe called everyone together to leave Aiden in peace. Mischa's hug lasted a little too long for Cassidy's liking again, but Aiden got hugged just as long by Joe so she kept a hold of her tongue. Theo and Holli gave out lots of hugs and kisses. Cassidy was treated to her own over the fence from them all too. Mischa's whispered, "She's a sweetheart. You might want to find out how much," was delivered along with a swift hug and kiss on the cheek. Joe nearly smothered her in his warm hug. Their leaving was boisterous and noisy but swift with the ease of practice of corralling kids and getting Mischa to shut up long enough to get in the car.

Cassidy wondered what was going through Aiden's head as she waved them off and then stood, hands stuffed deep in her pockets, watching the car go for much longer than was necessary.

"I'm betting you feel you've gone deaf now they're gone," Cassidy remarked cheekily. She knew all too well the volume of the Ballantynes was sometimes overwhelming.

"It was nice," Aiden said softly before turning around to her.

"You obviously don't come from a large family."

Aiden's eyes dropped. "I grew up in a series of group homes or foster placements. It was kind of like having a large family. It was just never really one of your own. I had to wait a long time before I was adopted. You learned to tune out the noise of the other kids. Today it was nice to hear them."

Cassidy felt her heart clench in sympathy. "Oh, sweetheart," she breathed, but Aiden shook her head to stop her.

"It made me who I am today, right?" Her eyes turned momentarily back to the road. "Today was fun though. It was nice to be included in a family like theirs. Even at my age, it felt good to be a part of that again." Aiden shook herself briskly as if ridding herself of the melancholy clear in her voice. "So"—she walked over to where Cassidy stood staring at her over the fence—"how did your day go?"

I spent it thinking of you the whole time, but I daren't admit that because of what it could mean. But seeing the loneliness in your eyes just now tore gaping holes right through my chest and has left me bleeding. If you come any closer I'm going to want to hold you, and I don't think you're ready for that, and I know I'm certainly not.

"I was studying my lines for next week's shoot. An actress's weekend is never her own."

"Well, your successful career shows your dedication. And *The Alchemidens'* popularity is proof enough too."

Cassidy was charmed. "That's not all on my shoulders though. Mischa brings the headline name to the show."

"But it's Karadine Kourt who carries a lot of the action and the hero's mantle."

Cassidy narrowed her eyes playfully at her. "You're more of a fan than you led me to believe, Aiden."

"It's a very well written show. I can appreciate talent."

Cassidy smiled at the non-committal comment. They both jumped when Aiden's phone rang out. Aiden grabbed it from her pocket and made a face at the caller ID.

"It's Karen. She's probably calling to make sure I'm putting my imagination to good use this weekend instead of playing hooky with a magical priestess and her wild and rambunctious family." Aiden made a gesture of her having to take the call and Cassidy reluctantly left her to it.

Once back inside her house, Cassidy looked again at the photo of Aiden with the children, and this time could clearly see the enjoyment on her face. Cassidy hated the thought of Aiden growing up without a family to love her. Cassidy knew though, whatever Aiden's upbringing had been like, it hadn't held her back from pursuing her dreams.

She typed out a quick message to Mischa. *"Thank you for the photos today. They were all wonderful. I'm all tucked in for the day here."* Knowing she probably would have been wiser to have just kept quiet, Cassidy set her phone aside and chose not to care. Seeing Aiden happy made her happy, and Cassidy was in need of some joy from any source. She sat down and picked up her script again. After a moment, she laid it aside and picked up her iPad to continue reading Aiden's book instead.

CHAPTER EIGHT

Twenty-seven years ago

Aiden's face was pressed up against the windowpane. From her bedroom window, she could clearly see the main road. She'd been silently watching as one of the other children in the house was going out to play with his friends. Some of the luckier ones were leaving to spend the day with prospective families that afternoon. Aiden's sigh steamed up the glass. She was seven years old and hadn't found a permanent home to stay in. She'd overheard one of her previous foster fathers talking about her at the last home she was in. Aiden was a "hard sell" child because she was unnaturally quiet and not as outgoing or gregarious as the other children looking to be adopted. She'd been moved not long after to live with her new foster parents, Frank and Trudy Woods.

Aiden rubbed at her arm and winced at the bruise that lay under her sleeve. Families also didn't want to adopt little girls who got into fights either. This latest bruise was from the known bully of the house. Thomas was a much older boy, one with as little a chance of being taken in as Aiden apparently had but for totally different reasons. Aiden disliked him immensely. He kept stealing from Aiden's meager collection of books that she hoarded like gold.

She'd searched everywhere for him just last week and found him ripping one of her books apart page by page. He was trying to light a fire in the yard between their house and the one next door. Aiden had been furious as she mourned the loss of yet another of her books to his pyromania. She'd heard that particular word used by Frank too, along with the comment that one night Thomas was surely going to burn down the home with them all in it if he wasn't straightened out soon. Aiden hadn't slept a night through since.

Her missing book was lying in the fire, its cover curling in the flames. The story was being burned away, precious words that Aiden used to escape in were being lost in every curl of smoke rising into the air. In that moment, Aiden hadn't cared that he was many years older than her and so much bigger. She'd thrown herself at him, swinging wildly and punching and kicking any part of his skinny frame she could hit. He'd beaten her down easily, splitting her lip open and twisting her arm to leave a wicked bruise that was now still tender to touch. She hadn't explained to Frank what had happened.

There was no point; he wouldn't really understand. She wouldn't get her book back, and that was all that mattered to her. Only her foster mother Trudy had asked with any understanding so Aiden had told her the truth. Trudy wasn't like the other foster parents Aiden had been passed around to; she listened. She was the only person Aiden trusted. She was the one person in Aiden's life who seemed to truly care what Aiden was going through.

Every second Saturday of the month, Trudy took Aiden out from the home and they went for a treat. There were usually a total of four children in the Wood house, and each child had a day that was classed as theirs alone. It usually meant something connected to sports for the boys who went with Frank to a local game. Second Saturday was the highlight of Aiden's life. Her whole world revolved around it.

School was a means to an end. The home was just a place to live in until they bundled her off somewhere else. The revolving door system of foster care made Aiden very unsettled. But every second Saturday was like Christmas and birthdays all rolled into one. She always dressed for the occasion in her best jeans and her cleanest shirt. She also made sure her sneakers were clean so she looked her best and didn't let Trudy down.

She recognized Trudy's car when it pulled up outside. Aiden took off at a run. She clattered down the stairs, jumping over the last three, and all but flew out the door. Trudy was laughing at her as Aiden dove into the car. Aiden fought to get both her seat belt on and close the door behind her, all at the same time.

"Hey, sweetie. Slow down there. We have plenty of time," Trudy said, still smiling. She directed the older kids who were unloading the car full of groceries to be careful with the eggs. Saturday morning was the week's grocery run. But this Saturday afternoon was all Aiden's.

"Hi." Aiden finally buckled herself in and flashed Trudy a smile with a missing tooth.

"Please tell me that tooth came out on its own and not because Thomas took another book." Trudy fixed Aiden with a look. "You had it last night if I remember."

"It was loose so I wiggled it out. Thomas hasn't found where I have my books hidden from him now."

"You still hiding them in the laundry room?"

"He won't ever go in there," Aiden said.

"You're a smart girl."

Aiden just shrugged that off, impatiently watching the groceries being carried into the house. She only relaxed when one of the kids slammed the trunk down and banged on the roof to signal they were done. "What are we seeing today?"

"The cinema is showing an older movie. I think you might enjoy it."

Aiden wriggled excitedly. "I can't wait. You always pick the best movies for me."

❖

The cinema was Aiden's favorite place of all to go. She stuck like glue to Trudy's side so as not to lose sight of her among all the other patrons. Aiden was terrified of being left behind. She never asked for popcorn or candy, but Trudy always shared whatever she brought. She told Aiden she couldn't possibly eat it all herself so always seemed to need Aiden's help to finish her sweets.

They found their seats and Aiden settled in.

"How old is this film, Trudy?" she asked, mindful of eating one gummy bear at a time instead of piling a handful into her mouth all at once. Aiden believed all good things should be savored.

"It came out in 1977."

Aiden scoffed. "That's really old. I wasn't even born then!"

The second the lights went down, Aiden hushed and sat perfectly still. Her eyes were glued to the screen ready for whatever story she was going to see played today. A fanfare of music assailed her ears as the movie began, and Aiden was proud of herself that she could read all the words that were scrolling up the screen. Her eyes widened as a huge star field was unveiled and then the biggest space ship she had ever seen seemed to fly right over her head and out across the screen. Her mouth fell open, and for a time she even forgot to blink. A silent "whoa" slipped from her lips as a space battle began.

Aiden was totally spellbound. She was transported to a galaxy far, far away, away from the less than perfect life she existed in. Captivated, she soaked up all the sights and sounds from these brave new worlds.

When the film finished, they stayed behind to sit through the credits as always. Aiden loved hearing the music but was also reluctant to leave the safety of the cinema. She wished desperately that she could take a step through the movie screen and enter the worlds she had just seen and never have to come back. Maybe, in whatever strange new world she found herself in it would be better than where she was now. She could have the chance to be anything she wanted to be there and not just be seen as Aiden the orphan. Maybe she wouldn't be bullied anymore and there'd be someone who would care enough to give her a home where her books were always safe.

"Did you enjoy the movie, Aiden?" Trudy asked from beside her.

Aiden threw her arms up into the air. "Best movie ever!"

Trudy grinned. "There are two more movies to this story."

Aiden's eyes grew large. "Really? There's more? Can we see them?"

"I'll make sure we can." Trudy shook the loose popcorn from her dress as she stood to leave.

"Thank you." Aiden slipped her hand into Trudy's as they left the room. "I want to do that, Trudy."

"Do what, sweetheart?"

"Tell stories so big they have to put them on a movie screen so everyone can see all the pictures I keep in my head. Can I do that?"

Trudy squeezed her hand. "I think you'd be fantastic at it. You'll have to study hard and practice all your spellings though."

Aiden made a face at that. "But then I can write about heroes and princesses?"

"You can write whatever is in your heart, little Aiden. You can show everyone what you're best at."

"No one can ever take away the stories in my head, Trudy. That's the safest place I know for them."

Trudy made the kind of sad face that Aiden didn't quite understand. Then she leaned down to plant a kiss on Aiden's forehead. "You're such a good girl. Can I treat you to an ice cream?"

Aiden considered this for a moment. "Is there a book written about this film?"

"I'm sure there is."

"Can I put the ice cream money toward that, please? I have some money saved from my chores. I'd really like the book instead."

"It's your birthday soon, isn't it?" Trudy guided Aiden through the cinema foyer and back outside toward the ice cream parlor that was conveniently placed next door.

"Yes, next month. I'll be eight."

"How about my gift to you is the book you want and you get ice cream today to make up for the wait?"

Aiden eagerly agreed. "Two treats?" She swung Trudy's hand in her own. "I love Second Saturdays best of all."

❖

The earlier foster homes Aiden had been placed in had not been entirely successful. She'd been passed from one home to another until she was finally placed in the more stable household of Trudy and Frank. Initially, Aiden had been fearful of Frank Woods on sight. All through her first week there she'd followed after Trudy like a little shadow. The whole time she'd been in his presence she'd all but hidden behind Trudy, using her body like a shield. With boys closer to her own age, Aiden didn't have a problem, but older men she was inexplicably frightened of.

It had been hard work for Frank to get her to trust him, but eventually, he won her round. It didn't help that they shared nothing in common. Frank was big on sports, so got on better when there were boys in the house. Aiden couldn't have cared less about anything connected to a bat or a ball. He had no interest in movies, which Aiden was relieved about because that meant Second Saturday was still strictly her and Trudy's treat.

Aiden believed that Frank was the kind of person who'd probably talk through a movie, and she didn't appreciate those kind of people at all. Trudy was always encouraging her to read and write. She championed Aiden to use her imagination and get her stories down on paper. Frank tried instead to get her to quit sticking her nose in a book and get out more in the fresh air. So Aiden took her book outside and sat on the swing set. She'd never heard him laugh so much in all the time she'd known him.

It slowly began to dawn on Aiden that Trudy had been trying to get her husband on board with the idea of adopting her. It wasn't long after she realized this that Aiden overheard a rather curious conversation. She had been coming down the stairs to get a drink and halted mid step when she heard their voices.

"We've had a lot of waifs and strays come over our doorstep, Trudy. What is it about this little girl that makes you feel she's one to keep?"

"She needs us. She needs the stability of knowing that no one is going to come and take her away again. She's constantly expecting to have to just pack up and leave, and I don't want her to. I love that kid. She's special and she's so damn smart when you get her to open up."

Aiden froze on the stairs. Were they talking about her?

"You know the other kids think she's strange as hell."

Aiden sat down on the stairs. *Yes, they're talking about me.*

"She's not strange at all," Trudy said. "She's probably still suffering from being traumatized so young and no one taking the time to help her with it. She had to watch her mother die in front of her when she was barely four years old. She was left with the body for days until someone found the poor little mite. She's been in and out of homes way too much for someone so young. She deserves a family."

"What if the perfect family is out there for her and our adopting her stops her from being in it? Have you thought about that?"

"I love that girl. *We* can be her perfect family," Trudy said. "She's changed so much since she's been here with us. She's come out of her shell a little. And she's clever. She's doing so well at school and she's settled here as much as she can." Trudy's voice softened a little. "Don't think I don't know what you're doing, Frank Wood. Don't you use those devil's advocate techniques on me. I know you like her too."

"I like the fact she kicked Thomas's butt. I barely had to say anything; the shame from bearing the bruises from a little girl are enough for him to carry. I did make it very clear to him that violence would not be tolerated in this house, especially against little girls. He's doing extra chores, and his money will go to Aiden's savings to replace her books he ruined." Frank paused. "I have a few concerns though. She has no interest in boys like the other girls we've had here, and I've seen the fight you have with her trying to get her to wear a dress. She even looks like a boy since you cut her hair the way she asked. What if she's queer?"

Aiden heard Trudy sigh. "Frank, she's eight years old. She's still working out who she is in the world without having to get serious about some silly boy in class. Or some girl, if that's the direction life takes her in. I don't care either way. We just keep raising her the way we are and she's going to turn out just fine, you mark my words. As long as she finds love, I don't care who it's with, boy or girl."

Aiden puzzled over that comment for a while. She was thinking about it a little too much and nearly missed what else was being said.

"So? Are we in agreement about this? Can we keep her?" Trudy's voice sounded happy. Aiden liked that sound. It usually meant dessert.

"She's not a puppy!" Frank said. "We'll have to sit down with her and ask her. She might not want to stay with us. You're a natural with her, but I'm…a little limited in what we can share."

"She likes it when you let her work on the watches you fix."

From her place on the stairs, Aiden nodded. She loved seeing all the tiny innards of the watches laid out. Frank knew how to put them all back together, piece by piece. It was like he was creating an elaborate jigsaw puzzle. The watches always started ticking again when he was finished. Aiden was fascinated by whatever magic he seemed to wield over the cogs and springs, bringing them to life to tell the time again.

"I've got her working on that pocket watch of your father's. She does seem to love that. She's got quite a fascination with the past," he mused.

"See? We can do this. We'll make her *our* daughter."

The sound of that made Aiden excited and nervous all at the same time. She really wanted to be a part of a family, one that she could call her own. And to be chosen was the best feeling Aiden could remember having. She'd been passed around too many times to ever think someone might actually want to keep her. She just hoped she didn't do anything to make them change their minds. Such as being found out listening in on private conversations. She snuck back up the stairs as quietly as she could in the hopes of not getting caught.

❖

Aiden wandered into the kitchen and found Trudy washing the dishes left over from lunch. Without being asked, Aiden picked up the dish towel and began to dry them for her.

"So how much did you overhear us talking about you?" Trudy asked, not turning around.

Aiden never ceased to be amazed at how Trudy seemed to know everything. She squinted at the back of Trudy's head to see if she could spot the eyes one of the other kids said Trudy had there.

"I heard a little, maybe," Aiden hedged, not wanting to get into trouble for eavesdropping. "Do you really want to keep me? I wouldn't have to go to another family anymore?"

"You'd get to stay here with us for as long as you like. Do you think you could be happy here permanently? With me as your mom and Frank as your dad?" She watched Aiden closely for her answer.

Aiden nodded. "I don't remember my real mom. Sometimes I think I might know what she looked like, but it's all jumbled up in my head now. I'd love for you to be my mom, Trudy. I'd really like that a lot." She liked the look that graced Trudy's face when she said that. "You're the only person who doesn't make me feel weird even though I am." She saw the look of chagrin as Trudy recognized Frank's words being repeated back.

"You're not weird, Aiden. You're remarkably creative, and that's what makes you special. That's what gives you that magical place in your head where all those stories of yours reside."

Aiden carefully placed the plates on the table and asked the question that had been niggling at her since she'd heard the word adoption. "If you adopt me though does that mean Second Saturday is no longer our movie treat? Because I really love you and I like Frank loads, but I really like going to the movies and don't want that to stop because you adopt me." She caught her breath after blurting all that out in one go.

Trudy ruffled Aiden's hair gently. "Second Saturday will always be yours, whether you are adopted or not." She laughed at Aiden's exaggerated sigh of relief. "I look forward to going to the movies with you too. Though, sometimes? I wish you'd move a little more because the first few times I thought you'd fallen asleep!"

Aiden grinned. "No, I just like watching and don't need to fidget because it's never boring."

"Your math teacher says you fidget a lot in her class."

Aiden grimaced at Trudy's look. The last parents' night at school had been favorable except for her inability to get through a math class without her mind wandering elsewhere.

"I like writing stories better. Math makes my brain hurt," Aiden said, wrestling with a saucepan to get it all dry.

"You'd better make sure you put that writing of yours to good use, young lady, if it's going to mean you can't ever do your sums right."

"I'll try harder," Aiden promised. "But Miss Taylor's voice is very boring, and she makes me feel sleepy so I have to keep moving to stay awake."

Trudy failed to cover her smile. "So, now that you know we'd like to adopt you, how about I take you to McDonald's for supper? The other kids aren't due back until later so it's just you and me for tonight. If you have any questions at all we can talk about them there."

Grinning, Aiden quickly agreed. "What about Frank?"

"He can make himself a sandwich when he's ready. He's settled in to watch one of the games on TV. That leaves you and I to go and celebrate wanting to be a family." She took the heavy saucepan from Aiden who was struggling with it and placed it on the stove. She reached for her purse. "I'm craving a large serving of celebratory fries."

Aiden considered her next words carefully. "Trudy, what's queer?"

A startled "oh" was her answer. Trudy quickly recovered. "Now, that is a question best dealt with over cheeseburgers and chocolate milkshakes, I think."

Aiden wasn't going to argue with that. Being part of a real family was going to be just fine.

❖

Present day

Sunday afternoon found Aiden seated at her desk staring at the words on her laptop screen. Unfortunately, her concentration wasn't entirely on her new story. Her head was too busy lost in the past. Snapshots of her childhood kept flickering in her memory, dropping her back into a life she had tried so hard to escape. Trudy and Frank had given her love and support, but Aiden had found it hard to be so imaginative in a world that tried its hardest to beat it out of her. Frustrated with herself, Aiden pushed back from the desk, her mood stormy and dispirited.

She barely remembered her mother, a seventeen-year-old girl who had gotten pregnant by a married man who had run off at the first sign of responsibility. Aiden had only just reached her fourth birthday when her mother had accidently overdosed on whatever drug she'd managed to steal the money for that night. Aiden had been found, days later, puttering around the apartment by her aunt who'd come over to demand back money she'd been owed. Instead, she'd gained Aiden. It had started off well. Her aunt had been happy to receive the payments she'd gotten for taking on the responsibility of her niece. The shine on that soon faded when her boyfriend got tired of her always having a kid under foot. So Aiden was placed into care. It was there her sense of loneliness and isolation grew.

Aiden sighed and rubbed at her eyes. Her gaze fell to the framed photograph among all the memorabilia. In it, Aiden stood on the red carpet of a movie premiere, looking handsome in a new suit and tie. At her side was Trudy Wood, looking older and grayer but still the only woman Aiden had wanted by her side for the occasion.

"Oh, Trudy. Didn't we have fun that night?" Aiden shook her head as she remembered surprising Trudy with an invitation to be her "and guest" at the premiere. Aiden had been one of two writers on the script for a small science fiction film that did very well at the box office. Aiden told Trudy that her being at the premiere was a long overdue thank you for all the movies she'd paid for Aiden to sit through. It had been wonderful to see Trudy being as spellbound at the premiere as Aiden had been at her first ever movie.

"I remember how hard you squeezed me when my name rolled up in the credits and how proud you were of me. It was the best night of my life and you were there to share it." Aiden brushed at a piece of dust on the frame. "I really wish you were here now."

Trudy had died just a few years later. While in the hospital, Aiden had taken to reading to her from the story she was working on. Trudy hadn't cared that it was a lesbian romance; she just wanted to know what happened next. She stayed alive long enough to hear the epilogue before succumbing to the breast cancer that had shown her little mercy.

"You were the first person to know about Hollister Graham and *A Pocket Full of Time*. You never got to see I dedicated it to you. I know you're still watching over me. I can hear you sometimes, urging me on and telling me I can do whatever I dream of." Aiden wiped away a tear. "Because I was your little girl no matter how many other children you and Frank looked after. You never treated any of them different from me, but I was your daughter by choice. I was adopted and loved. I couldn't have wished for a better mother than you. I just wish my earlier years hadn't molded me to be so desperate to hide or escape from an overwhelming world. I'm still weird, but it's a weirder world I live in now."

Aiden had to look away from the photograph. Her grief was always too painful to bear where Trudy was concerned. She missed Trudy's calming influence in her life every day.

"Look at all the books I have now." Aiden ran her fingertips over just one of the many bookcases she had crammed with all the books she owned. She touched the precious *Star Wars* book that had been her birthday gift from long ago. It was well worn from being read so many times. Next to it was a more pristine copy Aiden had managed to find years later. But she still only read the one Trudy had given her.

"And these! Look what I added to my collection."

Aiden would always be drawn to the heroes in a story. Thanks to Trudy, her passion for fantasy had been indulged at an early age and she'd been exposed to the sheer magic of those worlds. "I could never have had anything like these as a kid. It was hard enough keeping a book hidden."

The shelves in her writing room were littered with figurines—each statue a talisman she could touch and gain strength from. She had a Superman fixed in his strident pose. A Green Lantern with his magic ring. There was a Captain America, the man who had started off as a weakling but had taken on the hero's mantle to save the world.

"You'd like this one, Trudy. You always had a thing for the underdog." She touched his shield and smiled. "He's one of my favorites too."

Aiden drew strength from all these characters. She had learned most about life from her books and the films she saw. The escape Trudy had given her every second Saturday had helped shape Aiden's future. Trudy had made Aiden's young life bearable by bringing fantasy into it to take Aiden away from her reality. She'd never forget that.

"I wish you were still here, Trudy. You wouldn't believe the heroes we get to have now. Some of them are so very beautiful."

She turned back to stare at one of the posters on the wall. Karadine Kourt, one of the more recent additions to her hero collection. She could see Cassidy clearly in her favorite character's features, but Cassidy was nothing like the fearless fighter Karadine embodied.

Aiden was glad. She liked Cassidy too much as herself.

I may immerse myself in fantasy, but even I can eventually separate the character from the actress. And Cassidy is fascinating enough in her own right. But I'm not sure how well she'd take knowing how much I idolize who she plays on TV.

Aiden figured it was best to keep that information to herself for now. She reached for the white envelope lying on her desk. She flipped it back and forth between her fingertips. Inside was an invitation to Mischa and Joe's wedding anniversary. Mischa had given it to her yesterday with the plea to "Please bring Cassidy with you because we don't trust her to get here alone." Aiden was curious as to whether they had run that idea by Cassidy first. Either way, Mischa had pretty much made sure Aiden couldn't back out. Not that she wanted to. It had been a while since Aiden had made new friends, and Mischa was pushy enough to make sure Aiden stayed in touch. And if she was where Mischa was, usually Cassidy was close by, and Aiden liked the idea of that a little too much.

❖

Cassidy was screening her calls that day. She didn't want to be disturbed while she was memorizing her script. When her cell phone did ring, Cassidy paused to check the screen. She answered it immediately.

"Sorry to disturb you, but I was wondering if you'd received your invitation for Mischa and Joe's party?"

Cassidy's eyes flicked over to where she'd tucked the card into the edge of the room's large feature mirror. Cassidy never failed to look there, so she figured that would be the best place to put reminders.

"I did, Aiden. Mischa all but threw it at me with the instruction of 'You'd better buy me something expensive.'" She could hear Aiden's soft laughter down the phone.

"Mine was handed to me with a little less threat involved. I've been asked to see if you would care to accompany me?"

Cassidy was thankful Aiden couldn't see the face she made at Mischa's blatant meddling. "I can't believe they've roped you into making sure I go."

"Actually, she gave me the excuse because if left to my own devices I might have procrastinated way too long in asking you to please accompany me. If I promise we'll use my car would that make it easier?"

Cassidy closed her eyes at Aiden's query. *Oh, Aiden, like the car is necessary to sweeten the deal of going anywhere with you.*

"I mean, if you want to come with me, that is. I'm sure you could have someone else you'd rather—"

Cassidy interrupted Aiden's nervous rambling. "There's no one else I'd rather turn up with on my arm. Thank you for asking." There was an unmistakable sigh of relief from Aiden that surprised Cassidy.

"That's settled then. Now all I have to do is find a suitable gift for a couple I'm only just getting to know."

"Joe's a wine connoisseur," Cassidy said helpfully.

"Oh, that's great, thank you. Though I wouldn't know one wine from another."

"Not much of a drinker, Aiden?"

"I stayed for six months in a home where the foster father drank a little too much. I lived in fear of his temper and his fists flying. It put me off alcohol for life. For a long while, I couldn't stomach the smell of whiskey if anyone drank it around me. That thankfully eased the older I got." She paused and Cassidy realized that Aiden had probably not wanted to share that quite so openly. She waited, hearing what sounded like Aiden warring with herself. "Besides, as a writer I have such a tenuous hold on reality as it is without adding alcohol to the mix."

Cassidy could hear the self-deprecation in Aiden's quieter tone. She decided to spare Aiden from sympathies. "Oh, you writers are all so melodramatic!" she said and smiled when she heard Aiden's laughter.

"This from an actress?"

"Oh, darling, there's nothing mellow about my dramatics. I'm sure Mischa would be ecstatic with a signed book or two from you. After all"—Cassidy deliberately altered her voice—"you're my favorite author!"

Aiden laughed. "Please tell me Mischa knows you can mimic her so perfectly? That was fantastic!"

"She does know and it pisses her off to no end. Especially when I do it on set and pretend to be her moaning about her costume being too tight after she's just eaten off my plate again."

Still chuckling, Aiden said, "You know, I think I might still have a few first edition copies of *A Pocket Full of Time* and the others. Do you think that would be suitable? I don't want to look like I'm promoting my work at her party."

"Aiden, you'd make her day with a gift like that. A spa day, complete with a champagne lunch at the most expensive club, won't stand a chance against that kind of gift."

"Would Mischa go to a spa?"

"I hope so because that's what I decided to get her."

"Then I'm sure she'll love it, especially if you go with her."

Cassidy loved how diplomatic Aiden could be. There was a loud clanging noise that made Cassidy startle. "What are you doing?"

"Preparing dinner. I'm in the mood for Mexican tonight."

"You're cooking a Mexican meal from scratch?" Unbidden, her mouth began to water.

"Would you like to come over and see how authentic I can make it? I always make too much as you know."

"Well, I'd hate to be a nuisance..." Cassidy said, blatantly lying.

"You'd never be that. An invite is an invite, and it will be nice to have company for a while."

That decided it. "What time do you want me?" There was a long enough pause that Cassidy thought Aiden had changed her mind.

"If you come when you're finished whatever you're doing I can promise pre-meal entertainment and you can graze at the kitchen table while I cook."

Cassidy was up from her seat. "Give me five minutes."

"The front door is unlocked for you. Just come right on in."

Chapter Nine

Working schedules and writing deadlines meant Cassidy didn't get to see Aiden again except as she was racing off to work and Aiden was picking up her newspaper off her drive. All too soon, the night of the party was upon her. Excited for the chance to get out and cut loose, Cassidy applied her more elaborate makeup with a skilled hand. She sat before her mirror in just her lacy underwear. She was in her favorite bright red set of what Mischa called her "barely-there underwear." It complemented the dress Cassidy had chosen to wear. The sparkly dress was the color of rich red wine. It fit Cassidy like a second skin when she eased into it, smoothing it over her hips and centering the neckline to reveal just enough flesh to tantalize. Cassidy checked herself out in her mirror and fussed with her hair until she finally left it hanging loose around her shoulders.

"I hope Aiden appreciates all this," she said then berated herself for even thinking of her. "I do not have time for pursuing my extremely gorgeous looking, if a little geeky, neighbor. Even if she does cook like a dream and is kindness personified." Cassidy eyed herself in the mirror one more time. "No, I can't risk it, and I won't risk *her*."

The sound of the doorbell startled her. She ran down the stairs as best as her tight dress let her but paused before opening the door, ever mindful. She looked through the door's spyhole and was relieved to see Aiden standing outside. She opened the door and was instantly captivated. Aiden took her breath away.

Aiden was dressed in a black suit. It was matched with a crisp black shirt threaded with silver and a matching tie. Cassidy couldn't help herself; she reached out to touch the silver handkerchief peeking from Aiden's breast pocket.

"My, oh my. You're looking mighty handsome for a nerd." Cassidy tweaked Aiden's tie. She couldn't keep her hands off her. She let her fingertips flitter along the length of the tie and then ran them along the edge of Aiden's lapels, feeling the fabric of the suit. Aiden smiled as she let Cassidy's wandering hands take her all in.

"We nerds clean up real well when we're allowed out to mingle with the pretty girls." She held out a box of candy for Cassidy.

"For me?"

"I know it should have maybe been a corsage or something, but I'm getting to know your tastes quite well. So you have candies."

Cassidy's heart melted at the way Aiden was suddenly abashed.

"I mean, I know this isn't a date, but it's a special night and I just wanted to…thank you for accompanying me."

Cassidy placed the candy on the table by the door. "I'll enjoy those immensely as I intend to enjoy your company tonight too."

Aiden's head shot up and she grinned like a child at Christmas. "Now can I tell you how absolutely gorgeous you look?" Her admiring gaze took all of Cassidy in from head to toe.

"I'm very receptive to flattery." Cassidy could feel the heat from Aiden's eyes burning a path upon her skin. She slipped into a lethal pair of red heels and was sure she heard a stifled choke from Aiden. She barely hid her grin.

Aiden stepped back to let Cassidy leave. Out of habit, Cassidy quickly scanned the driveway and the road.

"My car is still in my driveway," Aiden said, catching her looking.

Cassidy closed the door behind her, locking it soundly, and hearing the fading chips of the alarm setting. She readily accepted the crooked arm Aiden held out for her.

"So, how crazy is tonight going to get?"

Cassidy laughed and squeezed Aiden's arm. "It's going to be loud and boisterous. There'll be people you'll want to speak to but a few more you'll want to steer well clear of. There'll be the obnoxious boors and the braggarts. And then the one or two who you'll probably want to stick near all night for fear they'll leave you to fend for yourself in the madness."

"I hope you're offering yourself in that role for me, Ms. Hayes."

"Well, your most devoted fan Mischa, who would kill for that role, will be expected to hang off Joe's arm, seeing as she's the celebrating hostess." Cassidy cringed at what sounded like petty jealousy in her own voice. She hated that she felt that way.

"Mischa said her sister will be there too."

The sudden rise of possessiveness burst through Cassidy like a roaring flame. She tightened her grip on Aiden's arm. "Then you'll have another fan there," she gritted out between clenched teeth. She hoped she looked like she was smiling and not grimacing like she feared. *Where the hell is this urge to yell, "Hands off. She's mine," coming from?*

"Promise me if I start hiding in a corner you'll come to my rescue?"

At the gentle plea in Aiden's voice, Cassidy's ire melted. She leaned her head on Aiden's shoulder.

"I won't leave you to the mercy of the party rabble, I promise." Cassidy was looking forward to being just a face among a crowd of friends tonight. Being left alone made her nervous, but being among strangers made her doubly unsure. Tonight, she'd be in the safest place.

She surreptitiously kept her focus on everything around her once Aiden got them onto the road. Cassidy sat back in her seat with a sigh. "It's a lovely night. They're used to me rolling up fashionably late. Let's take the scenic route there."

Aiden gave her a curious look then shrugged. "Just give me directions and we'll go wherever you please."

Cassidy rested her hand on Aiden's knee. "You're a sweetheart, and Mischa will accuse me of corrupting you, but just go straight over the next set of lights. We'll go a few blocks out of our way and then double back. What's the use of me wearing this dress if I can't make a spectacular entrance in it?"

Aiden laughed beside her. "You're risking Mischa's wrath."

Cassidy just waved a hand dismissively. "The spa day will make up for my being tardy. She's such a lightweight, after a few glasses of champagne, she'll forgive me anything."

"I'll chart our course by your lead, Ms. Hayes." Aiden flashed her a smile.

"Then let us follow the path laid out for us by the stars," Cassidy said but added, "but first, take the second left there on Elm to start us on our journey."

❖

The party was in full swing by the time Cassidy and Aiden arrived. Aiden helped Cassidy from the car and just stood in awe of the house Mischa and Joe lived in.

"It's like a palace," she said, staring at the rooftop and spying a face or two leering down. "Mischa has gargoyles of her own!" Aiden was tickled by this discovery. Cassidy tugged her toward the front door where the rhythmic beat of music and voices were vying for which could be the loudest. Aiden had never lost her sense of wonder at the splendor some people could afford to live in. She was perfectly happy with her own home. It was big enough for her needs, and she felt safe there. But this? Aiden was blown away by the ornate brickwork, the stained glass windows, and the gracefully carved topiary that had hidden the splendid house from view.

"This is just one of their smaller homes," Cassidy said as she led her through the door and literally cut a swath through the partygoers.

Aiden wasn't surprised by how many rushed to Cassidy's side for the ubiquitous air kisses that Aiden found meaningless and false. She craned her neck to see if she could spot the hostess anywhere. Mischa waved to her and made her way imperiously through her guests.

"Aiden, I see she finally let you arrive. What was it this time? A last-minute hair emergency, or could she not find her shoes?" Mischa hugged Aiden tightly and gave her a kiss on the cheek. She pulled back to smooth a hand over Aiden's suit. "You're looking mighty fine tonight."

"We took the long way around to get here. It wasn't like we were dodging the paparazzi so I'm really beginning to think she's fallen for my car."

The humor in Mischa's eyes faded. "Ah yes, well, Cassidy can never be too careful when out and about. You're both here now and that's all that matters." She squeezed Aiden's hand. "Mingle, mingle, and then we'll open the food hall and we can all watch Cass eat us out of house and home."

"I heard that." Cassidy hugged Mischa tightly from behind and kissed her properly on the cheek. "Sorry we're the last to arrive."

Mischa gave Cassidy a look that Aiden couldn't decipher. "You're here now so go say hello to everyone. *The Alchemidens* crew has taken over the seats by the fireplace so you won't miss them. Joe's holding court in the kitchen, and the kids are thankfully well out of the house at a weekend long sleepover. So Mommy Dearest here can partake in a glass or two…or five."

Aiden was still looking around, amazed at the building. "You have a beautiful home."

"Thank you, sweetheart. Cass, how about you go get yourself a drink? Aiden can come pretend with me that some of the more pompous actors and actresses were actually worth inviting, if only for the shallow gifts they brought me." She winked at them both.

Cassidy laughed as she looked to where the bar was set up. "Darling, I'm always worth an invitation."

"Cass, you're always top of my list, empty-handed or not." Mischa linked arms with Aiden. "How about I give this handsome young woman a tour of the house while I pretend to be the welcoming hostess to this rabble?"

Aiden managed to just spare Cassidy a quick look before she was steered away. Cassidy just waved her on with a resigned look.

"Go, I'll be fine. I'm sure I'll find someone to talk to while Mischa parades you and marks you as hers before the masses."

Aiden had to smile at how Cassidy had made sure only Aiden heard that comment.

"I'll come find you, never fear. Or you can find me grazing at the tables when she finally decides to let us loose on the nibbles."

Aiden was swiftly led away with Mischa providing a running commentary on her home, the people there, and what she thought of them. All this was delivered in her inimitable style. Aiden just went with her, though she was conscious of just how much she missed having Cassidy at her side instead.

CHAPTER TEN

A rmed with a tall glass of soda, Aiden found herself seated with the writers and the producer from *The Alchemidens*. Mischa had nudged her forward with an introduction then disappeared on her. She was welcomed into their huddle as they ate and drank and were trying not to talk about work. They were failing dismally. Aiden listened with barely restrained glee. She'd never had the opportunity to meet these people in her dealings with TV and film so she was having a wonderful time just being a fan. She loved that she was getting to meet them and learn their roles on the show.

"Can I ask you a question, Aiden?" Nicole Abnett, the producer of the show, shifted closer. The writers Rory Perlman, Janis Holmes, and Mike Pace all mirrored her move.

"Is it personal or do I need my agent involved?"

Nicole smiled. "Well, I might need your agent's number if you agree with what I'm considering doing."

Aiden's interest was piqued by their cautious manner as they huddled closer. "Ask away."

"You've been an adviser on a few shows, haven't you?"

"I've been asked to advise writers on how to write gay characters properly, yes."

The group all exchanged looks then leaned in further still.

"I'm considering a gay storyline in the show," Nicole said. "But I want to do it justice and not just have it as the plot for an episode and then glossed over."

"I'm glad to hear that. Sexuality shouldn't be used to just boost ratings or to draw in the gay viewers only to throw them aside later."

Nicole looked around, making sure no one was within earshot. "I want to bring out a main character. I feel it would work with our stories, and the character I want would be perfect for the reveal."

Aiden stared at her. "You'd better mean Karadine Kourt because she is the only one that it makes sense with."

"Mischa said you were a fan of the show," Rory said.

"You have no idea how much," Aiden said. "So, do you just want me to say do it, make Karadine come out? Because you do realize you're going to have to do more than just that, right?" Aiden knew she was going to get on her soapbox, but this was important. This was a mainstream TV show. It also starred a very famous actress who would be taking this responsibility on. A very famous *lesbian* actress who would be expected to bring more to the role than what she'd already developed in the first season.

"You need to realize what this will entail. Karadine can't just come out in one episode and everyone just nod and say okay and move on with the next adventure. You've written Karadine as the loner with no romantic ties, so that's in your favor. There'll be no sudden switching her interest from males to females. Let's give the lesbians someone to root for."

"You a gold star lesbian, Aiden?" Janis winked at her. Aiden knew straight away who she'd likely be working with if their plan came to fruition.

"It's the only thing I know. So, no sudden reveals. Also, you'll want to steer clear of the stereotypes too. TV has the terrible habit of over-exaggerating the masculinity of butches or making queens a figure of fun." Aiden looked at them all. "Have you spoken to Cassidy about if she's okay with this change in her character?"

Mike shook his head. "Season two is in production now. If we get the green light for a third that's where we'd like to make the change. We're still on the fence about whether to do it or not. It could make or break the series."

Sadly, Aiden knew how true that was. "If you do it, there's another thing you have to consider. Fans today aren't your quiet little followers of whatever you put on the screen. Social media has given them a voice, a very loud voice, and if you screw this up they will let you know. If you're going to court the lesbian audience, then with that power comes great responsibility. You're not going to want *The Alchemidens* to fall into the same tired clichés other shows before it have doled out. You need to do this right. But if you do? You'll have the most loyal set of viewers ever because we lesbians are crying out for something to watch that portrays us in a positive light. We need heroines that are strong, fearless, and vulnerable. We don't want to see one that constantly needs a man to rescue them to prove they're still the 'weaker' sex. And no queer baiting with subtext and maybes, because that's just lame writing."

Aiden could see they were hanging on her every word so she continued her list. "Don't kill them off just to further another character's story arc. If they're the villain, let them stay a villain but explain what got them to that place. I've dated some less than redeemable women. Not all lesbians are sweetness and light." Aiden shared a wry look with Janis who nodded emphatically back.

"And if we decide to go this path?" Nicole said.

"Then I'll hold up *Rookie Blue* as an example of great character evolving. They wrote a wonderful lesbian love story that developed over a few seasons. Sadly, there was no happy ever after for them, but their portrayal was written realistically and handled with as much care as the straight relationships in the show were given. And their actresses were very supportive of their fans and the characters they were portraying. I'll be honest; if I ever get the chance to write for Aliyah O'Brien? I'll kill for it. The woman is awesome."

Janis laughed. "Nice to see you're as much of a fan girl as the rest of us."

"Being a writer, I am drawn to well written and performed characters. You've already written Karadine as a heroine and the audience loves her. Now you've got to find a way to sell her as a lesbian to the straight population too. Not everyone is going to like it. You're going to have to go on record stating you haven't done it just because Cassidy is gay. You're going to be portraying a lesbian woman to children because kids and teens are in your demographic.

All of this has to be taken into consideration. A gay heroine can fight, bleed, and feel pain just like a straight one can. They can be funny, loyal, and fall in love just like anyone else can too. If you do it right, it will make sense to the viewer that this is just who Karadine has been all along."

Aiden took a sip from her glass and eyed them over the rim. "But I promise you this. If you think you have fans now, if you make Karadine a lesbian, you will draw a legion of new viewers from every corner of the world to her side. The superhero market is full of strong men with strong heterosexual genes. You'd be delivering a lesbian superhero for the gay geeks among us to aspire to."

"You too?" Nicole smiled.

"I've been involved in a lot of projects, but I'm still, first and foremost, a huge fan of science fiction and fantasy. I yearn for a lesbian superhero who can fight crime with her girlfriend cheering her on. We all need to see someone like us that can do things we can only ever dream of. I mean, I love Thor to pieces, but I can't identify with him. Sometimes we just need someone who says, 'I'm just like you and look at what I can do.'"

"We're aware we are taking on quite a challenge," Nicole said.

"Don't let the show's legacy be that you had the chance to do something great and instead you bent over for the powers that be and let them tell your stories. Write what's best for the character and what their story is telling you. Theirs is the loudest voice."

Nicole looked at her writers then back at Aiden. "Do you have your agent's number? I think we might have a place for you in our team if you'll consider it."

Aiden's hand shook as she reached inside her suit jacket to take out a business card. She'd never expected to be offered a job with her favorite show at Mischa's party. She assured them she wouldn't say a word about what they had discussed. "You need to talk it over with Cassidy though. She's the one who has to bring that idea of yours to life."

"Speaking of which, I think she's looking for you," Janis gestured to where Cassidy was sauntering around the room, obviously searching for something.

I hope it's me she's after, Aiden thought as she said her good-byes and stood up. Cassidy's eyes snapped to her, and the smile she gave Aiden took her breath away. For a moment, Aiden tried to see Karadine Kourt in the beautiful woman making her way toward her. For the first time, Aiden failed. All she could see was Cassidy, and that was all she desired.

❖

At some time during the evening, Aiden had been pulled aside again. She was now in the company of Mischa's sister Sorcha and some other literary fans. Cassidy was trying her best to feign disinterest, but her gaze constantly drifted back to where Aiden stood.

"Look at her, shamelessly flirting," Mischa said as she handed Cassidy a full glass of wine.

Cassidy frowned. "I don't believe that is Aiden's flirting face."

Mischa huffed at her. "Cast your eyes elsewhere for a moment and look at Sorcha."

Cassidy did and was surprised to see the smile lighting up Sorcha's usually serious face. She always looked surly and bored, but here, talking with Aiden, she looked positively giddy. Sorcha was a very handsome butch. She knew it too and played her role as a lady-killer to perfection. Cassidy remembered the first time they had met. Sorcha had hit on her, oozing charm and sensuality. Cassidy had shot her down kindly but bluntly. She preferred her women a little less masculine than Sorcha. Also, she liked her women less bossy, but that, apparently, was a familial trait.

"My sister usually falls for pretty femmes like you, Cass, but I swear, I wouldn't be surprised if she rolled on her back and spread for Aiden."

Cassidy nearly choked on her drink. "Mischa!"

Mischa just grinned. "I'm serious. Look at her fan-girling all over Aiden. It's indecent."

"This from the married straight woman who had Aiden's face in her cleavage on their first meeting."

"She's my favorite author."

"That excuse will wear thin after a while, darling."

"You're just jealous that I've had more boob action than you have," Mischa said. "Don't give me that face! I've seen how you look at her. That handsome nerd of a writer has you intrigued. You want to know if she's as nerdy once those glasses are off and she's between the sheets."

"She'd be more than just a quick fuck, Mischa. I can't afford that kind of involvement at the moment and you know it."

"You can't stop living, Cass, and you don't want to miss your chance with this woman if she's someone you'd give your heart to."

Cassidy was silent for a long moment. She watched as Sorcha engaged Aiden in what looked like an intense conversation. "Do you think Aiden would be susceptible to Sorcha's brand of magic?" She hated the fact she was jealous and she was powerless to stop the question from spilling out.

"No, I'd say Aiden is being the polite author and answering the same questions she told me she always gets asked." Mischa took a sip from her glass. "All while she's waiting for someone to ask that number one question."

"Which is?"

"Are the sex scenes you write in your books based on reality?"

Cassidy's jaw dropped. "Seriously? *That's* the question she gets asked the most?"

"All the time," Mischa said with a knowing smile. "I asked it myself."

Cassidy rolled her eyes in exasperation. "Why am I not surprised?" Her eyes were drawn back to Aiden. *Truth be told, she does write some very imaginative scenes.* "What was her answer?"

"She told me a writer never reveals her sources."

Cassidy laughed. "Very diplomatic." She discreetly tipped her glass at Aiden.

"As for Sorcha's wiles, or even her friend Eve's more blatant charms clearly being offered"—Mischa's head gestured to the more than ample cleavage on display in a tight black dress that barely fit where it touched—"I'd say Aiden is not interested in the slightest. In fact, she appears more interested in someone else entirely. She keeps looking over here."

"She's probably waiting for you to wade in there and join the literary discussion."

"Actually, her eyes have rarely left you all night. You may have noticed how solicitous she's been around you. She let you eat off her plate, for fuck's sake."

"What? You eat off my plate enough times."

"Yes, but I don't go fill the plate back up so you can continue grazing from it while you talk to people."

"I like my food," Cassidy said defensively.

"And she obviously knows that, hence her waiting on you tonight. She's a big name in her own right, Cassidy. She doesn't have to hold a plate for anyone. Yet she does it for you." Mischa nudged her none too gently. "So stop shooting daggers at my sister who doesn't stand a chance in hell with Aiden. Instead, look closer at Aiden because you can't miss the fact her heart is in her eyes when she looks at you."

Cassidy swallowed hard against the rush of fear that chilled her flesh. "Sooner or later, I'm going to have to tell her what's going on in my life."

"Let's hope its sooner so we can get down to what's more important in all this." Mischa flashed her a big toothy smile. "Double dates!"

Cassidy shook her head vigorously. "Are you insane? And have you monopolize her all evening? I don't think so. I wouldn't get a word in edgeways, and everyone will think she's dating you!" Cassidy fussed at Mischa's loud and boisterous laughter directed at her. Deep inside, she was excited by the feelings thoughts of them dating filled her with. To have someone in her life after being alone for so long would be blissful. She looked over at Aiden and found her staring back at her. Aiden smiled, and Cassidy felt her heart swell at the wealth of feelings that enveloped her. She waggled her glass at Aiden, silently asking if she wanted another drink. Aiden checked her own glass which Cassidy knew had been filled with soda all evening. It was empty. She mouthed "Yes, please."

I can look after her too. You just watch me. Cassidy studiously ignored Mischa's open-mouthed stare and brushed past her toward the bar.

CHAPTER ELEVEN

The signed and very limited first edition copies of all four of Aiden's Time series books had been the perfect choice for Mischa's present. She'd hugged them to her like they were precious babies and thanked Aiden profusely. It had been a great night out, and Aiden had enjoyed herself immensely. She'd made new contacts and had the opportunity to meet some of her favorite actors and actresses. She'd even met up with fans of her own work and had been able to give them a few tidbits on what she was working on now.

"Did you enjoy the party, Aiden?"

Aiden risked a look over at Cassidy while she was driving them home. Cassidy's hair was blowing in the night breeze, and Aiden thought she had never looked more beautiful.

"Best night I've had in ages. Mischa knows a lot of fascinating people." She glanced over at Cassidy. "Present company included."

Eyes closed and head held up to the stars, Cassidy smiled. "Thank you. I noticed Sorcha having a quiet word with you before we left and then she whisked you away. What was that all about?"

"She asked if I minded having my picture taken with her and her friends. So I was striking a pose."

"Sorcha's Facebook page will be splashed all over with those tomorrow. Good job it's a private one."

"She'd also taken a few I asked for copies of for myself." Aiden kept her eyes on the road. "There's one of you and me that she took earlier in the evening before I realized who she was. I thought she was the official party photographer, not Mischa's sister."

"One of us? I'd like to see that one. As long as I wasn't eating in it because Sorcha has way too many candid shots of me stuffing my face. She usually gets them at Mischa's barbeques. Sorcha even made up a board of them for me as a birthday gift."

"That was creative of her," Aiden said. "This one I remember was when she asked us to smile. We were by the fireplace at the time."

"Was that when I was messing with your tie?"

"Yes, you were repositioning it after a certain actress had tried to loosen it for me." Aiden knew exactly what Kristine Lang had been after. She'd been trying to persuade Aiden to get her a part in a film Aiden was rumored to be doing work on in the future. Cassidy had been silently seething beside Aiden while Kristine had poured on the charm.

"I don't like that woman. How she got that role in *CSI* I'll never know. If I'd have been on set I'd have shoved her into a morgue freezer and left her there for the entire episode."

Still laughing at Cassidy's uncharacteristic snarky comment, Aiden was waved through the gates at Oaken Drive as they returned home. Within minutes, she pulled up on her driveway and parked. "May I escort you home, Ms. Hayes?" She got out and walked around to help Cassidy from her seat.

"I had a great time tonight. Thank you for taking me, Aiden." Cassidy leaned her head to Aiden's shoulder.

The scent of her perfume drifted on the night air. Aiden closed her eyes momentarily as she breathed her in.

"What are you doing?" Cassidy's voice was barely above a whisper in the darkness.

"Trying to memorize everything about this evening so I never forget how I feel at this precise moment in time."

"And how do you feel?"

"Happy." Aiden opened her eyes and looked down into Cassidy's curious face. "Grateful."

"For what?"

"For you being the girl next door. I like Lori well enough, but she's nothing compared to you." The words slipped out of her mouth before Aiden could censor them. "I'm sorry. That was...I wasn't..."

They'd stopped before Cassidy's front door. She opened it, hurriedly turned off the alarm, then she pulled Aiden inside with her. She pushed her back against the door with a bump. It slammed shut behind her.

"I—" Aiden began, but Cassidy tugged her head down and kissed her. The gentleness of her lips blew Aiden away. The strength of Cassidy's hold on her was the only thing that kept her anchored to the ground. Cassidy tasted divine. There was the lingering tang of the fruity wine she'd been drinking, but the rest was all Cassidy. Aiden sank into her, returning the slow, sensuous kiss hungrily. Her hands settled on Cassidy's hips, smoothing over the curves under the fabric of her dress. Cassidy was moaning softly with each kiss she pressed fervently to Aiden's lips. Each moan heightened Aiden's arousal, and she pulled Cassidy closer still. Her hands slowly traced up Cassidy's spine. Aiden let out a moan of her own as voracious kisses stole her breath away.

So this is what it's like to kiss Karadine Kourt.

For a moment, Aiden stopped kissing her and pulled back a fraction. Cassidy groaned as their lips separated. Aiden saw the pout form on Cassidy's lips as their kissing was interrupted. Her eyes were still closed as she caught her breath. It gave Aiden a chance to *really* look at her. This wasn't Karadine. Aiden wouldn't want to be kissing her. That character was unobtainable, untouchable, seriously mission bound. A fictional character brought to life by the real woman in her arms. The actress C.J. Hayes was equally untouchable, held aloft by her fame. Aiden leaned forward and rubbed her nose against Cassidy's. She nuzzled closer and lifted her hands to cup Cassidy's face. Tracing soft kisses along Cassidy's cheekbone, Aiden marveled at her softness.

"Cassidy," she breathed, mesmerized by her silky skin. That's who she was kissing. Not the make-believe character, not the star, but the woman behind it all. She was exquisitely feminine, beautiful beyond compare, and *real*. Aiden pulled Cassidy firmly against her and kissed her hard. Her kiss was demanding, heated, and ardent with the passion that was burning inside her.

It was Cassidy who finally pulled away, gasping for breath and looking giddy in Aiden's arms. "You kiss like a dream," she whispered. She burrowed her head under Aiden's chin and pressed warm lips to Aiden's throat.

And you've been the star in so many of mine, Aiden thought as she rested her chin on Cassidy's hair. They clung together for a while.

"I wanted to do that at the party," Cassidy admitted.

"That would have been quite the photo opportunity for Sorcha."

"It could have been quite embarrassing for you."

"No, it would have let everyone see how very lucky I am," Aiden whispered in Cassidy's ear. She pressed a kiss there, then brushed back Cassidy's long hair to feather kisses down her neck. The pulse point she lingered over seemed to triple its beats beneath her lips. "I'd better go while I can still be chivalrous and pull myself away from you." Reluctantly, she loosened her grip and instantly missed the feel of Cassidy's warm body. She opened the door without breaking her gaze on Cassidy's face. She looked well kissed, her hair was mussed, and her breathing was still ragged. She watched as Cassidy wrapped her arms about herself.

"Good night, Aiden. Thank you for your company tonight."

Aiden took a few steps away then, as if pulled by an invisible force, she leaned in for one more kiss before finally dragging herself away out of temptation's reach. Cassidy pressed her fingertips to her lips when Aiden stepped back.

"Good night, Cassidy."

"Good night, Aiden. Sweet dreams."

Aiden smiled. *And I know every one of them will be of you.*

❖

Awake early the next morning, Aiden quickly set out to the local farmers' market. There she picked up all the ingredients for breakfast. She had the flower seller fashion her a marvelous bouquet of flowers of every color they had available. It was a rainbow explosion of petals and was almost too big for Aiden to carry. She loved it though. Its big, bold statement was perfect for Cassidy. She headed back home to start mixing up the batter for the pancakes she intended to start with. All to accompany a cooked breakfast with plenty of bacon and heaps of scrambled eggs. Aiden wanted to present Cassidy with a morning after the party feast. She hoped the surprise would be well received.

She headed over to Cassidy's, the huge bouquet in hand. She knocked on the front door, anxiously shifting from foot to foot, and waited for Cassidy to open it.

"Who is it?"

"It's Aiden." She held the flowers out in front of her so they'd be the first thing Cassidy saw. She heard the door open. "Look what I found with your name on it. It says they are from your secret admirer." She popped her head around them, but her smile faltered at the look of sheer terror visible on Cassidy's face. "Cassidy?" She was unceremoniously pulled into the hallway, the door roughly shut tight behind her. The multitude of locks were all slammed into place with speed. Cassidy leaned back against it as if holding back intruders.

"Oh God, he's found me. He's found me. Fuck, what now? Where can I possibly go now?" Her eyes fixed on the flowers. "Put those down quickly. You don't know what he might have planted in them or on them."

Aiden didn't understand what on earth was going on. "Cassidy?"

"Did you see who brought those? How long have they been out there do you think? Did you touch the card with them?" There was a very noticeable card sticking out from the blooms.

"Yes, I touched the card."

"Fuck! That was evidence. Why would you do that?" Cassidy was working herself up into quite a state. Her eyes were tormented, her face ashen.

Exasperated over Cassidy's heated rambling, Aiden ended up shouting to be heard. "Cassidy, *I* wrote the damn card. Of course I was going to touch it."

Cassidy finally stopped clutching at her hair. "*You* wrote it?"

Aiden held up the flowers she still had in her hand. "I've just gotten these for you. I wrote the card for you. I'm your secret admirer. Only I'm not so secret after all the kissing we did last night." The air was knocked forcibly from her lungs with a loud whoosh as Cassidy launched herself into Aiden's chest and squeezed her tight. Cassidy then began crying uncontrollably. With her free hand, Aiden smoothed her fingers over Cassidy's head, threading her fingers through her hair. "Sweetheart, please tell me what all this is about. I don't understand at all." Her ribs ached from Cassidy's death grip, but Aiden didn't let go. She held Cassidy as she cried her heart out, her body shuddering with bone-wracking sobs.

Eventually, the hysteria calmed and Cassidy's crying grew quieter. Aiden maneuvered slightly to put the flowers down on the hall table then wrapped both arms around her. "Hey, I have all the fixings for breakfast at my place just waiting for the short order cook to whip them up. I came over here to sweep you off your feet with the promise of good food and the lure of pretty flowers for a beautiful woman." Aiden pressed a kiss to Cassidy's heated brow. "How about you come back with me and I'll feed you and then, if you feel up to it, maybe you can tell me what's breaking your heart." She lifted Cassidy's head up and tenderly wiped the tears from her cheeks.

Cassidy sniffed and buried her head back into Aiden's chest. "I'm sorry."

"No. I'm sorry for whatever I did that triggered this. So you need to tell me what it was so I don't inadvertently do it again. I learn real fast, I promise."

Cassidy pulled back from the sodden fabric of Aiden's shirt. "I need to wash my face." She hurried off upstairs without meeting Aiden's gaze.

Aiden just watched her go. With a deep breath, she stumbled over to the stairs and sat down with a bump. She was still sitting there trying to puzzle out what the hell had happened when Cassidy came back and sat beside her.

"Thank you for the flowers," Cassidy said. "They're gorgeous." She rested her cheek on Aiden's arm. "You mentioned something about food?"

Aiden snorted. She loved how Cassidy's mind always fixated on what she obviously saw as the most important thing. "Yeah. I've got a shit load of pancake batter and enough bacon and eggs to feed an army." She nudged Cassidy gently. "Or satisfy you at least."

Cassidy finally laughed, albeit weakly. "I'm going to need something to fortify me while I tell you what you need to know." She stood and pulled Aiden up after her. "Bring my flowers please. I want to appreciate their beauty while I share something ugly."

CHAPTER TWELVE

Three years ago

No one ever paid much attention to Adam when he walked around the studio lot. Wearing his heavy tool belt, he made sure to be seen carrying some kind of lighting equipment. That way it always looked like he was on a job. He could pretty much go anywhere he wanted without having to flash his credentials at the guards. It was like being invisible. He blended into the background and no one looked at him twice.

His latest job was as the assistant to the key grip, which meant he was kept busy setting up the lighting and all the rigging for the sound stages. He also got to move the set pieces for the cameras to be put in position. That got him nearer to the actors and actresses waiting to retake their scenes. They never looked at him; he was invisible to them too. It was a precise job and he'd worked hard to get the position he now held. He had a specific goal in mind for his career, and today, on the set of the hospital drama *Heart Beat* it had paid off. The fates had smiled at him, providence had lead him exactly where he desired.

From his lofty position on the scaffold holding the lights, Adam began moving a light to hit the set below. Its beam of soft light fell upon the newest member of the show.

C.J. Hayes was in his spotlight.

He'd followed her career closely, *very* closely. He'd tried to get her attention with fan mail, love letters filled with praise for her beauty and her acting choices. He'd sent her gifts to prove his adoration, and at first, she'd acknowledged him. Eventually, he realized he was getting the standard notes of thanks and an obligatory signed photograph. He had a growing pile of those. But then even those stopped and he was ignored. Adam didn't take kindly to being dismissed by the woman he'd set his heart on from the first moment he'd seen her. He'd pushed to get work at the studio she was in. Her star was rising. She was moving on from bit parts in established shows and being offered bigger roles that showcased her talents. He needed her to see he was there for her. He wasn't going away.

From his position high above the set, he could watch her without being detected. She was so beautiful. He wished she hadn't chosen to ignore his advances. That only spurred him to try harder to capture her attention. His letters to her now were harsher, he admitted, venting his frustration at her not acknowledging his devotion to her. He knew she needed him. After all, he'd been there from the start.

Adam leaned against the rigging and marveled at how his lighting caught the highlights in her hair. He did that for her. Without him, she'd be left in the dark. Instead, he was the one in the shadows, watching over her, yearning for her, needing her to see him.

Always there, always watching, because she was his alone.

❖

Present Day

"He'd been working at the studios with you all those years and no one knew he was the one sending you the crazy fan mail? And now he's gotten into your apartment? Where the hell was your security?"

Aiden's voice was incredulous. The ever-tightening grasp she had on her coffee mug was just a fraction away from shattering it to smithereens. She was sitting beside Cassidy at the kitchen table. The remains of their meal were long forgotten, pushed aside as they sat cradling their drinks. Aiden was listening in a dawning horror as

Cassidy told her all about this man called Adam Bernett who was terrorizing her…and had been for *years*.

"The doorman said he never saw anyone come in that didn't have access to the building. The police surmised that Bernett probably slipped in when there was a shift change. Bernett is nothing if not a master of doing the impossible to achieve his own ends." Cassidy sat with her hands wrapped around her own mug. She was trembling from letting out her secret. Aiden was afraid to touch her. She knew Cassidy had needed to tell her story, had needed to get it all out before she broke down again.

"How did you know someone had been in there?"

"He'd tidied up in my living room. What kind of creepy-ass stalker does that?" Cassidy said, shaking her head. "That's how I knew someone had been in the apartment. I'm a bit of a devil for allowing clutter to grow into barely manageable piles. Seeing my mail all neat and tidy was a loud warning bell going off."

"Why didn't you just get out of there and call for help?"

"I'm a superhero. How embarrassing would it be to have me seen running screaming from my apartment in a time of peril?"

Aiden had to smile at Cassidy's reasoning, however crazy. "You *play* a superhero. No one really expects you to actually put yourself in a position of danger to save the day."

"Well, I was brought up in London, and we don't back down from a fight. Thankfully, the apartment was empty. Except for me and the culinary knife I was brandishing."

"There's a part of me that wants to ask if you were at least holding it by the handle." Aiden couldn't resist teasing her and was gratified to see a faint sparkle reignite in Cassidy's eyes.

"I was indeed, Little Ms. Master Chef." Cassidy reached across the table and threaded her fingers through Aiden's. "He'd left his message in my bedroom."

Aiden winced and Cassidy shook her head. "No, not like that. Oh thank God, no. I think he'd gotten his jollies by splashing red paint all over my bed cover and writing the words 'You're Mine' plain for all to see." She shuddered violently and Aiden tightened her grip. "Even weeks after, I still can't say what frightens me the most. The fact he got into my home and desecrated it, or the fact he still won't let me go. I'd at least had respite once the restraining order was filed. The police believe he left the state not soon after, and good riddance to him. But now he's back with a vengeance. He's even been posting threats against me on *The Alchemidens* fan pages. The studio is scurrying to delete them before the public sees them. He's relentless."

"Why hasn't this been publicized in the press?"

"Because the bosses at the studio don't want one of their leading ladies seen as anything less than an action heroine. Being stalked by a madman isn't the kind of publicity they want to generate around the show." Cassidy shrugged. "Besides, giving him the publicity that being linked to my name would generate is what the detective in charge of my case thinks he would enjoy."

"So you suffer in silence, looking over your shoulder all the time?" Aiden was not happy. "Do you even know why this Bernett is doing this? Apart from the fact he's obviously demented?"

"I wish I could say I know him, but I don't. When all this started, he was just another earnest fan writing me letters, but in time their tone changed. They got scarier with each one he sent and the more famous I got. That continued for years, and I ended up having someone else deal with my mail so I didn't have to think about him. Working as I do, there are always people around you doing their jobs. They fade into the background and I just go on and do my part. I never expected that the letter writer had escalated into stalking me and was literally with me every day on set. He could have walked past me and I'd never have known. Adam Bernett was right there under my nose all the time and I just didn't *see* him."

"You weren't going to know," Aiden said, thinking how vulnerable famous people were to anyone who wanted a moment of their time. Aiden knew enough about it from her book signings. People always believed they knew you when really they didn't at all.

"His letters were awful, full of threats and what he'd do to me when we met. Then the flowers started arriving, and the gifts. Who knew they were able to get on set so easily because he could bring them in himself and have them put in my room? You're taught very early on when you start acting that your rise in stardom is in large part down to the fans who support you. I'd been polite, sent out the thank you notes at first, but it got to be too much. I had to ignore the gifts, but I had no return address to have them sent back to him. The police ended up with a lot of them as evidence, along with the letters my assistant kept just in case. It was through those that they were finally able to track him down. They arrested him on the set. I just thank God I wasn't on call that day to see it."

Cassidy was silent for a moment, obviously lost in her own thoughts. Aiden waited for her to continue when she was ready.

"I had to face him in the court room as the judge issued the restraining order. His lawyer said we'd met on a film set and I'd apparently led him on." She made a wry face and pointed at herself. "Hello? Lesbian! There's just so many people involved in a project. You say hello to them every morning, but some become just another face behind the scenes, and by the time you move on to the next job there's a whole new set of faces to get used to." She sipped at her coffee before continuing. "He wasn't anyone I went out with, never even sat down with at the dining tables. But he's got all these fantasies about me in his head that are some crazy kind of reality to him. In his mind I'm his and he's determined to get to me to prove it."

"I won't let him anywhere near you," Aiden said. Cassidy's sad smile made her ache.

"You're a sweetheart, Aiden. I'm just waiting for him to make another mistake so the police can finally track him down."

"Fuck that!" Aiden shot out of her seat, startling Cassidy. "We'll get you away from here. I have friends in other states, other countries even. Lori has homes in every nook and cranny on this planet thanks to all her exes. You've got options; exercise them. Let's get you someplace safer than here." She fell to her knees beside Cassidy's chair. "You can't keep living like this."

"And what about my job? I can't be on *The Alchemidens* and be in hiding somewhere south of the equator. I'm hoping for a shot at a dream of a film role on the show's next hiatus. It's a big role, the biggest I've gone up for. I want it."

"And Bernett wants you."

"He's chased me out of my home and left me in fear for my life. He's not taking my career from me as well. I've worked hard to get where I am. Every bit part, every time I played just"—she made air quotes—"*the girlfriend.* This next role could be my big break into cinema, Aiden. That's more important to me than he is. I can't let him take that from me too."

Aiden didn't think she could be in any more awe of her. Now all Cassidy's nervousness when they were outside made sense. The "going out of their way" when they were driving. Cassidy never seeming to go anywhere but to work. Cassidy's nerves were still jangling, all because of Aiden's unintentional secret admirer screw-up. She mournfully eyed the flowers that were center place on the table. She hadn't meant to fuck up so royally on a gesture she'd meant to be romantic.

Cassidy cupped Aiden's cheek in her palm. "You couldn't have known that I would freak out. The flowers are really wonderful, and your card with them is so sweet."

"My delivery sucked, however." Aiden was still furious with herself.

"You couldn't have known." Cassidy tugged her closer by her shirt collar. "But now you do. You know the whole sordid tale."

"You know you're safe here, right? This gated community is very secure. And if you were ever worried you could just come stay with me."

Cassidy kissed her on the tip of her nose. "I'd eat you out of house and home in a day."

Aiden shrugged. "Then I'd just go out and buy more. You're always welcome here, Cassidy. Whatever I need to do to keep you safe, I will do it." Aiden meant every word. The feelings she had for her were wild and chaotic and beautiful. Aiden was falling for her, and falling fast.

Cassidy smiled her first real smile of the day. "You're wonderful. Do you know that?"

"And you're so very brave. I don't think I could be that strong."

"Sometimes I don't feel strong enough." Cassidy snuggled into Aiden's arms.

"Then I'll be strong enough for the both of us." Aiden shifted Cassidy out of her chair and up into her arms, cradling her close.

Cassidy gasped at the show of strength. "What are you doing?"

"The dishes can wait. I'm taking us somewhere more comfortable to sit where we can rest our meal, maybe talk, or just watch a movie together. We both need to chill out."

Cassidy patted Aiden's bicep appreciatively. "I like this fact about you."

"To be honest, there's not much to you." Aiden marveled at how easily Cassidy fit into her arms.

"So last night you could have literally swept me off my feet?"

"I'm sorry, but last night? I'd say you were doing that to *me*." Aiden walked into her living room where a large screen TV dominated a wall. "Do you want to pick the film?" She gently lowered Cassidy back to her feet. Cassidy didn't let her move very far. She reached back and snagged Aiden's hand in her own to keep her near. Cassidy perused the extensive collection of DVDs Aiden owned, picked one, and held it out to her.

"You really are a Harry Potter fan." Aiden put *Harry Potter and the Sorcerer's Stone* into her DVD player.

"It's always been about Hermione for me. After all, she's the smartest witch. I just love her character, both in the book and in the films. She's so feisty right from the start. And fellow Brit Emma Watson is such a pretty girl."

Aiden got them settled on the sofa, Cassidy tucked into her side. Aiden couldn't stop her mind from going over and over all the details Cassidy had shared with her. With Cassidy in her arms and a story of magic on the screen, Aiden was feeling a joy she had never truly experienced before. Her home seemed oddly complete with Cassidy in it. It gave Aiden a sense of peace that had always seemed to elude her in life. Aiden embraced it and lost herself to the warmth of Cassidy held close and the fantasy woven on the screen.

❖

The sound of the credits music playing brought Aiden slowly out of her sleep. Eyes still closed, she luxuriated in the warmth blanketing her body. Cassidy lay pressed up against her, her butt cradled against Aiden's hips. Aiden's arm was hooked under Cassidy's breasts, holding her close. She dimly remembered them lying down at some point to watch the film. The sofa had ample space to take both of them lying stretched out, Cassidy's back to Aiden's chest. She opened her eyes to find Cassidy cuddled in her arms, fast asleep, with a faint smile curving her lips. Aiden listened to her breathing, deep and even. She was enchanted by the opportunity to watch Cassidy so at peace after the upset earlier. Aiden was thankful Cassidy trusted her enough to be this exposed and vulnerable with her.

I promise you I will keep you safe if you let me.

Aiden had no idea how long they lay there, but eventually, Cassidy started to stir. She turned in Aiden's arms so she could face her. She looked up at Aiden with sleepy eyes.

"Do you always sleep with your glasses on?" Cassidy's voice was husky from her slumber.

"Not usually. I seem to remember us getting more comfortable here, and I know I saw Hermione doing the feather spell. I don't think I stayed awake much longer after that."

"You saw more than I did." Cassidy covered her mouth as she yawned. She nuzzled her face into Aiden's neck and snuggled in closer.

Aiden distracted herself by smoothing her hand through Cassidy's hair. The soft puffs of air Cassidy breathed against her skin were sending frissons of excitement throughout her whole body. When Cassidy's lips brushed against her pulse point, Aiden couldn't stop the whimper that escaped.

"Am I bothering you, Aiden?" Cassidy teased the tip of her tongue along the tense line of Aiden's throat.

"You're making me hot and bothered." Aiden shifted to give Cassidy more access to where she was now trailing soft kisses over Aiden's exposed flesh. Cassidy planted kisses down to where Aiden's shirt was unbuttoned. Playfully, she toyed with the next button.

"If you're hot then I think I should help you out of these clothes." She pulled at the button again. The look on her face asked Aiden for permission.

Nodding her consent, Aiden watched as Cassidy's nimble fingers slipped each button free. While Cassidy was occupied, Aiden pressed a kiss to her forehead. She lingered there, breathing in the floral scent of Cassidy's hair. "You're so beautiful you break my heart."

"I hope not." Cassidy shifted and helped Aiden sit up so she could pull the shirt off completely. It fell to the floor. Cassidy's eyes darkened as she stared at Aiden's exposed chest.

Aiden smiled at the look of intent clearly written all over Cassidy's face. She wondered if Cassidy's hearty appetites lent themselves to more than just food. Cassidy moved to straddle Aiden's lap. She removed Aiden's glasses and put them aside for safety. Then she moved in to give Aiden a kiss that shook her to her very core. Aiden slipped a finger under Cassidy's T-shirt to stroke over her stomach. She couldn't stop the grin from forming when Cassidy whipped her top off and threw it behind her.

"Holy fuck, you're gorgeous." For a moment, nerves got the better of her and Aiden froze. She wanted to grab Cassidy and kiss her senseless. She also wanted to take things slowly and savor every second touching and tasting her. She was torn over what to do first.

Cassidy obviously wasn't in the mood for waiting. She grabbed Aiden and kissed her fiercely. Her tongue snuck between Aiden's lips and deepened their kiss until Aiden's head spun. Aiden gave up on over thinking and just let herself be taken. She smoothed her hands over Cassidy's soft skin, relishing the feel of it. She ran her fingers over Cassidy's bra and soon made short work of the clasp. The loosened scrap of silk was trapped between their bodies until Aiden eased back to slide it down and off Cassidy's arms. She palmed Cassidy's breasts, loving the weight of them in her hands. Aiden brushed her thumbs over the taut nipples feeling them tighten even more. She could feel Cassidy's hands directing her head closer to where she wanted Aiden's mouth. Aiden ran her tongue around a straining nipple then sucked it into her mouth. She teased Cassidy, alternating between flicks of her tongue and gentle nips from her teeth. Cassidy was groaning by the time Aiden switched to her other breast to lavish it with the same loving attention.

Aiden's own desire was swiftly spiraling out of control. She wanted Cassidy so badly it was a fire raging out of control in her. Judging by the frantic lap dance Cassidy was all but performing, she wanted something more too. Aiden wrapped her hands under Cassidy's butt and stood up with Cassidy clinging around her neck. Aiden turned and lowered Cassidy back down on the sofa leaving her legs dangling off the seat. Aiden knelt before her and watched Cassidy's lips curve into an all too seductive smile. Cassidy's naked chest was already flushed with arousal, her breasts lifting with each ragged breath she took. Aiden pulled the shorts down Cassidy's shapely legs and off. The wisp of lace that remained barely left anything to the imagination. Aiden brushed her finger over a decorative swirl covering Cassidy's sex.

"These are very sexy. I promise I'll admire them more fully some other time, but for now they have to go." She hooked a finger on each side of the bikini briefs and pulled them off. Aiden eased back between Cassidy's spread legs. She smoothed her hands back and forth along the line of Cassidy's thighs, going only so far before trailing back down. She never took her eyes from Cassidy's face. Cassidy was biting her bottom lip, desperately trying to angle her hips so that Aiden's hands would stray closer to where her need was very much on show.

"You need to head a little higher before I touch myself," Cassidy said, spreading her legs a little further, opening herself up to Aiden's gaze.

Aiden wrapped her hands around Cassidy's ankles. She lifted Cassidy's legs up so her feet were planted on the sofa's seat but her legs were still spread wide.

"Don't you dare move those hands," Aiden said as she began kissing a path up each trembling leg. She caressed Cassidy from her feet to tickle behind her knees and then lingered over her thighs. She pressed and spread Cassidy's legs wider still, keeping her in place, and leaving her open and exposed to whatever Aiden desired. She could feel Cassidy trembling beneath her firm grasp as she leaned closer to Cassidy's center. Aiden flattened her tongue and ran it the length of Cassidy's sex.

The intoxicating scent of Cassidy's arousal, the taste, filled Aiden's senses, and she dove in for more. She kept Cassidy immobile, pinning her down. Languidly, she ran her tongue through the swollen flesh that was drenched with Cassidy's need. She flicked her tongue over Cassidy's straining clit until a moan burst from Cassidy's throat, rumbling long and low. Unable to resist, Aiden rubbed her cheek over the neatly trimmed hair that framed Cassidy's sex. She breathed in deeply the scent of Cassidy's ever increasing arousal. It intoxicated her.

Aiden ran her tongue around Cassidy's entrance then speared her tongue inside. She felt Cassidy's walls tighten around her. Cassidy bucked against Aiden's grip, straining to get Aiden in deeper and to get herself closer to Aiden's insatiable mouth.

Aiden lifted her hands off Cassidy's thighs to roughly brush her thumbs over Cassidy's aroused flesh. The thick lips of her sex were swollen and glistening. She framed Cassidy's rock hard clit with her thumbs and began to strum out a rhythm on and around the sensitive bud.

"Oh fuck," Cassidy yelped. She lay sprawled on the sofa, one hand buried deep in Aiden's hair while the other was twisting and pulling on her own nipples in desperation. Her body danced to the tune Aiden was playing upon her. "If you keep that up I'm going to come all over your face."

Aiden sped up her actions deliberately. With her legs spread, her body flushed, and her body tensing as she neared orgasm, Aiden had never seen Cassidy look more beautiful. She couldn't drink her in enough or get over the feel of Cassidy coming apart under every kiss and intimate lick Aiden bestowed upon her. It was every fantasy come true. But none of Aiden's lonely fantasies began to compare with the reality of hearing Cassidy crying out her name over and over as she began to come apart. She wasn't fucking a fantasy though. She was making love to Cassidy, the woman who was rapidly stealing her heart.

Aiden held on tight to Cassidy as she hit her climax hard and fast. She memorized every sound that spilled from Cassidy's lips as she peaked. Aiden's tongue was buried deep enough to feel the contractions taking Cassidy over the edge as she bucked against Aiden's face. Aiden lifted her head from between Cassidy's legs and watched as she rode out her climax. Aiden lowered Cassidy's legs so she wouldn't cramp and leaned in to lay her head on Cassidy's heaving breasts.

Cassidy clutched her close. "My God, Aiden. For someone who never speaks a harsh word, that tongue of yours should be classified as a lethal weapon!"

Aiden grinned against Cassidy's breast. "Can I remind you that as a writer I am also considered to be skilled with my fingers?" She laughed at Cassidy's moan and how her legs tightened around Aiden's waist to cradle her closer to her.

"God, you're good at that," Cassidy said with a smug smile. "I'd like to return the favor, but I don't think I can move just yet."

Aiden slipped out a little from Cassidy's hold. Cassidy grumbled and tried to pull Aiden back down. Aiden merely picked Cassidy up in her arms, holding her securely.

"How about we move this to a more suitable location?" She carried Cassidy upstairs.

"Are you whisking me off to your bed, Aiden Darrow?" Cassidy curled her arms around Aiden's neck and held on tight.

"Yes. If that's okay with you?"

"So polite. I want to know if Zumba strengthens your stamina. Care to let me test that theory out?" Cassidy's lips brushed over Aiden's collarbone making her shiver.

Aiden carried Cassidy into her bedroom and pulled back the sheets on her bed one-handedly. Aiden finally lay Cassidy down in the middle of the bed. Cassidy pulled her down upon her, her hands already racing over Aiden's chest to tug at her bra. Between them, Aiden was quickly naked, and Cassidy wasted no time getting familiar with Aiden's sensitive spots as she caressed and kneaded Aiden's breasts. She rolled Aiden's nipple between her fingers, tugging just enough to ignite Aiden's need to incendiary.

"If you keep doing that, your test will be over before it even had a chance." Aiden shivered as Cassidy pushed her over onto her back and her fingers dipped lower to play between her legs.

"You're very wet." Cassidy raised her hand to show her proof.

"Having my tongue inside you got me very excited."

"It worked the same magic for me too." Cassidy sucked her fingers into her mouth one at a time. She made Aiden ache with arousal with every teasing flash of her tongue licking each finger sensuously. When she'd finished, she pressed her fingers back between Aiden's lower lips and spread her open. "Think I need to get you any wetter?"

"Keep looking at me like that and there'll be no need at all." The want in Cassidy's eyes was crystal clear. Aiden had never felt so desired by anyone before.

Cassidy's answering smile was wildly seductive. It was totally different from any of the looks she wore when doing romantic scenes on the screen. Aiden loved that she was seeing something not everyone got the pleasure of witnessing in moments of intimacy.

"And what about if I look at you like this and touch you.... here?"

Aiden moaned, loving the feel of Cassidy's fingers as they stretched her open and pushed inside.

Cassidy grinned. "I'll take that as a yes." She leaned over to kiss Aiden, slipping her tongue inside so Aiden could taste herself. "I've read your books, Aiden. How much of what your Hollister likes from her lover is your preference I wonder?" She pressed in deeper and began to push a little harder.

Aiden lifted her hips off the bed to help Cassidy deepen her thrusts. She was amazed by how someone so slight could be fucking her so forcefully. Aiden loved it and caught Cassidy poised above her, watching her every expression greedily.

"I promise I won't kiss and tell that just like Hollister, you like to be taken just as passionately as you like to take."

When Cassidy moved lower to suck Aiden's clit between her lips, Aiden was past caring who knew how hard and fast she loved to be fucked. She just didn't want Cassidy to stop what she was doing.

"Cassie—" Aiden could feel her insides clenching as her climax was all but wrenched out of her by incredibly skilled fingers and a very talented mouth. Her whole body shook with the force of her coming undone, fast and furious. Shivering, she blindly reached out to draw Cassidy down on her to wrap herself around her. She needed to hold on to Cassidy and be reassured she wasn't alone. She was comforted by Cassidy's soft whispers of adoration she murmured into her ear. She smiled when she heard Cassidy chuckle softly and rearrange herself to fit in Aiden's tight hold.

"I'm sending Lori the biggest 'Thank you for letting me use your home and seduce your neighbor' gift I can find."

"I'll pay half toward it. I have some major gratitude to express as well."

Cassidy tugged the bed sheets up over them and snuggled in closer. "God bless that damn sprinkler system."

"Amen to that. I love it when you get wet." Aiden laughed as Cassidy retaliated by digging a sharp finger into her side. Still laughing, Aiden wrapped her arms around her and kissed the pretty pout right off Cassidy's lips. She lay back and savored the moment of lying in her bed with Cassidy in her arms.

She couldn't have written a better happy ending if she'd tried.

CHAPTER THIRTEEN

Cassidy was grateful she was on a late call to set again. She was loathe to even open her eyes. She was warm and snug in Aiden's bed, sprawled across Aiden's chest. Her head was tucked under Aiden's chin, and her leg was spread possessively over Aiden's thighs, pinning her down. She could feel Aiden's chest rise and fall as she slept on, blissfully unaware. Cassidy was now wide-awake. Her eyes traced over Aiden's body that she had spent the night feasting on. She moved her hand a little to rest it over Aiden's heart, loving the strong beat under her palm. Cassidy couldn't ever remember waking up in this position before. It was intimate. One of Aiden's arms was holding her tight, keeping her close. Cassidy hadn't expected that from her previous lovers; she'd been more interested in leaving and moving on. She sighed and snuggled into the crook of Aiden's neck. This was perfect.

Aiden had been a very innovative lover with an attention to detail that Cassidy had been thrilled by. She'd loved that Aiden had been equally as comfortable being fucked as she was being touched more softly and slowly. Cassidy spied the already darkening bruise she'd inadvertently left when she'd bitten Aiden's shoulder to keep her cries from ringing out through the neighborhood. Aiden's fingers deep inside her had made her almost embarrassed by how wet she'd become, and Aiden's kisses had left her breathless in so many ways.

From being this close to Aiden's nakedness, Cassidy could see faint scars on Aiden's arm. There was also something that looked suspiciously like a cigarette burn. Cassidy knew Aiden didn't smoke. Cassidy had played a police officer once in a TV show and had researched the role with a Special Victims Unit. She knew abuse when she saw it. Her heart bled for what Aiden had had to go through to become who she was today. She tightened her hold just a little more.

Aiden stirred finally. "Are you late for work?" she asked, rubbing at her eyes.

"No, I'm on a late start today so I can lounge in bed with this gorgeous woman I spent the night with."

Aiden wrapped her arms around Cassidy and hugged her close. "Good. I'd hate to have to rush this morning. I'm feeling decidedly lazy after such a busy night."

Cassidy touched the scarring on Aiden's bicep. The burn was high enough to be hidden by a shirtsleeve. "What happened here?"

"A foster parent got a little careless with her cigarettes one night after too many beers. She thought it would be funny to brand all the kids in her care. It worked out for me. I got sent to a new foster family where I ended up being adopted by them." Aiden rested her hand over Cassidy's. "It's old now, like many of the other scars you'll see."

"I'm sorry, Aiden."

"The past is the past, Cassidy. And it led me to you so it was worth it in the end."

"I don't like the thought of you being hurt."

"The pain is long gone now. She got suspended for it so the kids after me were safe."

"I want to kill her for hurting you." Cassidy wondered at the surprised look Aiden favored her with. "What?"

"No one's ever said that before." Aiden laughed humorlessly. "But then no one has bothered to ask about these marks either."

"I'm nosy like that. I want to know everything about you there is to know." Cassidy loved how shy Aiden suddenly appeared. She kissed her for it and was pleased with how eagerly Aiden kissed her back. When they finally pulled apart, Aiden reached toward the bedside table but came up empty.

"Crap, my glasses are downstairs somewhere."

"How poor is your eyesight without them?" Cassidy stared into Aiden's eyes, spotting tiny flecks of gold amid the blue.

"I'm blind as a bat without them. Thankfully"—she tugged Cassidy closer—"you're nice and near so I can see you perfectly and do this..." She sucked Cassidy's lower lip between her own. Cassidy felt herself get wet as Aiden's tongue slipped inside her mouth to deepen the kiss.

"I want to do more than this," Cassidy muttered, pushing Aiden back so she could rise above her. "We have time. If you're agreeable?"

Aiden laughed. "I'm ready, willing, and able, Ms. Hayes. And when we're done I promise to fix you breakfast and then drive you in to the studio."

Cassidy gazed down at Aiden's smiling face. She trailed her fingers over every feature lovingly. "You are perfect."

"Not in the least. I just don't want to waste a second I get to spend in your company. Now, let me do what I want with you."

"If you promise me pancakes you can do anything you desire." Cassidy squealed as Aiden tumbled her onto her back to look down at her.

"I'm holding you to that. I'll just satisfy your other appetite first."

❖

The kiss Aiden had left her with still lingered on Cassidy's lips. Self-consciously, she rested her fingertips against them, feeling the smile she was unable to hold back.

"About time you rolled up." Mischa came up behind Cassidy and startled her from her musing. She squinted at Cassidy, looking at her with an almost laser-like intensity. Her mouth dropped open with a gasp. "Oh my God," she drawled. "You fucked Aiden!"

Cassidy pulled her aside out of the earshot of anyone else. "Hush, you!"

Mischa didn't intend to be kept quiet. "You left my party and you took that woman home and you ravished her!"

"Actually, she was the perfect gentlewoman that evening and walked me to my front door, leaving me to spend the night alone I'll have you know."

Mischa snorted. "Cass, you have something going on because you have that 'just fucked flush' thing going on about you. I can see it in your eyes. I can always tell when you have a playmate, but this"—Mischa leaned in close as if she could look directly into Cassidy's soul—"this is different." She gripped Cassidy's chin and tilted her head left and right. "If I didn't know any better I'd say you looked loved up and a little shell-shocked by it all."

Cassidy glared at her. "You are too goddamn perceptive. Go read someone else, Mystic Mischa. I am not telling you anything."

"So there is something to tell," Mischa said. "You know I'll get it out of you sooner or later."

"Well, I'd prefer later because I want to keep this feeling to myself for a little while longer. Okay?" Cassidy wrapped her arms about her. She knew Mischa would want all the details and would drive Cassidy crazy until she gave her something, but she really wanted to just bask in the feeling Aiden left her with.

Mischa smiled. "Well, aren't you all dewy-eyed? Looks like that neighbor of yours found a way to bring some romance into your life after all." She grabbed Cassidy's arm before she could walk away. "Just tell me one thing."

Cassidy groaned silently but raised an eyebrow at Mischa giving her permission to ask away.

"Is she as good as her written work?"

Cassidy laughed. "Oh, darling, her books don't hold a candle to how fantastic she is." Cassidy's smug smile said it all.

Mischa clapped her hands delightedly and hugged Cassidy to her. "Good for you. Now go see Claude. He said he wanted to see you the second you got in."

Cassidy frowned at her. "Why am I being called to the big boss?"

"Who knows?" Mischa shrugged. "But if you're getting a pay rise you can buy me lunch today. Claude's hanging out with the producer and the writers."

Cassidy headed off to where she knew they all camped out. She wondered what she had been summoned into.

❖

Claude Saunders and Nicole Abnett took Cassidy aside the second she found them. The studio boss *and* her producer? Cassidy's heart began to beat double time. On a table lay a long white box. Nicole lifted the lid, and Cassidy spied the bouquet of dead and rotting roses inside. Their scent was putrid. The sight of the roses rotted on their stems made Cassidy think of the bright and cheerful blooms Aiden had given her. The contrast was unmistakable.

"There was a new man on the gate when these were delivered. He just signed for them and then had them brought here."

"It's Bernett. He's going to keep targeting the studio now I'm back here filming." Cassidy backed away from the table. She didn't want to even look at what lay in the box. "Was there a card?"

Nicole nodded. "You don't need to know what it says. We've already called the police. The cop assigned to your case is coming out to see you."

"And he'll do what? Unless Bernett has left a way they can trace back to his whereabouts with these, I'm still screwed."

"He's not getting that close to you. We'll get a bodyguard on set for you if we have to," Claude said.

Cassidy balked at the idea. "No, this is the only place I get to feel normal. It will disrupt filming and everyone else will be on edge. I won't have that."

"We'll do our best to accommodate you, but I'd really like you escorted on and off the lot." Claude's stern face brooked no argument. "If he's started leaving gifts here again he knows exactly where you are. We'll close the set and allow no one else in or out."

"Thanks to social media, everyone knows where I am. There's always someone taking a photo or posting my whereabouts. I'm a virtual prisoner in someone else's home because he broke into mine."

"You have to be safe. I just wish there was something more the police could do." Claude shook his head. "The guard has been severely reprimanded. He won't make the same mistake again with anything that comes here under your name."

One mistake is all he'll need, Cassidy thought, eying the dead flowers with a growing sense of dread. He must have had them for days to let them reach this level of decay. She left them to go to wardrobe to get kitted out as Karadine Kourt. She knew that the police would find her when they eventually arrived. Meanwhile, she still had a job to do before he tried to take that from her too.

Chapter Fourteen

Janis Holmes fell into step with Cassidy on the way to get changed and linked her arm through hers. Cassidy relaxed. Janis was her favorite of the writers.

"Hey, C.J. The guys and I had a fantastic time at Mischa's party the other night talking with that Aiden Darrow. We're all so excited about getting the chance to work with her."

Cassidy stopped dead in her tracks. "Excuse me?"

"She's going to be such an asset to the show when she comes on board. Your character will take the TV world by storm in her hands!"

Cassidy just stared at her. "Aiden's coming to work on the show?"

Janis held up her hands with her fingers crossed. "God, I hope so. She'd be such a coup. With her name on the credits it would give us some serious bargaining points among our competitors." She nudged Cassidy and gave her a saucy wink. "And she's easy on the eyes too. Much more attractive to look at than Rory and Mike." She brushed a kiss across Cassidy's cheek and headed off in another direction. She threw one last comment over her shoulder as she left. "Just you wait for what we have lined up for you next season!"

"Wait! What do you mean?" Cassidy called, but Janis was already scurrying off toward the set. "Damn it! What the fuck is going on?" *And what does Aiden have to do with any of it?* Her mind was already in turmoil by the unwelcomed gift left for her and now this cryptic message from Janis didn't help. She reached for her phone to call Aiden to ask what Janis was on about, but the wardrobe mistress hustled her inside before she had the chance to touch the screen.

All the while Cassidy was sitting in the makeup chair she was stressing over the symbolism of the dead flowers in the pristine white box and what message Bernett was trying to convey this time around. The fact he had been at the gates again was disturbing enough. He was violating every restriction the police had been putting in place to stop him from getting to her. Cassidy could feel herself trembling with barely suppressed fear.

Yesterday had been so perfect, a dream day spent in Aiden's company and bed. Once again, Adam Bernett had stamped his presence on her life. He was always there reminding her she wasn't free to live her life without having to constantly look over her shoulder for him.

Janis's words were troubling also. Had Aiden gone to the writers? She'd never mentioned anything to Cassidy about meeting them the night of the party. Admittedly, they had been caught up in better things to do than retread the party dealings. Cassidy wondered why Aiden's meeting with the writers meant something for Cassidy's role in the show. Cassidy barely interacted with the makeup girl who got her into character. Thankful she could leave herself behind for a while, Cassidy left the chair as Karadine, the woman who let no man call her "mine."

❖

By the time filming had finished, Cassidy was wrung out, edgy, and in a foul mood that had been building all day. Fight scenes had been scheduled for her, and she'd channeled all her frustration into the physicality of the scenes. She'd had to apologize to at least two of the stunt men for inadvertently hitting them when she failed to pull her punches. Her own bruised knuckles were less than forgiving. Cassidy wiggled her fingers on her right hand and grimaced at the pain.

"Way to go, Slugger," she muttered to herself as she found Mischa waiting for her.

"Claude filled me in on the latest installment with that bastard Bernett so I am your designated driver for tonight. We'll take as long a route back to your place as you need me to."

"Oh, Mischa." Cassidy bit at her lip to stop herself from crying. She was so tired of it all. "Today has been a lousy day, and it started off so well."

"Let me guess? You and our resident author sleeping like the dead after a night of hot and steamy page-turning sex?" Mischa led Cassidy out to where her car was parked.

Cassidy was grateful for the darkness that hid her reddening cheeks. "I'm still not saying anything and fueling your fantasies." She got in the car and tried to ignore Mischa as she busied herself with her seat belt.

"I guess it's still all too new and shiny for you, eh?" Mischa reached over to pat her knee. "You bask away in your knowledge of how sexy Aiden can be when she gets her motor running. I'll wait because you will eventually want to spill it all." She pulled the car out of the lot. "If only to brag when I'm complaining about Joe being a 'once a night man' and you can be all smug about lesbians not needing recovery time."

Cassidy shook her head at her. "Sorcha has a lot to answer for giving you lesbian books to read." She didn't acknowledge the guard on duty at the gate. Instead she slid down in the seat and made sure her face wasn't visible through the car windows. She reached for her phone and sent Aiden a message asking if she could go straight to her home. Aiden's reply was immediate.

Come right in. I'll leave the door unlocked for you.

Cassidy was envious of Aiden's ease with leaving her door unlocked at night. She'd leave that conversation for a later date. For now she just wanted to get home and into Aiden's arms.

"The police need to catch this guy, Cass. You can't keep going through this."

Cassidy couldn't have agreed more. "I'm so tired, Mischa. I just want my life back to how it was before this one person made it his life's work to make it a misery."

"Looking on the bright side though, it did lead you to meeting Aiden. That's one silver lining, yes?"

Cassidy had to smile at Mischa's optimism despite everything that was happening. "I have to wish it had happened with less of the threats and the stalking."

"For fuck's sake, Cass! Give you the girl of your dreams and you still want it a picture perfect fairy tale," Mischa said. "Don't you know all fairy tales have that element of evil in them?"

"And a hero who saves the day." Cassidy stared out the windshield, barely seeing the road ahead. "But *I* play the hero, Mischa. It's all on my shoulders."

"Maybe someone will sweep in at the end and whisk you away from this evil bastard's clutches."

"I'd love that," Cassidy sighed. Her body felt weary and she was so tired.

"Me too. Especially if it ends with him locked away from the outside world for the rest of his days."

"And we all live happily ever after."

"The End. Roll the credits." Mischa pulled onto Cassidy's block. "Now let me work my charm on the keeper of the gates at your community. I think he likes me."

"You are such an incorrigible flirt."

"I've got to keep in practice. Joe's not getting any younger, and I have to keep my options open."

❖

It had been so easy to figure out which of C.J's castmates was driving her to and from the studios once he'd ascertained she wasn't driving herself. All Adam had to do was watch the studio gates and pay close attention to the cars arriving with *The Alchemidens* cast inside. He'd quickly deduced she was hitching a ride with Mischa Ballantyne. He was aware they were good friends on and off screen. So when Mischa's car pulled out from the studio that night, Adam had simply pulled his rental car out behind her to follow them. C.J. hadn't been visible from his vantage point, but Mischa was talking to someone in the car with her so he made an educated guess as to who it was.

The gated community they had pulled into had been a surprise to Adam. It provided him with the headache of another set of guards to try to get past. He parked and watched as Mischa was waved through. He timed how long she was inside the gates to give himself some idea how far inside C.J.'s home was situated. Mischa didn't take long to leave, and Adam let himself smile.

Found you.

He took a photo of the entrance. He'd be sure to send it to C.J. so she knew he'd caught up with her in this crazy game of cat and mouse they were playing. Satisfied with his result, he headed back to his motel room to research the layout of the Oaken Drive Community. He'd always liked the idea of living in luxury. This place would be idyllic for the two of them when they finally settled down together.

CHAPTER FIFTEEN

Cassidy waved Mischa off then walked up Aiden's driveway. Sure enough, the front door was unlocked and Cassidy quickly let herself in and secured the door behind her.

"Aiden?" She couldn't hear any noise from the kitchen so she looked around downstairs. There was a light on in a room she hadn't been in before so she decided to check for Aiden in there. It was empty, but it was obviously Aiden's writing room because her laptop was on the desk. The lights in the room made it brightly lit and welcoming. Cassidy took two steps in and stopped. Her eyes were drawn to the large framed poster hanging on the wall in front of her.

"What in the..." Cassidy's own face looked down at her from under the trademark fedora of Karadine Kourt. She looked to the right and saw shelving filled to capacity with film memorabilia. She easily picked out the numerous superheroes in bust form or figurines. There was a Catwoman cowl, the Green Lantern's ring, a scale model of one of the many Batmobile incarnations. A Captain America shield stuck out of the wall, alight like a night light. Cassidy could hardly take it all in. So many pieces all lined up according to character. Another wall had signed photos that Aiden had obviously collected from the shows and films she had worked on. There was even a cast photo from *The Alchemidens*. Cassidy knew they all signed so many a month to send out to fans, but she hadn't expected to see one on Aiden's wall. She looked a little closer and saw

Mischa's familiar scrawl and a row of little kisses she'd included. It sparked Cassidy's memory. Mischa had shoved the photo under Cassidy's nose last week and asked her to sign it and then whisked it away. She'd been signing it for Aiden? Why hadn't Aiden told her? She looked back up at the poster. Why hadn't Aiden told her just how big a fan she really was?

"Cassidy?" Aiden's voice was tentative behind her. "I was just upstairs running you a bath. I thought you might like to relax."

Cassidy felt her heart lurch at how considerate Aiden was. She couldn't take her eyes from the poster. *But who is Aiden really romancing here?*

"Just how big a fan of my show are you, Aiden?" Her voice was soft, controlled. Inside, her stomach was churning with disappointment.

"Pretty big," Aiden admitted.

"And your favorite character?"

"I'd say the poster gives that away."

Cassidy heard Aiden take a step closer. She couldn't turn around yet. She couldn't bear to see that earnest face trying to explain this. "Were you ever going to tell me?"

"Yes. But we kind of moved so fast from the kissing to the sleeping together that I didn't really have time to show you around my house so I could share."

Cassidy spun around. "Were you going to tell me before or after you got the job on my show doing whatever it is they are so excited about that revolves around my character?"

"That's not something that has even been properly discussed yet, and—"

Cassidy cut in. "But you never thought to mention it to me?" She dragged her hands through her hair. "I thought I could trust you."

"Cassidy?" Aiden looked lost. "What exactly do you think I've done?"

Cassidy pointed at the poster. "Was it me you've been getting friendly with or was it Karadine Kourt? And by working your way into my life you've managed to not only get a spot on my show to add to your credentials but you've also managed to fuck your favorite goddamn character!" She waved a hand at the shelves. "What memorabilia from our time together will grace your trophy case, Aiden? I'm quite certain I went home with my panties back on! And the signed photo? You never thought to just ask me for one? If you'd said you were a fan I'd have signed it more personally, but let me guess. Your biggest fan Mischa was more than happy to do whatever her favorite author asked of her."

"I never asked for it," Aiden said. She stood unmoving against Cassidy's tirade. "I didn't ask for the writers to talk to me. I didn't ask for the photo. I didn't tell you I was a fan because I wanted to get to know you personally."

"I'd say last night you got to know me more than enough."

"Last night wasn't because I like your show." Aiden took a step closer. Cassidy threw her hand up to stop her. Cassidy couldn't help but notice that Aiden flinched at the gesture as if Cassidy was going to strike her. For a moment, Cassidy felt terrible for making Aiden think she'd resort to physical abuse.

"What is this?" Aiden asked. "I don't understand…"

"This is me leaving you to your fantasy girl. I hope you'll be happy with Karadine." Cassidy stormed past her and flung open the front door after struggling with the lock. "And next time? Don't fuck the leading lady just to get a spot on a show. It's beneath you."

She all but ran to her own home and slammed the front door behind her. Only when she was inside did it finally hit her what she'd just done and she began shaking violently. Barely able to hold her phone, she dialed Mischa's number.

"Can you turn around and come back for me, please? I need to stay with you a while."

Satisfied that Mischa was doubling back to come get her, Cassidy quickly ran up her stairs and began throwing clothes into a suitcase.

Why can't I ever be wanted for myself and not for who I pretend to be?

❖

Aiden was left standing in the middle of her writing room wondering what the hell had just happened. She went over and over their conversation trying to understand what Cassidy had been so irate about. Surely the fact Aiden was a fan of the show wasn't that much of a stumbling block? Mischa had been tickled to pieces that Aiden was an avid viewer who could rattle off lines and episodes at will.

Of course, she hadn't just slept with Mischa.

By the time Aiden got her wits about her, she was barreling out of the house ready to go confront Cassidy and ask her what her problem was. She was just in time to catch the taillights of Mischa's car driving off with Cassidy in the passenger seat.

Aiden stood in the middle of the road, watching the car disappear.

History repeating, Aiden thought as she turned back to her home.

Everyone leaves.

❖

Cassidy had refused to talk to Mischa once she'd driven her to her home. So Mischa had just directed her to the guest room and settled her in. She barely left her in peace before she was back armed with food, an unopened bottle of wine, and two glasses. In silence, they had sat together, eaten their fill, and drank way too much. When Cassidy started crying into her pillow, Mischa had just held her until she fell asleep.

Cassidy knew Mischa wouldn't remain silent forever. She'd sat through the noisy Ballantyne breakfast, cradling her head in a hand and gratefully accepting the aspirin Mischa shoved her way. The children were excited to see her and used her as their own personal climbing frame while they ate bites of their breakfasts and dripped juice all over the floor.

The silence of the drive to the studio was sheer heaven to Cassidy's pounding head. It didn't stay quiet for long.

"I don't know everything that happened yesterday, but I do know the Bernett side of it. What I don't get is you needing to leave your home within minutes of me dropping you off there. He hasn't found out where you live, has he?"

Cassidy shook her head. She had to talk to someone about how betrayed she felt. "Aiden has a poster of me up on her wall and numerous photos from our show."

"And?"

"A poster, of me as Karadine Kourt, is center stage in her writing room."

Mischa shrugged. "So? Every writer needs her muse."

"But she'd kissed me, we'd..." Cassidy stumbled to continue.

"Fucked," Mischa stated baldly, never taking her eyes off the road.

"We *made love*." Cassidy was silent for a moment hearing the words come from her mouth. *We made love.*

"Love, eh?" Mischa looked over at her with a smile. "That's more like it. So what's the fuss about this poster then?"

"She never told me she had one."

"You know she's a fan, right? She did mention she knew your work."

"She knows it better than she admitted." Cassidy's tone was sulky and she wasn't proud of it.

"Well, yes. I know this because I spent time with her on our set and the woman is a big fan of the show. Maybe she didn't tell you so you wouldn't think she was only being nice to you because you're some famous actress and she was starstruck." The silence was deafening. Mischa's gaze left the road again. "Oh, fuck me raw. That guilty look says it all. You thought it, didn't you?"

"I might have mentioned it too," Cassidy said shamefaced. She felt terrible but had been assailed by a riot of terrible emotions all yesterday. Aiden had unfortunately fallen foul to the lot.

"You told Aiden you thought that of her? For fuck's sake, Cass, what the hell got into you?"

"I don't know. How about a delivery of dead flowers, with a note telling me I'm going to be my crazed stalker's bitch or die?

Oh, and maybe there's the fact he could get close enough to the studio again. Add that to a poster of me in my new lover's home that I didn't know about. It struck me a little too much like Bernett's apartment wall they found covered with all those pictures of my damned face. And *you* had me sign a photo of the cast for her and didn't even tell me who it was for either!"

"I didn't tell you because I was in a hurry. I don't usually have to ask for permission when I pester the cast to scribble on a photograph. It just happened to be for Aiden this time."

"Why didn't she ask me for one?"

"Maybe she didn't want you to think she was using you for a fan request," Mischa said pointedly.

"So she asked you?"

"No. I did it as a thank you. She had no idea I was going to do it for her. She wrote my kids a story for me to read to them. It's her first ever children's tale. A signed photograph doesn't even begin to cover how fucking priceless that story is to us." Mischa shook her head. "I have to read from it to them every night now. We're already on our second read through and the kids are still spellbound by it. Aiden wrote them into an adventure story where they are the heroes. It's fucking brilliant. I admit I cried when she gave it to me. She did that for a *fan* of *her* work."

"Janis told me that they were in talks with Aiden to write for the show."

"Really?" Mischa sounded honestly surprised.

"Specifically my character."

"Ooh, do you think they're going to make Karadine gay? That would explain why they'd want Aiden involved." She looked over at Cassidy excitedly.

"I don't know. I'm the last to know, apparently. But I'm more upset by the fact Aiden went behind my back to the writers and wrangled herself a job."

Mischa frowned at her. "Says who?"

"Janis said they talked with her."

"Yes, at my party. They'd found out about Aiden's interest because of me showing her around the set. The writers were very excited to meet her. I introduced her to them, and they must have spoken to her there about their ideas." She tapped at her phone that was cradled in its car dock. "Let's get this cleared right now." She tapped it again to switch to speaker.

"Who are you calling?" Cassidy wasn't ready to speak to Aiden just yet, even if it was facelessly over the phone.

Nicole Abnett answered. "Hey, Mischa, what can I do for you?"

"Rumor has it that you guys are looking to outside sources to change up a character on the show."

"Christ, you can't keep anything from being leaked. How the hell did you hear that?"

"Your own writers have loose lips, Nicole. You might want to batten down those hatches if you don't want to cause panic among the cast."

Cassidy could hear Nicole grumbling to herself about killing Janis. Mischa wasn't finished, however.

"So, what's happening? All my girl Cass here knows is that Karadine Kourt is being singled out for some reason. Spill the beans, girl."

Nicole's sigh was clearly audible over the line. "You were going to be told properly, C.J., I promise you. We've been considering making Karadine a lesbian. Meeting Aiden Darrow at Mischa's party was perfect timing. We were able to ask her some questions about her help with other shows and if it was something worth us considering doing."

"So Aiden didn't approach you?" Cassidy couldn't help herself. She had to ask to be sure.

"Hell no. We had Mischa bring her over so we could ply her with questions. She was very professional. She was also adamant that we checked all this with you first, C.J. She told us that just because you're gay doesn't mean we should assume you'd be comfortable playing it on screen."

Mischa gave Cassidy a "See? Told you" look. Cassidy nodded at her, feeling rotten enough already. "So, *is* Aiden writing for us?"

"Not yet. We'd have to contact her agent and set up meetings to get it all legal and aboveboard first. This was just an idea we were floating around for season three. Personally, though? I think it will be a great storyline to explore."

"I'd have preferred hearing this in a more professional setting than as gossip, Nicole." Cassidy was still smarting from finding out the way she had. Also for how she had used it against Aiden in a way she hadn't deserved. *How the hell do I apologize to Aiden for that?* Cassidy felt sick inside. She'd screwed up beyond any hope of forgiveness. How could she possibly face Aiden now?

She heard Nicole apologizing again and that they'd talk as soon as they got to the studio. The ringing of her other phone had Nicole having to sign off.

"A certain writer will have her ovaries handed to her for spilling the beans on that particular plot spoiler," Mischa said, leaning back in her seat. "So, now that you've heard it from Nicole's lips, how are you going to clear this with Aiden?"

Cassidy lowered her face in her hands and sighed. "I honestly have no idea. I fucked up so bad."

"Yeah, you kinda did," Mischa said.

"She may never forgive me. *I* wouldn't forgive me." She whined pitifully and buried her head deeper in her palms.

"Good thing she's a nicer person than you then, isn't it?" Mischa smacked at Cassidy's hands to bring her head back up and pointed to her phone. "While you've been camped out at my home, crying into your pillow all night over some stupid ass 'poster-gate,'" Mischa grumbled as she snatched up her phone and one-handedly tapped on the screen. She refused to let Cassidy butt in on her rant. "Letting this woman down because you're too frightened about just how much you feel for her that you'd rather push her away with lame excuses of not dating a fan. And why? Because she might know your lines better than you do from the show?" Mischa laughed harshly. "The woman writes what we'd kill to star in. I'm honored she's fascinated by my character and can talk to me about her because that's what I worked so damn hard to achieve. Now…" Mischa waved her phone at Cassidy. "Within minutes of me picking you up last night, I received a text." She dropped the phone in Cassidy's lap. "Read it."

Cassidy did so.

Please keep her safe.

"This is from the woman you'd just accused of using you for your fame to further her own. I can see why you'd think she was so devious." Mischa rolled her eyes in derision.

Cassidy pushed the phone aside. "I'm aware of what a complete asshole I've been."

"I understand you'd had a bad day, but really? Why take it out on her?"

"I was thrown by seeing that she had Alchemiden stuff hidden away. It struck a chord at the wrong time. She's never once acted like a fan except, now that I think about it, around you. And then I thought she was just being polite because you're so goddamn pushy."

"I had the best time with her on the set. She's sweet and funny and loves the show. She loves the characters and appreciates it all, both as a viewer *and* as a writer."

"I never gave her a chance to explain. I know now I should have listened to her."

"But you didn't want to listen. You wanted to run and she gave you the opportunity by letting you see something of *her*. The collector of stuff you wouldn't be interested in but to her is priceless, and each piece probably has a story involved. All you saw was your TV persona staring back at you." Mischa shook her head sadly. "If you could only have seen the way her eyes followed you around the room at my party. It wasn't lust. It was total adoration. You weren't Karadine freakin' Kourt that night. You were Cassidy Hayes. That girl has got it bad for you."

"She won't be safe around me. If Bernett finds out how much I care for her he'll go after her too. I can't put her in that position." Cassidy finally admitted to herself that a big part of her deliberately letting loose on Aiden was to make her step back so as not to be put in danger over being with her.

"Oh, Cass, you fool. Don't you realize Aiden would rather be by your side no matter what?"

"She deserves someone without the humungous stalker baggage I'm toting around."

"She deserves you groveling on your knees to her," Mischa growled under her breath. "But enough about you now. I'm done trying to sort your love life out. Let's get back to this poster business. Did she happen to have one of me at all adorning her wall?"

Cassidy's head whipped around to pin Mischa with an incredulous look. "*Seriously*? No, she didn't."

Mischa made a face. "There's one of me available. I'll have to tell her because it's an excellent shot of my"—she brushed a hand over her cleavage to smooth her dress down—"considerable charms."

Cassidy couldn't help but laugh at Mischa's irrepressible behavior. "I'm thankful you're my friend, but sometimes? You're totally bat shit crazy."

"I have to be to put up with you, my dear. Especially after last night when you drank a whole bottle of one of my best vintage reds like it was soda pop while you bawled like an infant into your glass. So can I text a certain someone, who is understandably worried about you, to say you'll be home sooner rather than later?"

Cassidy sighed. "Maybe…just not yet. I know I owe her an apology if she'll listen to me."

"Well, when it finally happens, I'll want details of how wild your makeup sex was for my trouble."

Cassidy shook her head at her. "Maybe, if I'm that fortunate, the highlights can be in Aiden's next book."

"I want to hear about it the next day, not wait that long for her to tackle her next story! If she's going to be working for *The Alchemidens* it might be ages yet. You owe me details, Cass. Big, explicit details. I earned it after sleeping with you last night, Little Miss Bed-hog."

"Your guest room only has a single bed. It wasn't built to fit both of us. I didn't invite you to sleep with me. You took advantage of my weakened state."

The studio appeared ahead, and Cassidy began searching the sidewalks for the familiar haunting face of Adam Bernett. She welcomed the sight of the gates. Once inside, she was safe from the reality of the outside world and could lose herself in the fantasy instead.

There were days where her profession truly kept her from losing her sanity.

CHAPTER SIXTEEN

The photograph mailed to Cassidy at the studio wrecked any plans she had of returning home and talking to Aiden. It was a shot taken of the wrought iron gates and the guardhouse of Oaken Drive that kept Cassidy's new home safe from unwelcome visitors. Or so she'd hoped.

"He knows where I'm living now." Cassidy's heart dropped, and she slumped in her chair. "I can't escape him."

Mischa rubbed her hand over Cassidy's back, trying to comfort her as they sat watching Detective Peter Whitmeyer bagging up the newest piece of evidence. They were all sequestered in an office, far away from prying eyes. Cassidy knew that the sets would be buzzing with gossip, as they'd all seen her being pulled from the set yet again.

"You can't go back to your previous apartment. Bernett has already been seen back there hanging around. He was recognized and fled before we could get there to apprehend him."

"He's looking for me in every place he knows I could be. My home, the studio, and now my new home." Cassidy ran a hand through her hair. She knew the makeup lady would be livid, but there was nothing Cassidy could do to stop herself. He was getting closer and closer; she could almost feel his breath on her neck. "What happens when he finally tracks me down, Detective? I don't think he's just going to hand me a valentine."

"We're trying to stop him before that happens," Whitmeyer said.

"But you can't find him. Yet he's everywhere Cassidy is, like a tick on a dog's ass." Mischa scowled at the detective. "And you really can't do anything until you even find him."

"You know our hands are tied while he remains hidden," Whitmeyer said.

"So, while this lowlife is tracking Cassidy, you keep searching under every Dumpster and park bench. You've got to have access to all the fancy tech to trace calls. Track him when he keeps calling trying to be put through to her here."

"He's oddly elusive for someone who manages to keep excellent tabs on Ms. Hayes. He's out there somewhere. Unfortunately, we haven't been able to pin him down. But he'll surface again. He can't resist coming after you."

"That knowledge doesn't make me feel any safer," Cassidy said. "He's just one step behind me all the time."

"Where are you staying now?"

Cassidy looked at Mischa. "I *was* staying with a friend, but I'm not putting her or her family in danger just like I wouldn't before. If he can follow me to the gated community I've been staying in, then he can surely find me where I am now. They don't deserve being dragged into this any more than they already have been."

"Cass—"

"No, Mischa. At least back at Lori's house I'm reasonably secure with the guards that patrol there."

"Let us put extra protection in place at the house before you return," Whitmeyer said. "It's the best I can offer seeing as you won't let me post someone on you twenty-four/seven."

"If you can find me someone who isn't going to expect to live in my house with me then I'll agree. My life is screwed up enough without someone trailing after me at all hours of the day and night expecting me to cook them breakfast." Cassidy wanted her life to feel as normal as it possibly could with a stalker dogging her every movement. She didn't want a bodyguard who made her feel even more trapped.

"You're staying with us until they've tricked your house out." Mischa's tone warned Cassidy not to argue. "I'll tell your neighbor not to worry about the maintenance crew showing up at your place too."

Cassidy nodded. She hoped that by the time she returned to her home, she had finally found the words she needed to say to Aiden.

❖

Late Friday night, Cassidy was chauffeured back to the gated community by a burly man who appeared to take up most of the car with his intimidating size. Aiden watched as Cassidy was cautiously released out of the vehicle's rear seating. Her newly appointed driver dutifully checked the road before finally allowing her to step foot on the sidewalk. Only then did he catch sight of Aiden. His stare was a deadly weapon in itself, and he held Cassidy back with a massive arm across her chest.

Aiden was sitting on Cassidy's front door step. She smiled at the guy, hoping her checkered shirt and tailored shorts screamed anything but "stalker" to his narrowed gaze. She caught Cassidy obviously say something to him that made him lower his arm, but it didn't change the steely look on his face. He stepped back into the car still eyeing Aiden stonily.

Cassidy walked toward her, and Aiden was enthralled by how beautiful she looked. Her hair was loose and fell around her shoulders. The simple red dress she wore accented every delicious curve that graced her body. Aiden couldn't help but smile at her. Cassidy appeared nervous, and she slowed her pace the closer she got to where Aiden sat.

"Aiden..." she began nervously, her voice trailing off when Aiden stood up.

"I think we need to talk, don't you? I'd like you to come back to my house please."

"I need to inform my bodyguard. I warn you, he's likely to park his car on your drive. Then, no doubt, he'll do a recon of your whole yard."

"He's welcome to do that. I'll even supply coffee if he's in need of a caffeine fix." She escorted a compliant Cassidy to her house. Aiden couldn't miss the nervousness radiating off her.

"How did you know I was coming back?" Cassidy asked, her voice soft in the quiet stillness of the evening.

"A little bird might have told me," Aiden said with a grin. She'd received Mischa's text with much relief. She knew how long it took to travel from the studio so had settled herself on Cassidy's porch to wait.

"Mischa." Cassidy sighed.

"She knows I've been worried about you." Aiden steered Cassidy through her front door and closed it behind them. Cassidy could barely meet her eyes.

"After all I said, why would you even care?"

Aiden hated the resigned timber of Cassidy's voice. Aiden curled a finger under Cassidy's chin and lifted her head so she could look into her eyes.

"Because I care for you." She took a deliberate step back and held out a hand. "I think we need to clear up some things between us before we go any further." She waved her hand for Cassidy to shake it. Cassidy's slender hand was cool to the touch when she finally took the hint. "Hi, I'm Aiden Darrow. I've been following your career for some time now and I'm a huge fan of *The Alchemidens*." She shook Cassidy's hand firmly.

"Aiden," Cassidy said, but Aiden tugged on her hand before letting it go.

"I should have told you that the moment I met you, but I was too interested in getting to know you. I figured you wouldn't want to have anything to do with me once you knew I was just another fan."

"You couldn't be *just* anything if you tried," Cassidy said with a small smile.

"Well, I would like to state, for the record, that I am seriously pissed over the fact you'd think I would use you to bolster my own career." She held up a hand to forestall Cassidy's hasty words she could see ready to spill from her lips. "I've done pretty damn well on my own merits, thank you very much. Just like everything else in life that I have accomplished. Through *my* hard work, *my* talent, *my* success, all earned, not given to me." She noticed Cassidy's eyes widen at her unusually harsh tone. Cassidy looked so suitably contrite that Aiden sighed.

"Can you ever forgive me?" Tears began to fill Cassidy's eyes.

"That depends. What took you so long to come back when you had to know how worried I'd be? It was hard enough knowing you had walked out on me, but you left your safe place. If nothing else, Cassidy, you need to be safe. Especially as he's obviously ramping up his attentions."

Cassidy stared at her. "How do you know that?"

"Because you wouldn't be having extra security added if nothing had changed. And you have a bodyguard outside the door." Aiden wanted to ask more about what had happened, but Cassidy looked so fragile. Besides, Aiden had something else she wanted to get off her chest. "You can fill me in on that later if you want to. There's something I'd like to show you first." She led Cassidy toward a familiar room.

"I've seen the poster and the memorabilia shelves. I have the less than fond memories of making a total fool of myself in there." Still, Cassidy followed after Aiden's lead.

"I know you've seen it, but you didn't see it through *my* eyes. I've never had to explain myself to anyone before but you're not just anyone. So let me show you the other world *I* inhabit."

CHAPTER SEVENTEEN

Aiden pulled her chair out from under the desk and settled Cassidy in it. Then, opening her arms wide, Aiden gestured around the room. "This is my writing haven. In here I work on all my stories, the TV scripts I'm involved with, and the screenplays I receive. Some writers need a window to look out of while they work, some like blank walls, and some, like me, prefer to be surrounded by things that have significance to them."

She took a deep breath. She'd never spoken to anyone about what she was about to reveal to Cassidy. *Please don't let her run again because of this.* "You have to know that, as a writer, I pretty much live in a fantasy world most of the time. I'm always going to have one foot in this world while the other is firmly planted in my imagination and the worlds I inhabit there. I can't switch it off. People joke about writers 'hearing voices.' It's true. Characters talk to me all the time, feeding me their next lines. But for me, it's not all in here." She tapped at her head. "I need visual stimuli because I get great comfort from being surrounded by certain objects."

"You don't have to do this," Cassidy said. "I'm sorry for what I said. You didn't deserve any of it."

"I know. But I need to share with you why these things are important. Otherwise you'll never understand. And I'd like you to understand them, and me." Aiden pointed to her shelves. "When I was growing up, I could never have had anything like this. Firstly, I couldn't have afforded even one of these figurines. And secondly, the bigger kids would have taken them from me and smashed them. I lost count of how many of my books they ripped up or used as kindling for the little fires they set. I became an expert at hiding stuff and soon learned to travel light because anything I had was never mine for long. Story of my life that," she muttered, acknowledging to herself that no truer words had been spoken concerning herself.

"My one foster brother, the car thief? He'd bring me comic books he'd stolen and I'd devour them like a starving animal. I recognized something of myself in the characters. You'll note that nearly all of the superheroes we know and love have lost their parents or their guardians. I identified with that. I knew what they were going through, the struggles they had to fit in, and the fact they were pretty much always left alone. And, sadly, I'm *still* waiting for my superpowers to kick in."

Aiden gave Cassidy a self-deprecating smile. "Anyway, my foster mother, Trudy, used to take me to the movies. That was my special time with her and my treat once a month. She thought I'd love the escapism. And I did. I'd watch those stories play out on the screen, and no one could take that away from me. I could lock the movie away in my memory and replay my favorite scenes over and over again. When I got bigger, I learned to make my own worlds, create my own stories. They became my safe places, a place where I was free. No one could hurt me there or touch my stories.

"I was adopted by two very patient people, and I believe that saved me from things being so much worse. But I still had problems fitting in with the other kids. School was such a trial for me. Contrary to belief, you *can* feel isolated when surrounded by people. I finally left home and eventually got a home of my own. To be honest, I didn't know what to do with it. I'd never had a real home before that didn't involve others sharing my space. I was totally lost. I needed something that made me feel safe in it. Something that made it mine. One day, I found a Batman poster. He was one of the protectors I'd always dreamed of who'd come get me out of the bad homes and rescue me."

She ran her fingertips along the edge of the shelf. "I've added a few things since then. Things that inspire me, or remind me of the story the movie portrayed. I no longer have to keep it all in my head, now that I can reach out and touch these things. I need to know they are real."

"Your car is one of those things as well, isn't it?" Cassidy said with a dawning understanding.

Aiden smiled. "Yes, that's my biggest collectible. One that I can drive every day and for those moments be reminded of *Thelma and Louise* and how I felt when I watched it."

"By any chance are your glasses one too?"

Aiden snorted with laughter. "Well done, Ms. Lane! I do indeed have Clark Kent frames for exactly that reason. That, and the hope they'll make me look smarter. The jury is still out on that though."

"So, are you really hiding a superhero persona behind those geeky glasses, Aiden?" Cassidy said softly.

"Oh, I wish I was. I would love that so much. I have a deep and abiding love for all things superhero. Finally being able to indulge myself in that has been so much fun. Their stories made me want to be a better person. I was surrounded by thieves and abusers and very little love until I was taken in by Trudy. I wanted a different life from that, and my imagination gifted me it. My being able to use it for my career makes my life as close to perfect as I can get it. I get to write words that my favorite actors recite. As a kid, I wished I could step through the movie screen and enter whatever world I was watching. Anything to get away from where I was." Aiden tapped her laptop lid. "I get to do that now. My writing is me stepping through into that other world and playing there for as long as I wish."

"You've got a fantastic imagination," Cassidy said. "I'm in awe of what you can do with it."

"I can't imagine not being able to write. I think it would kill me if I lost the ability to bring characters to life in worlds of my making." She looked up at the poster prominent in the room. "I'm drawn to strong characters. I can't help it. I need the fantasy they bring as much as I need air to breath. TV or movie, I can lose myself in a well written story populated by characters who make me care enough for them." Aiden smiled at Cassidy. "Karadine Kourt is one of those at the moment, so she rightly found her place in my room."

"I understand that now," Cassidy said. "I'm really, really sorry."

"This woman here?" Aiden pointed at Cassidy as Karadine Kourt. "I think she's amazing. She's willful, so bold and beautiful. She's all the things in a superhero that I admire." She reached down to pick up a picture frame from beside her laptop. It had been positioned at an angle so Cassidy couldn't see it. Aiden turned it around for her.

"But this woman? This is the woman I'm falling in love with because she's also beautiful, but she's also funny, tenderhearted, and so fascinating she makes me appreciate that life is worth living." The photo in the frame was the picture Sorcha had taken of Aiden and Cassidy at Mischa's party. They both had smiled automatically for the camera at Sorcha's request, but Cassidy's hands were still on Aiden's tie. It was an oddly intimate moment caught in time. Cassidy's breath hitched audibly.

Aiden drew her attention again to the poster. "This woman is a fantasy. A glorious heroine who fires my imagination." She lifted the photo and held it out for Cassidy to hold. Aiden tapped on the glass. "But this woman is the one who finally makes me grateful that I live in the real world. Because where she is? That's exactly where I want to be."

Still clutching the photo, Cassidy flung herself into Aiden's arms. Aiden held her as close as she could, burying her face in Cassidy's hair and breathing in her familiar scent. It soothed her aching soul.

"I missed you so much," she murmured, pressing her lips to Cassidy's head. She could feel Cassidy crying against her shoulder. "Don't cry, sweetheart. Please don't cry."

"How can you be so understanding when I was such a bitch to you?" Cassidy wailed, hiding her face in Aiden's shirt.

"Because I know you and I know you don't really think I was with you just because of the show you're in. I'd hope you really know me better than that."

"I was stressed. I was so stressed and I just…lashed out at you when I saw the poster and everything. It was stupid of me."

"You've got to admit, it's a fantastic poster of you."

"Mischa's pissed you don't have one of her on display."

"Your character in the show was the one that caught my attention from the very first episode. I adore the show, but she was the draw for me to it and remains so."

"I won't say a word." Cassidy lifted her head from where she'd dampened Aiden's shirt with her tears. "I need to talk to you about Bernett, but not tonight, please? There'll be plenty of time tomorrow."

"Okay, not tonight. I'd like you to stay here with me, please? I just need you near. I've missed you desperately."

Cassidy pulled Aiden's head down for a long, lingering kiss that left them both breathless and shaking in each other's arms. Carefully, she placed the photo back on the desk, then Cassidy ran her hands up Aiden's back to take fistfuls of her shirt. She freed it from Aiden's shorts. Her warm hands on Aiden's skin made Aiden groan with need. Their first night hadn't been enough for Aiden to temper her desire for Cassidy. But tonight wasn't going to be about sex. Tonight it was about being able to reassure herself that Cassidy was there for her like she wanted to be for Cassidy.

"I should never have left you that night," Cassidy admitted. "Everything had gone to hell that day and I just wanted to get back to you. The poster and what it stupidly reminded me of just seriously fucked everything up."

"I should have told you."

"And I should have given you the chance instead of storming out like a diva."

"No more secrets." Aiden kissed her gently.

Cassidy reached up to remove Aiden's glasses and popped them on the desk. "No, *Clark*, no more hiding yourself from me any longer either. And I promise I won't ever be foolish enough to accuse you of being with me to further your career when it's painfully obvious you don't need anyone's help to rise to the top."

"I just need *you*." Aiden kissed her again, longer this time, taking her time to trace Cassidy's lips and just taste her. "I made you dinner," she said quietly and was taken aback by the stuttering sob that rose from Cassidy's chest. Aiden just held on to her. She rocked her gently while she cried herself out and clung to Aiden as if she were the only thing keeping her upright.

Guess I need to get used to being with a temperamental actress.

❖

"This really wasn't my intention for tonight."

Aiden's words came out breathy as she panted with exertion. Cassidy had three fingers buried inside her, and the pleasure from each thrust was flooding Aiden's senses. Cassidy was poised above her, her face so close that she was able to rub her nose along Aiden's. It was a sweetly tender gesture, at odds with the sturdy press of her fingers within Aiden's tightening walls. Cassidy scattered soft kisses over Aiden's face. The contrast between the soft teasing lips and the strength behind her fingers made Aiden all but whine beneath her. Cassidy was finding all her well-kept secrets tonight. Aiden had been thrilled when Cassidy had realized she liked her nipples licked rather than sucked. That and extra fingers deep inside her would make Aiden beg for release. Cassidy's eyes were so focused on Aiden's that Aiden was certain she could see directly into her soul. She could feel herself begin to shake, clenching tighter around Cassidy's fingers as she started to explode.

"Come for me, Aiden," Cassidy breathed in her ear.

With a tortured howl, Aiden let go. Her hips bucked erratically. She could feel her wetness flowing as she climaxed. Cassidy never let up on her movements and, caught up in the sudden addition of a twisting wrist that forced Cassidy's fingers even further, Aiden came a second time. Her shout of surprise broke the air, and she shook as if fevered while the aftershocks ripped through her and left her boneless.

Cassidy settled herself over Aiden's sprawled body. She slid her fingers free and placed her wet hand over Aiden's heart. Then, tucking her head under Aiden's chin, she began tracing lazy patterns on Aiden's chest. The wet trails glistened on Aiden's already damp skin.

Finally, when she was able to move, Aiden wrapped her arms around Cassidy and hugged her closer still. "I may never leave this bed again. You wiped me out." Aiden could feel Cassidy's smug smile against her skin. "You have magical powers, Cassi. I never come more than once."

Cassidy pressed a kiss on the rapidly pounding pulse that beat in Aiden's neck. "That's because you've never had a girl like me before."

"There's *never* been anyone like you," Aiden said. Cassidy lifted her head to look at her.

"You're the one with the dangerous powers. I keep telling myself to stay away from you. That you're not safe around me with that bastard still on the loose, and yet here I am, back in your arms because I can't stay away from you."

"We'll work something out. I promise," Aiden said.

With a sigh, Cassidy settled herself back down at Aiden's side. "I'm going to be swamped at work this week because we have a heavy shooting schedule planned. Then this coming weekend I've got a charity event I have to attend. The weekend after that I'm at a convention to publicize the show's new season. We got a late inclusion after another show pulled out due to them being cancelled midseason."

"You're doing Nova-Con?" Aiden knew the convention well, so named because it was always held in the month of November.

Cassidy nodded. "Yes, the whole cast, the writers and our producer are all going. It should be fun, but conventions are so tiring. So many people wanting your attention all the time. And you can't let your mask slip because they don't want to see you tired or annoyed because you've just been asked the same damn question three times in a row."

"I'll be there too. I'm part of the panel *From Written Word to Movie Screen.*"

Cassidy's face lit up. "Seriously? How exciting! I hope we're not on at the same time. I want to see you work a room. What will you be talking about?"

Aiden grinned. She was so proud of her latest accomplishment, and it had been a nightmare being sworn to secrecy from announcing her involvement. "You can't repeat a word of what I am about to tell you. Not even to Mischa," she said. Cassidy nodded. "The convention is where the official announcement will take place."

Cassidy leaned up on an elbow to stare at her. She jabbed a finger into Aiden's shoulder. "Don't keep a girl in suspense. Spill!"

"I'm to be the official screenwriter for *Guildanan's Quest*," she announced proudly.

Cassidy's mouth dropped open. "Oh my God! That's huge! That's like the biggest selling book in ages, and the buzz all over Hollywood has been about which studio was going to secure the movie rights. You're going to adapt that book into the movie?"

Aiden nodded, knowing her own excitement was shining from her eyes. It was a fantastic opportunity and one she intended to do justice to.

Cassidy flung her arms around her and squeezed her tight. "Congratulations! That's fantastic! Oh, my darling, you're going to do a wonderful job on that story."

"I hope so. It's a book I really enjoyed, and they wanted someone who wouldn't be coming to the story cold and had some experience writing fantasy period drama. I think they just wanted someone who wouldn't balk at the idea of dragons and titans and sea monsters." She laughed as she thought about the storyline. "Big sea monsters that can come ashore. I wish the special effects guys good luck with that because I am not losing that fact to shave money off the budget. I'll try my hardest not to change the story too much. I want it to remain true to the book, and the author knows that. He's a good friend anyway and has told me he trusts me to bring his book to life."

Cassidy looked suitably impressed. She kissed her, a swift press of her lips to Aiden's smiling ones. "I'm so proud of you I could burst."

Aiden grinned then watched as a curious look flickered across Cassidy's face.

"You know, my agent has been saying I need to get a higher profile in movies. She's kept on that when they filmed *Guildanan's Quest*, I'd have to put myself forward for the role of Cassiopeia. I've been waiting for the call to go out."

Aiden tried not to let her thoughts show on her face. She knew Cassidy would be perfect for that role. She'd even brought it up at the meetings for the movie she'd already sat in on. All well before she'd even met Cassidy.

"We'd heard talk of it being filmed next year. I'm praying for it to be in the show's summer hiatus because I want that role so bad."

Unable to resist, Aiden pushed Cassidy onto her back and loomed over her. "Is that what this evening was about, Ms. Hayes? Were you sleeping with me to soften me up to secure the leading lady role?"

The look on Cassidy's face would have been funny if it wasn't for the fact her eyes were ablaze with a furious flame.

"How dare you!" Cassidy began, struggling to get out from under Aiden's hold. Aiden only tightened her grip, smiling the whole time until Cassidy stopped thrashing and finally realized she was being given a dose of her own medicine. She fell back with a thump against the pillows. "Touché, Aiden," she said with an edge. "I guess I deserved that." Her eyes, still darkened with annoyance, gradually softened as Aiden nuzzled her to get her smile back. "Does this mean I can't ever be involved in something you do?"

"Of course not. It just means you'll go through the same hoops as any other actress to get the role. I won't let my bias for your talent go against what the studio decides." Aiden tugged Cassidy close. "But you'd better work your ass off to get Cassiopeia because I've seen you in that role from the second I read the book."

Cassidy nodded then sobered. "And this is the last either of us talks about using the other to further their career. That subject dies here and now."

"I agree." She yawned abruptly. "I'm sorry, but you wore me out."

"Two orgasm lightweight," Cassidy said and reached down the bed to pull the sheet up over them. "Go to sleep, Aiden."

"Will you still be here when I wake?"

"Yes. I'll need you to get me up and ready for work though because the orgasm you dragged screaming out of me earlier this evening has left me a little tired too."

Aiden fumbled for her clock and set a time. "I'll make you breakfast and kiss you off on the doorstep when your big, bad driver comes to pick you up."

"You're so domesticated. I never thought I'd want that."

"And now?"

"Now I'm amazed at what I want where you're concerned. But..."

Aiden hushed her softly. She snuggled them both down. "Shhh, no more talking tonight." Aiden kissed Cassidy good night with a sweet, lingering brush over her lips. "It's all going to be all right."

"Promise?"

"If you'll let me, I'll promise you everything and more besides."

Cassidy stared at her, stopping Aiden's hand from turning out the light. "I love you, Aiden."

A curious feeling of peace and euphoria suffused Aiden's chest. She smiled down at Cassidy's beautiful and oh-so-serious face. "I love you too." She turned off the light and relished the feel of Cassidy in her arms. *I'll do everything in my power to bring about our happy ending.* She held her dream girl close. Not the heroine who kept the city safe on TV but the real woman Cassidy Hayes was. The woman Aiden loved and was loved by in return.

Aiden closed her eyes and fell asleep, safe in the hold of someone who wanted her. Someone she could maybe build a home with, a home with someone to share it with. Finally, a forever family all of her very own.

CHAPTER EIGHTEEN

A few nights later, Detective Whitmeyer stood in the middle of Cassidy's living room. He looked rumpled and tired as befit the hour he was visiting. Surreptitiously, he was checking out the décor. From the look on his face, Aiden thought he was finding it as overpowering as she did. The whole house was an explosion of color. Aiden was convinced Lori was colorblind because the living room alone was migraine inducing.

"I have to say this place is nothing like your apartment, Cassidy." He accepted the coffee Aiden had made and all but drank half of it down in one gulp.

"None of this house is done to anything like my particular tastes. Lori does seem to have an eye for the eclectic. Though I'm not quite sure what she's going to make of all the high tech surveillance equipment dotted around her property." Cassidy nudged Aiden gently. "And here I was just worrying about how to get the wine stain out of her sofa before she returns."

Aiden was sitting beside a clearly nervous Cassidy. She was purposely close enough so that her knee touched Cassidy's to remind her she was there. Whitmeyer had requested a meeting with Cassidy outside of the police station and out from under the watchful gaze of the studio heads. Aiden couldn't help but feel that didn't mean good news.

He pulled out a file from his briefcase and slid it across the coffee table to them.

"Bernett is still sending you letters to the studio. These are the latest batch. They've been arriving at a rate of one a day again for the past week. I have to say, they're not pretty."

Cassidy ignored the file, but Aiden wanted to see for herself what they were dealing with. The first words she read shocked her.

You dying in my arms is all I can dream of now.

Her head snapped up to catch the sympathetic wince Whitmeyer gave her. She read through the rest of the letter. She'd been a writer for many years and knew the power of words. These weren't the kind words from a devoted fan. These words poured his hatred out through the ink. The cruel vitriol stained the white lined page. It was such innocuous writing paper for such an evil message to be written on. For a moment, Aiden fancied she could all but see the words dripping their poisonous venom. The man who wrote these things wasn't just obsessed. He was seriously deranged. She picked up another letter, then another, reading them through quickly and finding his theme. *He wants her dead and won't stop until he's achieved that goal.* "Tell me you're employing more people to watch her."

Cassidy whined. "I already have Marks shadowing me like a bad smell. I don't need any more babysitters following me around like sheep."

Aiden shook a letter at her. "Even if you won't read these, Cassidy, you have to know what they say. You've lived with him in your world long enough now. There's no return address on these letters, but the postmark clearly points to him being right on your doorstep. He's *here*. Right where you are. You know he's only gotten more dangerous and you're the one he wants."

"I know full well I've moved on from being his one and only to being the one he wants dead and buried." Cassidy's hand shook as she reached for her coffee cup. "He's been singing that tune for a while now. Ever since I got signed to *The Alchemidens*. But there really isn't anything I can do. I just want to get on with my life the best I can."

Aiden was amazed by how determined Cassidy was to continue living as normally as possible, despite Bernett stalking her every move. Aiden looked to Whitmeyer for an answer. "You didn't come just to show Cassidy these letters tonight, did you?"

He shook his head. He drew out his phone from a pocket, placed it on the table, and pressed play. A man's voice, talking almost conversationally in his tone, filled the room.

"When I find you, I am going to kill you. Slowly at first, to draw out the agony. It will be just like how you slowly led me to believe you were true only to me. Maybe I'll cut you a little, to have the satisfaction of watching you bleed. Then we'll see if you share your character's tolerance for pain because I intend to hurt you until you scream. It seems only fair to exact such a price for all the suffering you have caused me. You've ignored me for too long, C.J. I've devoted my life to you. Seems only right for you to pay that debt to me with your own."

Whitmeyer paused the recording. "This was left on one of the studio's answering machines last night. That's just part of the message. He eventually loses how rational he sounds here and starts screaming." He looked up at Cassidy. "Believe me; you don't need to hear that." He pocketed his phone. "I'm putting another man on the gates here in case Bernett tries to come after you at home. I've been made aware you're living both here and next door with Ms. Darrow." He gave Aiden a glance. "We've been in touch with your security providers. We have both your homes under our watch now."

Aiden wasn't sure if she liked that he'd done all that without asking her permission first, but for Cassidy's safety, she wasn't going to argue.

"Marks is staying right beside you, no matter how much you hate it. I'm also posting another guard at the studio." Whitmeyer held up a hand at Cassidy's objections. "It will be a woman this time. I think she'll blend in more, but don't be fooled by her pretty face. She's more than capable of bringing a man down and subduing him."

"Finally, there will be some benefits to constantly having someone under my feet. At least a woman will hold my purse when I ask and not look quite so pained doing so." Cassidy flashed Aiden a wry smile.

Whitmeyer continued. "This charity event your show is running? I want you to cancel your appearance."

Aiden wasn't in the least surprised when Cassidy chose that to reveal her temper over.

"No, I won't. This is the first event my show has taken part in. It's got sponsors and everything set up. I have to be there. I *will* be there."

Aiden reached out to wrap her fingers around Cassidy's clenched fist. "The studio would surely understand why you had to pull out."

Cassidy shook her head. "I won't let him dictate what I can and can't do in my life. I have obligations. I am under contract, and that means I have the obligation to participate in certain events. Besides, I *want* to do this. The publicity alone from the shows involved will bring in a huge amount of money for the charities we're collecting for. If I have to turn up ringed by a bevy of policemen, I will. He's not stopping me from living."

"Then can we negotiate the convention in November?"

Cassidy cut him off again.

"I'm going to that too. I have fans, Detective. They are sending me Tweets saying that they are flying in to meet me. For some of them it's a once in a lifetime trip to make. These are my real fans. They are the ones who love my character and want to see me because I am her. They want to get their brief moment in time with me to get a photograph, or have me sign a picture for them. These are the fans I'm doing it for. The shy little geeky girls who can recite all my lines inside and out. The older ones who dress up like Karadine because pretending to be her empowers them. I am not letting Bernett stop me from seeing them. They are far more important to me than he ever will be."

"It's going to be a fucking nightmare," he grumbled, clearly unhappy.

"Then please try to make it less so," Cassidy said. "These are the last two big events to publicize the new season we're currently working on. The big bosses need us to push the show out there to make sure our audience doesn't forget us and are ready for when the show returns in the spring." She looked at both Whitmeyer and Aiden, needing for them to understand. "I have to be seen. It's what I've worked for."

Aiden marveled at how impassioned Cassidy was about her career. She admired that in her. It wasn't about the fame and fortune for Cassidy. She cared about the character she played and the story she told. That didn't stop Aiden from being absolutely terrified for her. Aiden had read his words now. She'd heard his voice. He wasn't some shadowy threat hiding in the shadows ready to jump out. He had a voice and a message to deliver. He had taken on form for Aiden now; he was *real*. And he was dangerous.

"We need you to find him, Detective." Aiden squeezed Cassidy's hand reassuringly and felt her slowly unclench her fist. Cassidy threaded her fingers through Aiden's and squeezed her in return.

"We're doing our best, Ms. Darrow. I can assure you of that."

He had a few more details to discuss with Cassidy concerning her guards, but all Aiden could hear was the threatening voice of Bernett.

When I find you I am going to kill you.

Aiden willed his voice out of her head, but the chilling words kept repeating over and over. The threat was all too real.

Welcome to Cassidy's world, she thought. What price was being paid for all the glitz and glamour now?

Mischa, as always, was the life and soul of the party Cassidy was hosting. People's laughter at her scandalous comments drifted above the music playing. Cassidy searched the busy room for any sight of Aiden. She couldn't see her among the throng surrounding Mischa and she wasn't anywhere near the dancers either. Cassidy checked at the buffet table, still nothing, and the bar would be the last place for her to be hanging out.

Cassidy took a step into the crowd. For a moment, it seemed like the number of people in the room doubled. She squeezed past them, trying to get through. They acknowledged her but then went straight back to their conversations, effectively shutting her out. Cassidy was trying to reach Mischa. It was a losing battle with the press of the partygoers hemming her in. Mischa waved her forward, but every time Cassidy got nearer Mischa appeared to be farther away.

"Mischa, what's going on here?" Cassidy yelled over the voices that were growing in volume.

"Fabulous party, darling!" Mischa raised a glass in her direction then drank it down. Her empty glass refilled instantly, and Mischa held it up again for the exact same toast.

What the hell? Cassidy took a step back in surprise. Someone grabbed her hand and yanked her from the crowd. She was spun around and pulled against someone's chest.

"Dance with me!" Chris Garrick said. Oddly, he was wearing just half of his monster costume for Ragnor Rhodes. He began spinning her around to the music. The quickness of the steps made Cassidy giddy and she begged for him to stop. The whole room was spinning now. Cassidy wasn't even sure her feet were touching the ground. The music made the air throb and her ears pulse. Then, as suddenly as the dancing had started, it stopped.

Cassidy found herself in the dark. There was just a thin sliver of light coming through a gap in front of her. Cassidy reached out her hand and realized there were curtains hanging there. She pulled them open. She smiled as she recognized a familiar view from the window.

Home.

She turned around and was thrilled to find herself back in her apartment. She wandered around, familiarizing herself with her furniture, touching everything she had been forced to leave behind. She smiled as she checked inside the fridge and found a takeout box from Maria's restaurant. Happy to be back in her own home, Cassidy leaned against the breakfast bar and just drank in her cozy little apartment. Her TV, her stereo, her coffee table with all the mail…

The mail was carefully arranged, piled up all neat and orderly.

Cassidy froze. Her head whipped around toward the hallway.

"Aiden?" Cassidy's voice barely broke a whisper. She reached behind her to draw out the biggest knife from the block. She called again down the hallway. "Aiden?" Nothing but silence greeted her. She worked her way down the hallway to stop at her bedroom door. "Aiden?" Cassidy pushed the door open and took a tentative step inside. Red rose petals decorated the floor leading up to the bed.

There, on the white sheets, lay Aiden. Her eyes were open, her handsome face contorted in a silent scream. The white shirt she wore was stained with blood and her heart had been cut out. It wasn't missing. It lay resting on the pillow that Cassidy always slept on.

"You're mine."

Before Cassidy could even draw in breath to scream, a brutal hand covered her mouth. His other hand snatched the knife from her and then swiftly slit her throat.

❖

Aiden was startled from an uneasy slumber by the sound of her name being screamed. She bolted upright, her heart pounding in fear. She found Cassidy sitting straight up in bed, clutching at her throat.

"Cassidy?" Aiden kept her distance and her voice steady. She'd had to talk many a foster child down from a nightmare. "Cassidy, it's Aiden. I need you to wake up, honey." She moved a little closer to check Cassidy's eyes. Cassidy was staring blindly out into the room. Her breath was escaping in short bursts. Aiden needed to get her fully awake before she hyperventilated. She shifted slightly to lean against Cassidy to let her feel her presence. "Wake up, Cassidy."

"I'm awake." Cassidy's breathing evened out. "Thank God, I'm awake." She dropped her hands from her neck and seemed to try to wipe something off them. She turned to Aiden and grabbed her face in both her hands. "You're here."

"I'm right here beside you." Aiden didn't move as Cassidy ran her hands over her face. She rested her palm over Aiden's chest, right above her heart. It was then that Aiden caught sight of the tears slipping down Cassidy's cheeks. They glistened like silver caught in the moonlight that shone through the gap in the curtains.

Cassidy buried her face in Aiden's neck and clung to her. Aiden could feel her tears dampening her skin and her body trembling against her. "Bad dream?"

"Worse dream." Cassidy didn't let go even as Aiden helped lower them both back down to the bed so she could wrap Cassidy around her. "I thought I'd lost you."

Aiden's heart clenched at the distraught edge to Cassidy's voice. She stroked Cassidy's hair, soothing her, and keeping her close. If Cassidy wanted to tell her about her dream, she would when she was ready.

"I'm right here, sweetheart." She continued to stroke Cassidy's hair. "I guess it's a testament to the good soundproofing of these houses for the fact we haven't got Marks banging on the door downstairs, trying to get in. Of course, he could be dithering on the doorstep wondering whether your shouting out my name was because of something he shouldn't ever come knocking about." She felt Cassidy's huff of amusement against her skin. "Try and go back to sleep, Cassi. The morning will come soon enough."

"I'm frightened to close my eyes. Tell me something, anything, to take my mind off what I dreamed, please."

Aiden considered what to share. "I spent my whole childhood wanting to escape. Being adopted by Trudy and Frank gave me the love and stability I'd been desperate for. But it also made me a target of jealousy from some of the other foster kids that came into their care. It meant I was bullied at home and I was still bullied at school by other kids. I stood out too much." Aiden smiled wryly. "I was a geek way before it was considered cool. And on top of that, I was gay. I went through hell being different and I desperately wanted to get away, anywhere, so I could be left alone and be myself. My books and films gave me that escape. And it's got me thinking."

"It is way too early in the morning for you to be doing that," Cassidy said.

"What if all I went through when I was growing up was part of my hero's journey? In every fantasy tale, your leading character has to undergo a quest. They face trials and great monsters to battle against before they can reach their goal. What if all I went through in my childhood was my trial through fire to lead me to this exact point in time? I could have taken the easy way out many times. Suicide in teens was and still is not uncommon, and I'll admit there were moments when it all felt too much to cope with. But I didn't. I stayed the course no matter what was put in my way. It made me stronger. It made me fight back. It made me who I am today. I'm still a geek, still a little shy around people, but I own it."

"I may be considered biased, but I think you're wonderful exactly as you are."

"What if I went through all that to be strong enough to take my place by *your* side to help you as you go through your trial now?"

Cassidy lifted up to look at Aiden. She was speechless for a moment then kissed her softly. "I love how your mind works. I can't think of anyone else I'd want by my side."

"It won't always be like this. You'll get your life back and we'll be able to move on. The only thing that will stay the same is I'll be right beside you every step of the way."

"I love the sound of that." Cassidy clung to her a little more.

"So do I." Aiden kissed her forehead. "Just close your eyes now. I'll keep you safe tonight, I promise."

CHAPTER NINETEEN

Baseball. As an activity for Cassidy to be involved in and willing participate in, baseball would have been so far down on Aiden's list that it would have been non-existent. Aiden lay half sprawled on Cassidy's bed. She was watching Cassidy change into her new baseball uniform and enjoying Cassidy's serious face as she pulled on the unfamiliar clothes. Aiden couldn't help but smile as Cassidy concentrated on making sure her shirt was falling just so. Cassidy getting dressed in her sports gear was almost as entertaining as watching her slide into a dress and stockings. Both had their merits.

"Are you laughing at me?" Cassidy stood before the large mirror in her room and turned to every angle to check out her reflection.

"No. I'm merely marveling at how you can make even a sports uniform look so damn sexy." Aiden couldn't stifle the moan that escaped her as Cassidy smoothed her hands down over her tight fitting pants. "You need to stop with the preening right this second. You are tempting me to rip all that off you, and something tells me you want to make it to the game on time today."

Cassidy grinned at her. "Mischa would never let me live it down, or you for that matter, if I arrived late because we took a 'time out' before the match."

"Game, sweetheart, it's called a game over here. I had to listen to Frank drone on about it often enough for that fact to embed itself in my brain. Just how much do you know about baseball?"

"Mischa's been coaching me since it was decided that *The Alchemidens* would put together a team to play. From what I can gather, it's very much like the game of rounders I used to be forced to play in school. There's a bat, there's a ball, and you run around. I remember that much at least." She looked up from where she was tying the laces on her pair of spotless Nikes that color coordinated with her uniform. "I'm required to hit said ball and then, to quote baseball guru Mischa Ballantyne, run like the very hounds of hell are snapping at my heels."

Aiden shook her head, but she could hear Mischa saying that all too plainly. "Sometimes it's hard to separate Mischa from Miriva. Sometimes, I think she is more the priestess than her character."

"She'd better be on her best form today." Cassidy stood and gave Aiden a very showy twirl, revealing her name and team emblazoned on her back. "Because *The Alchemists* are up against *The Majestics*."

Aiden had been fascinated to hear how the gathering of various TV show casts in a baseball game had come about. It was all done to raise money for different charities. The venue was a local school that was letting them use their baseball diamond for the day. The stars brought in the spectators, the charities brought their causes before an audience, and the studios garnered a huge amount of publicity for their cast and show. The team that won would feature all over social media. It was a publicist's dream.

"And *The Majestics* are the cast from *Towers Majestic*, right?" Aiden had heard of the show. It was one she intended to catch up with via boxed set. It was another show in the same vein as *Game of Thrones*. Which meant it was shown an hour later than Cassidy's show because of the gratuitous nudity and the blood and gore and violence depicted in its medieval period.

"They're who were picked out of the hat to face us. I was hoping we'd get to play against the cast of *Agent Carter*," Cassidy said. "Hayley is such a darling. It would have been nice to hear a familiar accent." She gathered her hair into a ponytail and tied it up. Then she put her baseball cap on and threaded her hair out the back.

Aiden couldn't tear her eyes away from how gorgeous Cassidy looked. She was wearing very little makeup and looked so much younger. Aiden thought she looked adorable.

"Don't get any ideas, my darling. I see that look in your eye. I refuse to get all hot and sweaty before I even get a chance to pick up a bat."

Aiden lay back on the bed with a thump. "You're no fun. I know so many other games we could play together." She lifted her head to catch Cassidy smiling at her. "You wouldn't even have to change. That uniform is quite the turn-on."

Cassidy laughed. "Stop teasing me. You know I'd much rather be alone with you given the choice." She grabbed Aiden's hands and tugged her off the bed. Face to face, Cassidy laid a soft kiss on Aiden's smiling lips. She took a step back and pushed Aiden's glasses back up to the bridge of her nose. "You may act innocent, but I see the real you behind that mild mannered exterior, Aiden Darrow."

"And just who is the real me?" Aiden nuzzled her nose against Cassidy's.

"Someone who's a sucker for a girl in a costume."

Cassidy kissed Aiden long and hard. Aiden gladly surrendered to her. She loved the feel of Cassidy holding her tight like she'd never let her go.

"I'm a sucker where you're concerned," Aiden said when they finally stopped for air.

Cassidy snuggled in closer. "Please tell me you're going to wear the baseball shirt I got you for today. Or are you still trying to decide if you can get away with adding it to your *Alchemiden* collection?"

Aiden knew she'd been caught out. She felt the damning flush heat her cheeks. "I'm really torn. It's got the show's logo on it and your name on the back. It's a one off. It's invaluable to me."

"I'll make you a deal, darling Aiden." Cassidy pressed kisses along Aiden's jawline. "If you wear it today I promise I won't tear it off you when we come home to celebrate *The Alchemidens'* victory."

"I'll be proud to wear your name," Aiden began but was interrupted by the sound of Cassidy's phone going off. Aiden picked it up from the bed. She groaned at the screen. "It's your bodyguard."

"That's him telling us it's time to go, so get your shirt on and come support your woman. Especially as she is probably going to embarrass herself in public with her lack of sporting prowess." Cassidy sashayed from the room, leaving Aiden behind smiling at her playfully silly side.

Aiden changed into her shirt quickly. She was thrilled that they were printed up specifically for the family and friends of the cast.

I'd better not get ice cream down the front of this.

"Hey, Cassidy? Is Marks sitting down in the dugout with you?" She hurried down the stairs, finding Cassidy waiting for her armed with a gym bag.

"Unfortunately, yes," Cassidy grumbled. "He's going to try to look as inconspicuous as possible every time I take to the grass. I'd rather you were down there instead, being my cheerleader."

"They don't have cheerleaders in baseball, Cassidy."

"Do you think Marks would consider carrying pompoms to detract from the fact that no matter how casual he is attired he still looks like a bodyguard?"

"You can ask. I don't think he'll go for it though."

Aiden really wanted to talk Cassidy out of going, but she knew Cassidy was determined to do her bit for the charity her show was supporting. Aiden admired that she refused to let Bernett dictate how she lived her life, but it didn't stop her from being anxious. His threats hadn't made for cheery reading. Aiden was understandably worried for Cassidy's safety the second she stepped outside her front door.

"Stop with the frowny face, Aiden. We're going to have fun today. I'm going to show how much Karadine Kourt's agility is down to acting talent while Mischa is going to try to shamelessly court your attention right in front of me as usual." Cassidy's phone dinged again. "That's our cue. Let's play ball."

❖

The star-studded baseball game was a complete sellout. That came as no surprise to Aiden considering the publicity machine she'd seen going into play to publicize it. The bleachers were already filling up with people eager for the game to begin and more were streaming in, searching for their seats. There were refreshments on sale, and just about every kind of fast food available. The smell of hot dogs was making Aiden's stomach growl. Everything was geared toward the day being perfect. Aiden wasn't worried about the entertainment. She was more concerned about the chance of Bernett making his move there. That thought loomed like a big black cloud spoiling the day.

Aiden checked her ticket to make sure they were heading in the right direction toward what had been designated as family seating. She was trailing after Joe Ballantyne as he and Theo led the way. Aiden held little Holli in her arms, keeping her safe from the crowd of adults blocking the steps. Aiden hadn't much experience with toddlers. Trudy and Frank had very rarely fostered infants. They'd mainly taken in older children because they were the ones usually left behind. Holli, however, seemed perfectly content to be with Aiden. She was clutching the neck of Aiden's shirt in a sticky little hand. Aiden had resigned herself to the fact that any chance at keeping her new shirt in any kind of pristine condition was pretty much doomed from the moment Joe had placed Holli in her arms. Holli chuckled at her, and Aiden decided she didn't really mind.

"Are you going to watch your mommy play ball today?" Aiden hitched Holli up a little more in her arms. Holli nodded and rested her head on Aiden's shoulder, hiding her eyes from the bright sunlight. Joe handed a small baseball cap to Aiden who dutifully stuck it on Holli's head. "Better now?" Holli nodded again but left her head where it lay.

"She'll probably be fast asleep by the third inning." Joe dropped the bags he was carrying and settled Theo into his seat. Holli had her own seat reserved too, but Joe had warned Aiden she'd probably switch from his lap to hers like a baby yo-yo. For now, he took her from Aiden and sat her beside them.

Aiden looked down at Holli. She'd never get over the fact Mischa had named her daughter after the lead character from her books. "She's the image of Mischa," she said, taking note of the shape of Holli's little face and those wide, expressive eyes. "Especially with all her curly hair."

Joe smiled, no doubt used to hearing that a lot. "I know. How lucky can one man be? I've got the love of my life in Mischa and then she gives me this gorgeous mini-me of herself." He turned to ruffle Theo's hair. "And then there's this handsome little man who's my brightest boy. I am blessed and I know it." He sat in his seat and handed Holli a book to play with. "Holli is a little angel and I adore her. Even when it's three o'clock in the morning and she comes into the bedroom, scrambles up on the bed, tramples all over my unmentionables, then lays on my face because she misses me and just wanted to come say hi." He wore a resigned expression that only a truly besotted daddy could possess.

Aiden laughed at the image of family life he painted. Joe and Mischa were the most perfect, well-matched couple she knew. She caught the sly look Joe directed her way and braced herself. Neither of them had much of a filter on what came out of their mouths.

"Are you and Cass thinking about having children of your own now you're an item?"

Joe's question caught Aiden completely by surprise. She had no idea how to answer him at first. She'd never given children much thought. She'd always concentrated on her career first and foremost. But then Aiden had never expected to find someone like Cassidy to share her life with.

"I don't know. It's not something that we've discussed yet. We're still getting used to there being an 'us' at the moment." She shrugged. "To be honest, I don't know if I would even want kids. I had a very unsettled childhood until I was finally adopted. And then I was surrounded by a steady stream of kids coming in and out the house, some of whom really needed help. I just don't know if I have the mindset to be strong enough to raise a child when I struggled so much with being a child myself."

Joe made a grab for Holli who was slowly slipping from her chair in a bid to escape. He gave Aiden a wry look. "Well, while you are thinking over that life-changing decision, Mischa and I will be more than happy to loan you ours for practice."

"That's very kind of you. Just don't get any ideas about me loaning out my car to return the kindness."

"Damn it," Joe grumbled. "Can't blame a guy for trying."

After making sure Holli was back safely on her seat, Aiden turned her attention to the field. The teams hadn't stepped out yet, but the crowd was buzzing with anticipation. She and Joe sat in the lower half of the bleachers, directly behind home plate. They had an excellent view from that position. Aiden twisted around to look up and into the sea of faces surrounding her.

How are we supposed to know if Bernett is here among this many people? There are so many strangers. He could be any one of them. Aiden scanned the rows as best she could. She searched for the face she'd memorized from the few photographs the police had of him on record.

"She'll be fine," Joe said, obviously guessing what she was up to.

"I hope so, because he isn't going to leave her with any peace of mind if he can help it."

"She doesn't deserve this happening to her. Cassidy's a good woman, a gentle soul. I love her like a sister. Admittedly, a sister with a mighty weird accent, but a sister none the less."

"She's the most amazing woman I have ever met," Aiden said. "And believe me, her real accent is downright sexy on certain occasions." She grinned at Joe. She had no doubt that particular comment would come back to bite her in the butt, courtesy of Joe telling Mischa and Mischa teasing Cassidy with it. Aiden didn't care. She knew Cassidy was well aware of how much power she had over Aiden with a well-chosen word or two whispered seductively in her ear.

With the sun beating down, Aiden was thankful for the shade her baseball cap afforded her. However, the glare was making it difficult for her to see the top tiers of the bleachers. She had been able to spot a few of Detective Whitmeyer's officers dotted around on the different levels. She was impressed by how well they blended into the crowd. She only knew their faces after seeing them parked in her driveway when covering for Marks and the new girl. There was also something about how they were dressed for the part of being a fan but that their attention was anywhere but on the field.

"You can't police this whole ballpark, Aiden. You have to let the real police here do their job. You need to turn your eyes to the field. Wait until you see my Mischa in her baseball uniform." His grin spread. "How pretty does Mommy look today, Theo?"

"Very pretty, but she wanted to wear her heels and not her sneakers to play in," Theo said. "I told her she couldn't run as fast in her heels and she needs to run very fast to win."

Aiden couldn't help but smile at the thought of Mischa strutting out onto the field in her highest of heels. "Thank God I didn't have that trouble with Cassidy. She just had to find a pair of Nikes that were the exact same color as the uniform because she refused to have anything clash." She shook her head. "I'm not going to complain. She looks gorgeous."

"She knows absolutely nothing about the game she's going to play. Did she tell you that?"

Aiden nodded. "I'm sport-impaired too, Joe. I'll freely admit that most of what I know about baseball comes from my reading the Charlie Brown comics."

Joe choked on his laughter. "Oh my God, you two are perfect for each other. Be prepared to be suitably educated today." He had to raise his voice to be heard over the sudden roar from the bleachers as the players stepped out onto the field.

The teams looked very professional decked out in their baseball attire. The Alchemists were resplendent in a strikingly rich purple uniform with a neon blue trim. The Majestics were dressed in a bold golden yellow with a black trim. They waved to the crowd, and the volume of noise rose.

Aiden focused on Cassidy among the lineup. The crowd went wild as the announcer for the game called out the names of each player on The Alchemists. Cassidy's name got a rapturous reception.

Aiden could see her bright smile shining clear across the field. The Majestics were then introduced. They played to the audience by bowing or curtseying as befit their royal status.

Will Evanson, usually the quietest of *The Alchemidens* cast, had been elected to speak on behalf of the charities they were playing for. He gave a brief explanation of what the charities were in aid of then thanked everyone for buying the tickets and supporting the people who would benefit from the donations. The actors and actresses were all donating their time and money to the causes too. The hope was to raise a lot of money in one day and make the event a resounding success.

Aiden listened to his speech, but her eyes never strayed from Cassidy. She could tell Cassidy was nervous about playing. No matter how much time between filming Mischa had spent coaching her, Cassidy had confided to Aiden she was still no better than she had been playing sports at school. She also knew how frightened Cassidy was of being out of her comfort zone and exposed on the field with so many eyes watching her. The constant threat of Bernett making an appearance made every moment Cassidy spent away from the protection of Oaken Drive a living hell for her.

"There are some of the most recognized actors and actresses out on that field and yet you can't keep your eyes off her." Joe had leaned around Holli to speak in Aiden's ear so she could hear him over the sound of Will on the mic. "It's a beautiful thing to see. I foresee it's just a matter of time before you're exchanging rings and buying a station wagon."

Aiden laughed at his persistence. "I am not trading my car in for a mom mobile, Joe. Be there rings being placed on fingers or otherwise. You're just going to have to get your own *Thelma and Louise* mobile to drive."

His eyes sparkled with mischief. "Care to make a little wager on our women to add a little spice to the game?"

"Mischa's obviously played before so it would hardly be a fair bet that Cassidy could beat whatever score Mischa racks up." She joined in the applause as Will's speech came to an end. "And I'm not betting my car for anything so don't even go there."

"How about a simple bet that, if I win, you and Cass babysit the kids so that I can take Mischa out for a meal that doesn't include chicken nuggets on the menu?"

"And what do I get if I win?" Aiden knew she was being set up. She didn't mind though because she knew it wasn't being done with any malicious intent. Joe was irrepressible like Mischa was, and he liked to play just as much.

"My brother owns a restaurant. One that's very private, very exclusive, *very* expensive. I'll wager a romantic dinner for two, all expenses paid. You two deserve a moment away from all that is happening with this stalker business."

Aiden was duly impressed by the prize. "And the wager itself?"

"I bet Cass misses her first ball and that Mischa hits hers."

"I haven't seen Cassidy play so I'm not entirely—"

"It's just a bet. There's a fifty percent chance she'll hit it, and a fifty percent chance she won't. As long as the bat touches the ball you win."

Aiden considered his offer while watching the teams take their positions. The Alchemists were up to bat first. She looked over at Theo who was cheering his mom on and down at Holli who was foraging for snacks. "You're on." They shook on it.

Chris Garrick was up first. He was goofing off at home plate, playing to the crowd. He made a production of positioning his bat just so before he finally settled down. The crack of the ball hitting his bat startled Aiden. It sounded like a shot being fired. She fought to calm her racing heart.

Mischa was up next. She was a lot more professional than Chris had been and didn't waste time clowning around. Aiden hated herself for hoping she'd miss the ball. She wanted their team to win, but there was a bet at stake over this play. A romantic dinner might be just the distraction Cassidy needed to take a little time out for herself. She groaned as Mischa hit the ball way past the outfielder who had to take off running to retrieve it. Joe was cheering loudly and dancing in his seat.

"That's my girl!" he gloated as Mischa managed to reach third base before the ball was back in play.

Cassidy strode out next. The crowd went wild and she gave them a wave. She looked into the crowd and unerringly found Aiden. Cassidy flashed her the biggest smile. Aiden felt the ballpark disappear. In that moment all that existed for her was that smile warming her heart.

"Come on, baby, you can do this," Aiden whispered, willing Cassidy to do well. Not for the bet but for her own self-esteem.

Cassidy stood at home plate and raised her bat a little awkwardly. Aiden stopped breathing as the pitcher wound up to throw. He deliberately threw a fastball. Aiden heard Cassidy's squeal in response. She brought the bat up in front of her to ward off the blow. Instinctively, Cassidy held it in a defensive pose. Just like Karadine Kourt brandished her katana so many times before in a fight. The ball banged off the bat, almost knocking Cassidy back with the force. The catcher behind her toppled over, startled by her lurch backward. Cassidy looked down as the ball rolled aside. The pitcher just stared at her. For a split second everyone was frozen until Mischa screamed, "RUN!" and Cassidy took off like a shot. She ran toward first base at full speed with Aiden cheering her on. The pitcher had to scramble down from the mound to scoop up the ball. The elderly catcher was still stuck on his back like an overturned turtle, hampered by all his protective gear. Cassidy touched base and hugged the woman who stood there laughing with her. Everyone was cheering as Cassidy's purely unintentional bunt sent Mischa home.

Aiden turned to a flabbergasted Joe. She pointed out to the field where Cassidy was still dancing at first base. She was clearly jubilant while the pitcher walked back to the mound, shaking his head at her.

"That's *my* girl. And I believe you owe us one fancy assed meal."

❖

The victory party thrown by The Majestics looked set to go on for quite some time. Cassidy didn't want to stay much longer.

She was tired, and she was getting antsy being among so many unfamiliar faces. It wasn't just the teams who were packed into the school's main hall where hospitality had been laid on for them. The friends and family of the players were included. Cassidy had dutifully been signing autographs outside for the fans until she and the rest of the actors had been ushered inside. There she'd signed more when requested and posed for pictures with fellow actors. She's even managed to get someone to take a photo of her with Aiden. It was only when she got her phone back that she found they had been photo bombed by Mischa.

The Alchemists might not have won, but they'd given the other team a hard fought game. Aiden had told her not to feel bad. Two of the cast from *Towers Majestic* were known for their sporting prowess, so going up against them and only losing by three runs was an amazing feat in Aiden's estimation.

Cassidy looked across the room to where Aiden stood discussing something with one of the actresses from the other show. She must have been staring over there a little too long because Mischa leaned in to whisper in her ear.

"Audrey Green was in *Thornmere*. Aiden spent a lot of her time on that set because the director was a bit of an ass. He kept adding scenes that he needed her to write dialogue for."

"And you know this how?"

"Because I'm a fan girl of *your* girl. I may have mentioned she's my favorite author." Mischa laughed when Cassidy said it right along with her. "Well, she is and I am unashamed of my adoration. And now that I know her, it just makes me love her even more."

"You're unashamed, period." Cassidy took a small sip from her glass. "And believe me, once you get to know her? Falling in love with her is all you can do." Cassidy couldn't help but frown. "She's worried about Bernett getting near me. This is exactly why I didn't want a relationship, Mischa, because I can't do anything about her being involved in this crazy stalker business."

"Tell me if you could honestly let her go now."

Cassidy shook her head, feeling wretched at the mere thought. It had been hard enough being away from Aiden the few days

Cassidy had stupidly blown up over something as trivial as a poster. She didn't want to go through that ever again.

"She's yours now and you need her beside you. I've seen you two together. It's like both of you have found the most important piece you were missing all your lives. If the situation was reversed and she was the one with a stalker? You'd be stuck by her side like glue."

"Fortunately for me, the only crazy stalker my Aiden has is *you*."

Mischa's answering laugh was loud as always. From across the room, Aiden's head turned at the sound. She grinned at Cassidy who just rolled her eyes at Mischa being…Mischa. Audrey followed Aiden's line of sight and waved at Cassidy. Cassidy waved back.

"Doesn't she play a queen who seems to spend most of her time flat on her back in varying degrees of nudity instead of running her realm?" Cassidy kept her voice low for only Mischa to hear.

"I think it's safe to say that there's a good portion of the people in this room that aren't on our team that we have seen naked on the screen at one time or another."

Cassidy's gaze fell back on Aiden.

"Oooh, your mind just went to a very naughty place, Ms. Hayes. It's written all over that smug look you're now wearing. Are you corrupting my favorite author?"

"Every chance I get." Cassidy held up her glass and Mischa clinked hers against it.

"She won the bet, you know." Mischa's attention was drawn to the other side of the room where Theo and Holli were playing with some of the other children. Joe was chatting amiably with Will who had his daughter with him.

"Joe couldn't resist, could he? Please tell me she didn't bet her car in order to protect my honor?"

"No, no amount of his usually persuasive wheedling got her to put that particular dream machine on the table. You, my dear, are going to Jacob's for an all expenses paid meal, courtesy of loser Joe. It's an open reservation until you can find a space in your schedule to book it. Just let me know when and I'll give Jacob a head's up."

"Wow, that's some prize. Did he forget he's accused me multiple times now of trying to eat him out of house and home when I come to visit? Jacob's restaurant is a veritable playground for someone like me whose appetite is healthy…and even more so when I'm not paying the bill."

"I think he was testing Aiden's loyalty like the dumb male he is."

"What was the bet?"

"That you wouldn't hit the ball on your first pitch."

"I told you he shouldn't have been allowed to watch us practice. I heard him sniggering. He could have been a spy for the other team and sold me out to them."

"Actually, he was much more devious than that. He was trying to con your girlfriend into babysitting the rug rats."

Cassidy stared at her. "*That* was his side of the bet? Us babysitting?"

"What can I say? He's devious but remarkably simple with it."

Cassidy shook her head. "Next time just ask me and I'll do it with pleasure so it gives you two some adult time alone. Anything to keep you a happy woman. Because grumpy Mischa on set is a total diva."

"As I should be, darling. I'm top billing, that affords me a little diva action. Add to that the fact I should be the recipient of the MVP for today." She gloated unashamedly, hamming it up as always to Cassidy's amusement.

"You were marvelous out there, Mischa, just like you told me over and over you would be. You kept us from being severely embarrassed by the sneaky ringers on the opposing team."

"You held your own, Cass, distracting them so that we could steal bases. We just need to practice more so that you hit the ball a little farther than somewhere in the vicinity of first base where they can tag you out. Now, what's the golden rule of baseball I taught you?"

Cassidy held her hand up like a child answering in class, playing along. "Oh, I know! I know! If you build it, they will come!"

"That's the second rule. What was the thing I warned you about in baseball and thankfully you didn't do?"

Cassidy grinned and rattled off dutifully. "There's no crying in baseball."

"We'll make a player out of you yet, my child." She slung a protective arm across Cassidy's shoulders and asked more seriously, "Did you have fun though?"

Cassidy nodded. "I did. For the first time in a long while, I was able to get a taste of normalcy again. Just being out in the sun, hanging with my friends, being able to introduce Aiden as my girlfriend to you all. For once, I felt protected enough to put that damn man aside for a moment." She could see Audrey was now showing Aiden something on her phone.

"Oh God, Audrey's flashing the baby photos. Doesn't she realize getting her tits out is more entertaining than endless snapshots of a gummy baby dressed like a cat?"

Cassidy had to cover her mouth to stop her laughter from escaping and attracting any more attention their way. "Mischa! Your tits are out and proud every week on our show."

"Mine are decoratively framed by my gorgeous priestess gowns. There is no nip-slip happening with these babies." She cupped her generous bosom and all but held them in Cassidy's face.

"I swear, I leave you alone for a few minutes and you've got someone flaunting their wares at you." Aiden appeared at Cassidy's side. She gave Mischa a censorious look. "Put those things down. They could be armed and dangerous."

Cassidy laughed as Mischa did as she was told.

"Seen enough babies for the day?" Mischa kissed Aiden's cheek and left a lipstick stain there. Cassidy huffed and wiped it off, much to Mischa's amusement, judging by her smirk.

"Seen enough of everything, I think," Aiden said. "I've come to see if you're ready to go home."

Cassidy nodded. "I like the sound of that." She kissed Mischa good-bye and then stood by while Mischa hugged Aiden until she had to be told to let go. Cassidy sighed. "Mischa, it's a good job you're my friend." She pulled a laughing Aiden free from Mischa's teasing grip.

Cassidy and Aiden wound their way through the room saying their good-byes and then stepped out into the school's hallway.

"God, I hated school so much just being here makes my stomach ache." Aiden looked around in disgust. "I was bullied from the beginning to the end. I can't tell you how many times I wished one of my heroes would come to my rescue and take me away from it all. I'd have had him beat all the bullies down for me first and then we could have escaped. That was my wish every year as the new school term started."

Cassidy tightened her grasp on Aiden's hand in sympathy.

"School was okay for me. I knew what I wanted to be from a very early age and set my sights on achieving that. If I did poorly in any classes it was usually because I couldn't exactly see where trigonometry was going to assist me in my acting career." She bumped Aiden's shoulder. "I wish I'd known you back then."

"I spent my school years hiding, Cassidy. I was torn between wanting to be left alone and wanting so desperately to belong."

"You belong with me now. There's no more hiding for you." Cassidy tried to ignore Agent Marks as he fell into step behind them. "So, you never said you know Audrey Green."

"I worked with her a few years ago. Even introduced her to a guy I knew who was totally smitten with her. They married within a year. I was invited to the wedding as the official matchmaker."

"And she has a baby now according to Mischa."

Aiden nodded. "She showed me pictures. Lots of pictures. What is it with people testing my limits with children today?"

"Care to expand on that, Ms. Darrow?"

"When we're safe and sound in the car, yes." Aiden yawned. "I am so tired and I wasn't the one running around those bases like you were." She hugged Cassidy to her. "I was proud of you today. You did fantastic for a total novice."

"Bet-winning fantastic so I'm led to believe too."

Aiden grinned. "You're always a winner in my eyes." She checked around and then kissed Cassidy. "I'll tell you all about that too once we're settled in the car. I'll help you take your Nikes off as well. I can tell by your face your feet are killing you."

"And that is why I'd never bet against you, my darling. You're always right."

Aiden toyed with the brim on Cassidy's cap. She was looking at her with such affection Cassidy couldn't help but want to crawl into her arms to be held. She always felt safe with Aiden. "You ready to run the gauntlet?"

There were a few people hanging around outside the school gates. Aiden released Cassidy and stepped back so that Marks could step forward to do his job. Cassidy quickly signed a few autographs before the waiting car took them out of the reach of the hovering paparazzi. It took them just a few blocks away to where Marks had his car parked. That way no one at the school got to see the vehicle that was driving Cassidy home. She was grateful for that. She just wanted to go back to Aiden's house and enjoy the rest of the weekend with her without giving a thought for the outside world.

❖

With Saturday spent on activities Cassidy wasn't used to and that her body took exception at, it was unanimously decided Sunday was to be a lazy day spent in bed. Cassidy and Aiden barely moved from under the covers where they indulged in activities Cassidy found much more satisfying. The simplicity of snuggling under the sheet with her hand on Aiden's chest was, in Cassidy's mind, sheer unadulterated bliss. She never wanted to move.

The call from Detective Whitmeyer in the very early hours of Monday morning was an unwelcome intrusion into the little bubble of joy Cassidy was hoping to stay inside longer. Marks was standing behind him when Cassidy opened the door to let them both in. Judging by the dour looks on their faces, this wasn't a courtesy call.

"What is so important that you have to see me before I am due on set? You know I keep ridiculous hours. It's barely five a.m."

Whitmeyer just headed toward the living room where Aiden sat with her coffee. He gestured for Cassidy to sit down. He opened a large manila envelope that held something sealed in an evidence bag. He set it on the table before them.

The photo had obviously been taken with a zoom lens. But it wasn't a scene from the baseball game. This was a candid shot of Cassidy with Aiden *inside* the school. Aiden was looking down at her, caught in a moment with her fingers resting on Cassidy's baseball cap. Cassidy knew exactly when and where that had been taken. Judging by the look on Aiden's face, she remembered that exact moment too. But that wasn't all. Someone had gone to great lengths to score hundreds of lines with a very sharp object on the print. They had totally scratched Aiden's head from the photo without ripping clear through. Cassidy's face, however, had been left untouched. Except for her eyes. Those had been brutally marked with crosses, erasing them from the picture.

"So he knows about Aiden now," Cassidy said, grabbing Aiden's hand and holding on to it tightly.

"From the angle it's taken, I'm guessing it didn't really show a great deal of her. I'm showing you this to warn you. He's apparently changed his appearance because he slipped right by us. We need to be doubly on your guard. Everywhere you go, he's there. We're just not seeing him."

But he can clearly see me. Cassidy's protective bubble burst as an all too familiar despair returned.

Chapter Twenty

T he convention center was packed solid. All manner of people wandered the halls, from the regular fans to the diehard cos players. Aiden was thankful her panel had been one of the early ones. The announcement that *Guildanan's Quest* was going to be made had gone over incredibly well and had left Aiden very aware of her great responsibility to its story. The fans of the book wanted the film, and they wanted the book *on* film.

Aiden had done her best to assure them that she was going to do her best to honor that because she wanted nothing less herself. She'd been heartened to see Cassidy and Mischa in the room while she'd done her Q&A session. Mischa had asked a question that had left Cassidy staring at her in astonishment. Aiden loved it when Mischa got her geek on and lost her famous persona. She had become just another fan desperate to know if Aiden was going to bring her own books to live action. Aiden had, as professionally as possible, told her that if she heard anything she'd make sure Mischa was one of the first to know. Mischa's answering squeal had made the audience laugh.

Aiden was stretching her legs before *The Alchemidens* panel was scheduled to start. She'd spent most of her time keeping Cassidy from getting over anxious before she went on stage. The cast was being briefed on what they could and couldn't reveal while on stage. Aiden didn't want to know any spoilers herself so had taken the chance for a breather. She hadn't told Cassidy she was also going to check if she could see Bernett anywhere in the vicinity. She had his photo on her phone, but his face was burned in her memory. It didn't help he was so ordinary looking. Medium height, brown hair, not really handsome but not ugly either. He was nondescript. He was also elusive if he was there. So far, all Aiden had seen was a fascinating array of costumes. She was in awe of the obvious time and dedication some people put into their portrayal of their favorite character. She felt rather underdressed in just a pair of black jeans and a T-shirt with Karadine Kourt emblazoned on the front. Cassidy had rolled her eyes dramatically when she'd seen what Aiden was wearing.

"You're going to get grief from Mischa for not wearing her, you know that, right?"

Aiden had just kissed her and ran her hand over the design. "It's my favorite shirt with my favorite character on it. Of course, when I brought it, I never dreamed I'd be looking forward to Kourt's alter ego taking it off me later tonight!"

Aiden smiled to herself as she dodged past a couple of women dressed as Root and Shaw from *Person of Interest*. Aiden was a fan of the show and loved the pairing. She gave them a thumbs-up as they passed her and the shorter of the two gave her a swift "I'm watching you" gesture with her fingers. Laughing, Aiden brushed past a group of men in their Halo Spartan costumes and got in line for a soda.

She found a stretch of wall to lean against and just watched the colorful parade of people go by.

"I swear, Princess, if you don't stop messing with your boobs I'm going to rip them off and beat you to death with them!"

Aiden looked up at the duo who had stopped right in front of her. They made for an unusual couple. Both were incredibly tall for a start. The one with *his* hands cupping his false breasts was dressed all in white as *Star Wars: A New Hope's* Princess Leia. His costume was perfect, the dress fit him impeccably, and he wore an ear bun wig that finished the look. The fact he also had a very long beard braided into a plait only detracted a little from his otherwise perfect Leia Organa.

Aiden looked closer at the person he was fussing beside. She looked more masculine than her cohort did and was dressed handsomely as Han Solo. Aiden recognized the clothing from *The Empire Strikes Back*. The dark blue jacket covered a white paneled shirt. She wore brown trousers with yellow blocks running down the seam. Aiden was envious of her boots that were exact copies of Han's footwear. A replica blaster and holster hung rakishly from her hip. However, cradled against her chest was something Han Solo never had to contend with. In a carrier snug against her front was a baby. A little girl who was fast asleep, with her thumb firmly in her mouth. She was dressed adorably as an Ewok. She had a fuzzy romper on with little padded feet, and the ensemble was completed by a Wicket the Ewok headdress with little teddy bear ears poking through. A felt spear stuck out beside her in the carrier. She was the sweetest thing Aiden had ever seen.

"Trent!" Leia stopped messing with his falsies and tugged his dress back in place. "I just want to look pretty."

Trent snorted at him. "Sure, Elton, because all that facial hair is exactly what Han found himself waking up to after they defeated the Empire."

"Hey! I love Carrie Fisher just as much as you, but I lost a bet. I wasn't shaving my hard grown facial fuzz just because your girlfriend proved to be a card shark."

Trent grinned. "Just be thankful she picked that outfit as your forfeit. You would have been strutting your skinny stuff in the metal bikini if you'd lost to me." They stared at each other then burst into laughter. Elton eventually sobered first.

"Dude, I can't believe Juliet and Monica begged off coming here with us. This is the highlight of our Californian trip."

"Elton, they're grown women. They'd rather hit the shops for clothes and last-minute Christmas gifts than try to find treasures here."

"They're still coming tomorrow, right? I've paid to get my picture taken with the *Sleepy Hollow* cast."

"They'll be here. Monica said she'll be on standby if you faint seeing Ichabod Crane in the flesh for the first time."

"He's my hero," Elton said in his defense. "And I'm not wearing the dress tomorrow to meet him either."

Aiden watched as Trent switched her attention to the child shifting against her. She dipped her head slightly to press a kiss on the baby's forehead, soothing her.

"I can't believe you said we'd take Harley and I'm the one left carrying this." Elton held up an R2-D2 shaped backpack doubling as a diaper bag. "But I'm glad you did. She's a chick magnet."

"She's no bother and you know it. Besides, Juliet wouldn't be able to shop with Harley Q snuggled to her like she is on me."

"You know people are going to think that's our kid, right?"

"No, they're more likely to think Leia cheated on me with Chewbacca and this is the result."

"She's awfully adorable in that suit," Elton said, shifting to look at the sleeping child with a tender gaze.

"Harley's beautiful, just like her mommy. I'll need to feed her soon, then change her, and then we can go back to the gaming section. I really want that *Assassin's Creed* Sword of Altair we saw." She brushed at the crop of wispy blond curls that were escaping from under Harley's hood. "Elton, take our picture so we can send it to Jule. That way she can see I haven't traded her in yet for the *Bayonetta* Scarborough Fair gun I told Juliet I wanted for my Christmas present from her."

Aiden couldn't help herself. She stepped forward as Elton was getting his phone. "How about I take one of all of you so the princess here is included?"

"Thanks. I really appreciate that," Trent said with a smile. She and Elton crowded in around Harley who snuffled then squeaked as she let out a tiny yawn. Then she snuggled in closer to her mother's chest and began snoring softly. Trent caught sight of Aiden's T-shirt. "Hey, that's a great show you're wearing. Karadine's my favorite too. You can't go wrong with a gorgeous woman who has kick ass skills. I love her character."

Aiden fiddled with the phone to frame them just right. "I love her too," she said with a wry smile and took the picture. She handed the phone back to Trent and Elton who agreed it was an excellent shot.

"Thanks again," Trent said, sticking her hand out to shake Aiden's. "I need to go eat now before Harley here wakes up and wants whatever it is Mama has in her hands. Her other mommy says she's too young to eat pizza, but apparently Harley isn't aware of that fact yet."

"No, no pizza," Elton said, shaking his head vehemently. "I can't get sauce on my dress."

Trent just stared at him then deadpanned, "You are such a princess."

Aiden hid her laughter behind her hand as she waved them off, watching as they cleared a path all the way down to the food hall. She checked her watch. It was nearly time for the afternoon sessions to begin. *The Alchemidens* panel was the first of the three sessions on stage that afternoon. Aiden wanted to make sure she got a good seat. She knew Cassidy was nervous and more than apprehensive about being on stage if Bernett was indeed in the building. So far they hadn't had any sign that he was anywhere near.

Aiden was all too aware Cassidy was living on her nerves. She hadn't slept well all week due to the stress of what Bernett was doing to try to get her attention. She'd been nervous and edgy every time she set foot out of the safety of her home or Aiden's. She jumped at every single noise and was getting to the point where she only felt safe on set or with Aiden. The convention was only going to drain her strength more as she had to perform as if she didn't have a stalker making her life an utter misery. Luckily, Mischa loved getting "down and dirty" with the fans so Aiden knew Cassidy was hoping to take a backseat while Mischa entertained the masses.

Personally, Aiden was just excited to be seeing her favorite show's cast in action on the stage. And the woman she loved doing what she did best, being a star. And woe betide anyone who meant her any harm while Aiden was by her side.

❖

Cassidy's distraction meant her grip on her coffee cup was making it burn a patch on her palm. She didn't realize until the pain finally filtered through to her brain, and she hissed, nearly dropping her drink. She kept watch on the door of the hospitality lounge the cast was all situated in as she waited for Aiden to return. Her nerves had increased ten-fold the second Aiden had left her presence. Her whole body felt like a taut wire, every sound a discordant pluck of the string, making her vibrate at every change in the air. She was conscious of the fact she was shaking. It was a barely discernible trembling, but Mischa had finally spotted it and had shifted closer to hold Cassidy's free hand in both her own.

"If he is here, Cass, they'll find him." She tried to soothe Cassidy's obvious distress. "Whitmeyer sent you two cops to add a police presence just in case and there are more wandering the halls. That asshole won't get past them. They're outside the door now."

"Have you seen how many people here have their faces painted or hidden behind helmets or masks? He could be standing right in front of me and I wouldn't recognize him like that."

Mischa patted her hand. "Did you give Aiden the shirt she's wearing?"

Cassidy wasn't surprised in the least that *that* was what Mischa chose to use to distract her. "No, I didn't. Apparently, it's part of her collection."

Mischa hummed in response. "She does know there's one of me as Meriva, doesn't she? You need to buy it for her."

Cassidy let out an amused breath, albeit a shaky one. "I'll get right on that, shall I? Somewhere in between me appearing on stage and being stalked."

"Please do. After all, I did let you sleep over at our house. Seems only fair you should have your lover wear a shirt with my gorgeous visage on because of that."

Cassidy leaned in and laid her head on Mischa's shoulder. "Don't ever change."

"I have no intention of doing so," Mischa said. "Aiden will be back soon. It's nearly time for us to go on stage. I think she really stepped out to go check in with the security here to make sure no bastard low-life scum has managed to slip by."

"She's so worried."

"She's worried about *you*, not herself. That woman loves you."

Cassidy smiled. "I know. She told me." Her head was rudely nudged from off Mischa's shoulder.

"And you're only *now* telling me this?"

"I'm still getting used to it myself." Cassidy loved the feeling she had just knowing how much Aiden truly cared for her.

"So when did this happen?"

"Sometime after she accused me of sleeping with her to try to get a role in *Guildanan's Quest*," she admitted dryly.

Mischa's eyes widened and she let out a loud, boisterous peal of laughter. "Well, good for her for turning the tables on you." She bumped Cassidy with her shoulder. "Do you think I stand a chance of getting an audition if I slept with Aiden too?"

Aiden answered from behind before Cassidy could say a word.

"Well, you could try, but the studio still gets last pick of the talent. Besides, I think my girlfriend and perhaps your husband might have something to say about you trying to get me on a casting couch."

Cassidy slipped from her seat and wrapped her arms around Aiden's waist. "Where have you been? I've been frantic."

"I was just checking around," Aiden said noncommittally. "I met a fan of yours and her gorgeous little daughter who was dressed as an Ewok. Cutest thing I've ever seen."

"Did the security guys have any information?" Cassidy was almost too scared to ask.

"They said they haven't had anything reported back so far, but they're stretched thin just making sure only those with valid tickets get in. So we remain vigilant. And you've got Whitmeyer's team keeping watch as well as Marks beside you." Aiden kissed her, and Cassidy melted into her arms. "I'll be in the audience the whole time. I'll keep an eye on the crowd for you."

"I love you." Cassidy leaned in for another kiss. She jumped in Aiden's arms as another pair of lips buzzed her cheek.

"I love you both too," Mischa said, kissing Aiden's cheek as well. "But unless you two are going to reenact a scene from one of Aiden's racier chapters for me to watch, then I have to remind you that we are due on stage in ten minutes. So you need to wrap this up. Go pee, grab a water, and then get ready to be asked about those fucking gargoyles." Mischa patted Aiden's cheek condescendingly. "You're not the only geek who expects the gargoyles to be real, my dear."

Chapter Twenty-one

Adam stood partially out of sight behind a standee opposite the room that was going to host one of the afternoon's panels. He knew this particular one would have the cast and crew of *The Alchemidens* inside. He couldn't stop grinning in his excitement. She was so close he could almost smell her perfume. He scratched at the prickly facial hair he'd been growing to alter his appearance. Earlier that morning, he'd walked right through the ticket booth without anyone even looking at him twice. He ran a hand over his cheek. Who knew, maybe C.J. would find him even more attractive with this more rugged look. Silver-framed glasses sat high on his nose, and the hideous false teeth he wore to complete his disguise totally reshaped his mouth. Both of those would have to go once they'd served their purpose of getting him near her. He'd hardly recognized himself in the mirror as he'd dressed to melt into the masses.

He watched as two men positioned themselves at the main doors of the room, purposely making the attendees file in in an orderly fashion so they could be scrutinized. Adam's eyes narrowed as he checked them out. For undercover police hoping to blend in, they stood out in their woefully plain clothes amid all the costume finery and obligatory geeky T-shirts. The jackets they wore did little to conceal their weapons underneath. Adam shook his head at their ineptness at blending themselves better among the crowd. He'd have been more impressed if they had dressed as Stormtroopers. He considered his options with this new information at hand. Convention security wasn't armed. These two men obviously were, and he was sure he'd spotted a few plainclothes police walking around. He shifted a little, reached into his messenger bag where there was a small box hidden inside and something else less innocuous. The cold metal of the gun was cool against his hand. He caressed the weapon and let a small smile escape.

He was confident he had enough bullets for everyone.

❖

The panel was energetic, humorous, and highly informative. Aiden's eyes were torn between scanning the audience for trouble and watching the cast win over their audience. Her gaze lingered on Cassidy who was being highly entertaining if a little restrained, to Aiden's eyes at least. She was currently telling tales mostly at the expense of Chris Garrick who had been telling some stories of his own, much to his castmates' embarrassment. He took over again to regale the room about a Will Evanson and Mischa wardrobe malfunction. Aiden's attention was drawn away by the sound of a muffled commotion somewhere outside. The doors to the room had been closed once the session had begun. Aiden rose from her seat to go investigate. She joined Officer Willis, one of the undercover police Whitmeyer had furnished them with, when he stepped outside to talk to his partner, Officer MacCauley.

"Any problems here, gentlemen?" Aiden asked.

"Just a latecomer who wouldn't take that the room is full for an answer and tried to push his way in," MacCauley said. "He should have gotten here sooner."

"Did he look like our guy?"

MacCauley hesitated. "The Bernett we're after is a clean-shaven man. This one had a week's growth of stubble, glasses, and the worst overbite I have ever seen. Squirrelly kind of guy though, clutching a box to his chest like it was something precious. When I asked about it, he said it was for his favorite actress, and he'd only give it to her in person. I told him he'd have to wait. I'll keep an eye out for him though if he tries to swing by again."

"It was probably doughnuts," Willis said with a shrug. "Fans are a weird bunch."

Aiden looked up and down the hall trying to see if this man had stayed close by. "What was he wearing?"

"A black tee, oddly enough like what you have on. But that's no different from many of the folk here. He was nothing out of the ordinary. I'm sorry, but all these geeks look the same to me." MacCauley shrugged. "He just didn't look like the photo we've been given."

"Bernett has worked in the industry for years. He's got to have picked up enough knowhow to change his appearance." Aiden searched the area again.

Willis glared at his partner. "Why the fuck didn't you grab the son of a bitch when you had the chance?"

"Because he didn't match the description we have. If I'd have laid a finger on him and he's *not* the guy we're after? We'd have had some nerd screaming police brutality bringing forth hundreds of wannabe heroes armed with lightsabers to save his scruffy ass!"

Aiden knew it wasn't MacCauley's fault, but she was still resentful. If this *was* Bernett then Cassidy was in danger. She stepped aside and took her phone out. *I'm not taking any chances with Cassidy's life.* She waited for her call to be answered. "Detective Whitmeyer? You need to get more people to the convention hall. I'm getting a really bad feeling about this."

"Has there been any sighting of him yet?" Whitmeyer asked.

"Not one that's conclusive. But your men have just stopped a man trying to sneak in to where the cast are on stage."

"Is there any chance we can pull her out of there?"

"No, she's on stage at the moment and then it's the photographs and the signings. You know she can't leave until she's fulfilled that obligation."

"I'm coming down there myself. And next week? I'm going to sit down with the heads of her company. I'll explain some things to them about keeping their investments safe if they want to keep raking in the dollars they make off them. They should be keeping her out of the spotlight now, not forcing her further under it."

"Yes, well, tell that to the studio heads who made her come here in the first place. I'm going back in and I'm not leaving her side." Aiden took another look around her. "If he wants to get to Cassidy, he's going to have to come through me first."

❖

From her seat on the stage, Cassidy watched Aiden return to her seat. The look on her face made Cassidy's heart plummet.

Oh God, he's here.

She lost track of what was being asked by the audience members and just stared at Aiden. Aiden wasn't looking toward the stage; instead her focus was on watching the back doors. Cassidy did the same though she didn't know what she was expecting.

Mischa leaned back unobtrusively. "What's wrong?" she whispered out of the range of the microphones in front of them.

"I think Bernett's here. Something has happened because Aiden is on alert."

"You need to get out of here."

"I can't leave until I finish the signings. I was told I had to promote the show by The Powers That Be."

"When was the last time they were stalked? They're all old farts with beer bellies hanging over their belts." Mischa caught Cassidy's hand under the table. "You'll be okay. I'll rally the troops and we'll keep you safe."

"None of you are putting yourselves in danger for me," Cassidy said.

"I'll kill him myself if he gets near you."

Cassidy stared at her. "I know you would, but I'd rather you didn't have to. Maybe he just wants to talk." She smiled wanly. Mischa's hard look shut her up.

"You don't believe that any more than I do."

Shaking her head, Cassidy had to agree. She had the horrible feeling Bernett wanted more from her than she'd ever be willing to give.

Chapter Twenty-two

Camped out in the hospitality room, Cassidy waited for Aiden to get backstage to her. Mischa had all but carried her bodily off the stage when their session was done and had been glued to her side ever since. The rest of her colleagues had been told that they feared something was up and now they all sat huddled around Cassidy like a human shield.

Aiden stepped into the room, and Cassidy ran to her.

"He's here, isn't he?" she asked, knowing the answer already from the wary look in Aiden's eyes.

"There's a man who was acting suspiciously that tried to push past MacCauley while you guys were doing your panel. Apparently, he has a box he's carrying around and he'll only give it to his favorite actress. He was wearing your T-shirt. MacCauley wouldn't let him in the room because it was full so no one knows where he currently is. So it's either another attentive fan or it's him. I've phoned Whitmeyer. He wants you out of here right away."

"You know I'd leave right this minute if I could, but I'm contracted to do this." Cassidy said with a disgruntled huff. "And I can't let the fans down either. You know, the *real* fans who don't feel the need to hound me to death."

Aiden's face fell at her choice of words. "Don't even joke about that, Cassidy," she pleaded. "He's obviously unstable. His phone calls and postings have attested to that. We know we can't expect him to be polite toward you if he gets the chance to engage with you." Aiden eyed Marks, who was keeping guard. "You need to stay by her side no matter what. If he's here, he's going to come for her. He's been building up to this. The fact Cassidy is here in the open is the opportunity he's been waiting for."

Cassidy fussed with the collar of Aiden's T-shirt. "I need to put my game face on. I have photos to look amazing in." She felt her bravado slip, as did her smile. "I am so terrified," she whispered.

"It's going to be okay. We're watching for him and Whitmeyer is on his way. You're going to be surrounded by so many people soon you won't be able to move."

Cassidy swallowed back a sob. "I'm so afraid," she said in Aiden's ear.

"I know, baby, but I'm right here with you. You're being so brave. You're amazing."

"I don't feel very brave." Cassidy tucked her head into Aiden's shoulder, holding on to her for dear life. She felt like she was shaking apart, and only in Aiden's arms did she feel she wouldn't shatter to a million pieces.

"You're my hero," Aidan said softly. "And I love you so much. I won't let him get near you. I promise you that, Cassidy."

Tightening her grip, Cassidy clung to her until one of the convention runners came in to tell them it was time for their photo ops. Cassidy didn't want to leave Aiden's arms. She was grateful Aiden stuck close to her as she was escorted from the room, but Aiden had to step aside from the cameras. Cassidy felt her loss keenly. She dug deep inside her to pull out all her acting talent to pretend to be light and bubbly and happy to be hugging total strangers who all felt they knew her intimately. She smiled for the camera, but between every shot she feared for who was next in line.

❖

Now that he knew the police would recognize him in this disguise, Adam felt more certain of the next stage of his plan working. *The Alchemidens* were due to do a meet and greet and sign autographs for their eagerly awaiting fans. The guy Adam had hassled earlier was firmly situated outside the doors again, his eyes scanning the lines and the people milling back and forth along the halls.

Adam needed a diversionary tactic. His opportunity wasn't long in coming.

"I just need twenty dollars more and I can get that Final Fantasy artwork. It's signed and everything." A young boy walked by Adam and was whining to the man at his side. "Come on, Dad. Loan me the money and I can get it."

"I've already loaned you all your next month's allowance." His father stopped to look for something.

"But I want it!"

His long-suffering father smiled at him. "Want away, son. You're not getting any more money from me today." He pointed across the room. "I'm hitting the bathroom. Stay here, do not dare to move a muscle, and quit your whining."

Adam watched the boy scowl at his father's back. He couldn't have been more than eleven years old. Old enough to know how to manipulate but still young enough to be manipulated. A perfect candidate for what Adam needed.

"I can help you get your artwork," he said. The boy whipped around to face him. "I'm here with my friend and he's being a pain in my ass. See that guy over there? The big one with the gray T-shirt and the bald head?"

"I see him."

"I will give you thirty dollars"—Adam smiled inwardly as the boy's eyes lit up at the extra cash—"if you go over to him and say you've just seen me going through that door over there that leads to where all the stars are hanging out." Adam grinned at him. "That way, I can do what I want to do without him dragging me out of here to do what he wants first."

"Aren't you a little old to be playing kids' games?" The boy's eyes narrowed at him shrewdly.

"I brought my DVDs to have C.J. Hayes sign them for me, but he doesn't want me to waste time standing in line. My friend there thinks he's LL Cool J from *NCIS: Los Angeles* and is trying to stop me from joining the line. I think he deserves to be sent on a wild goose chase so I get to see my favorite lady up close and personal." He winked and the boy laughed. "Are you up for it?"

"Thirty dollars? For real?"

"Just pretend you think he's a cop and tell him you've just seen a suspicious guy with a box going into the hospitality lounges. Give him my description as best you can."

"You're kind of goofy looking," the boy said with a grin.

"Then when you describe me he'll have no problem knowing exactly who you mean and he'll go running off in the wrong direction."

"I can do that." The boy pushed his way through the crowd to deliver his message.

Adam watched as the cop left his post and took off up the hall to search out the rooms backstage. With a satisfied smirk, Adam drew out the necessary bills from his wallet.

"I did it!" The boy sprinted back to Adam's side and happily accepted the cash.

"Just tell your dad you found it on the floor somewhere."

"Thank you!" The boy stuffed the money into his pocket. "Are you going to sneak in line now?"

Adam reached up to remove his glasses. "I'm going to hide in the best place I know." He pushed his way through the crowd, taking out the false teeth, and slipped into line at *The Alchemidens* signing. He tugged on a baseball cap this time to complete his new look. "Right in plain sight."

CHAPTER TWENTY-THREE

The long line of tables set up for the autograph signing was troubling Aiden. The table was a barrier between Cassidy and the fans, but it also meant no one could stand before Cassidy to stop anyone from getting overly familiar. Aiden could tell Cassidy was feeling the strain. She had Marks standing right at her shoulder, but the rest of the cast was spaced out so that they had plenty of room to welcome their fans.

Aiden was hovering as close to the table as she could without getting in anyone's way. Thankfully, they had put Cassidy on the end so Aiden wasn't stuck blocking the lines and getting in the fans' way. She ended up excusing the fact she was right by Cassidy by offering to take photos with the fans' cameras or phones for anyone who came to have Cassidy sign something. Once they realized they got a close-up memento, no one grumbled about Aiden being right at their side. Some even recognized Aiden and chatted with her while Cassidy personalized her picture for them.

Aiden kept looking for Whitmeyer, but she couldn't see him anywhere. Before the photographs had even been half done, she'd received a text from him that he was trying to get extra manpower approved and he'd be there as fast as bureaucracy allowed. Aiden was beside herself. The security staff at the convention hall were being great, but Aiden wanted the knowledge that Cassidy was being protected by more people armed and prepared to use their weapon.

The room was filled with people on an endless procession of moving down the tables to get their autographs. Aiden took another look around. It was then she saw him. Her breath caught in her throat.

Bernett.

He was standing at the back of the room, a baseball cap tipped low on his forehead, but from Aiden's position, she could see under it. He was motionless, his eyes fixed directly ahead of him. Aiden knew who he was staring at. Cassidy was directly in his line of sight. Aiden caught the attention of Marks as he did his own recon of the room. Before the next fan could step in front of Cassidy, Aiden leaned in.

"He's here." She glimpsed the look of sheer terror that fell on Cassidy's face before she schooled her expression and just nodded stiffly. She continued signing the photos as if nothing had changed.

Aiden kept him in her sights. *Do I call out to him and startle him into running? Can I reach him before he does anything? And if I get to him, what do I do? Grab him? Hit him? Sit on him until the police take him away?*

Aiden didn't get a chance to do anything. Bernett made his move. He drew his gun and shot Willis at point-blank range. The noise brought the room to a standstill with no one quite sure what had happened until Willis fell to the floor. Bernett pushed his way through the startled lines of people, roughly knocking them out of his way. As he did, Marks gathered Cassidy up from her chair to get her out of there. Bernett held up his gun, and the room went insane.

"Don't you touch her!" he shouted over the screams of the terrified people who either scattered out the room or stood petrified at what they were witnessing. "She's mine. Always has been, always will be. I told you, C.J., you're mine, but you keep having the police keep me away from you. That's not how it's meant to be. I tried to be nice to you, but you keep pushing me away!" His voice got louder until he screamed the last and pointed the gun directly at her. "You're mine, and if I can't have you no one will."

Cassidy screamed at him. "Why can't you just leave me alone? I don't even know who the hell you are!"

Aiden saw something flicker in Bernett's eyes. As he brought the gun up level with Cassidy's chest, Aiden didn't even think. She just reacted. She dove between him and Cassidy, effectively blocking his shot.

There was a deafening crack as Bernett pulled the trigger. The first bullet slammed into Aiden's shoulder, ripping through her flesh like a furnace and rocking her back on her feet. The pain that followed on its heels was sudden and excruciating. She dimly heard Cassidy scream, but the second bullet exploded into Aiden's chest and slammed her backward across the table with its force.

"NO!" Bernett roared, obviously furious Aiden had gotten in his way and taken the bullets he'd meant for Cassidy. His face purple with rage, he flung a box onto the table. It skidded across the photos to stop before Cassidy's seat. He lifted the gun again, and Aiden braced herself for the hit. Instead, there was a thud as Bernett was tackled to the floor by a very large man in Punisher garb. The bullet went high, missing its intended target. The gun was knocked from his hand as the man's fists rained down on Bernett's head, clubbing him nearly senseless. The baseball cap went flying. Bernett was finally unmasked. Through eyes blinded by pain, Aiden watched Bernett struggle desperately to get free. He skittered across the floor on all fours, grabbed up his gun, and ran out of the room, brandishing his weapon so that no one dared go near him. Aiden could hear the commotion that followed his escape. MacCauley was somewhere outside yelling at Bernett to freeze and drop the weapon. Screams filled the halls and echoed around the whole building.

Marks leapt over the table to give chase. Cassidy scrambled around the table, scattering her blood-spattered photos everywhere. She grabbed at Aiden as she slipped to the floor. Aiden sat down hard as her legs finally gave out. Aiden's hand clutched at her chest; she slowly held it out to look at it. Blood dripped from her fingers and pooled out around her on the ground. Cassidy held Aiden tightly to her chest. She begged for someone to call for an ambulance, to find a doctor, anything to help Aiden who was bleeding to death in her arms.

Aiden wondered how many were filming this on their phones, capturing her last moments and Cassidy's agonized wails. Her eyesight dimming, she could feel herself fading in and out of consciousness. She swallowed against the harsh metallic taste of blood in her mouth. She could feel it escape on every breath she took, the blood trickling out between her lips and down her chin. Cassidy just cried harder as she held her close.

"Research into being shot never said how much it fucking hurts," Aiden said with some difficulty. "It stings like a bitch." She tried to smile, but she was too tired and her face didn't seem to want to cooperate anymore.

Cassidy pressed Aiden's face to her chest, hugging her. "Don't you dare leave me, don't you dare. I've just found you and I'm not letting you go." In the distance, there was the sound of another shot going off somewhere in the building. "Oh my God, what has he done?"

Within seconds, Marks came running back into the room. "It's all over." He knelt beside Aiden. "We need to get pressure applied to these wounds. She's bleeding out."

Aiden winced as Marks pulled off his jacket and shoved it into her chest. She moaned out loud and her head fell back. She could see Cassidy's face up close. "You're finally safe. I told you I wouldn't let him touch you." She slipped lower on the floor. There was a strange buzzing sound in her head, and she could hardly keep her eyes open. And she was cold, so cold. She shivered with what little energy she had remaining.

"Aiden! No! Don't close your eyes. You look at me. You saved me, you crazy idiot. I didn't need Superman, or Steve Rogers, or even Karadine Kourt. *You* were the hero today, do you hear me?" Cassidy's hold tightened as Aiden started to grow limp. "All this time when you wished for a hero to swoop in and save you? You never truly needed one because you were a hero yourself all along. It's always been you. You're *my* hero, Aiden. Mine. *You're mine.*"

Mischa knelt beside them and pressed her hands against Aiden's shoulder. Aiden groaned as the pain intensified and she coughed up more blood. Cassidy just peppered kisses on her forehead, a warm touch on Aiden's rapidly chilling skin.

"Don't you leave me. You have work to do here, Aiden. Heroes live to fight another day, so fight! Fight, damn you, because I love you."

Aiden managed to open her eyes a fraction to see just how beautiful Cassidy was. "You were my every dream come true. I got my happy ending with you. You're safe now, Cassi, and I love…"

The last thing Aiden remembered was Cassidy screaming out her name and the feel of scalding tears mingling with the blood drying on her face. She slipped mercifully into unconsciousness, thankful to be escaping the pain but wanting desperately not to leave Cassidy behind.

Her last thoughts were of Cassidy and the feel of her lips as the blackness dragged her away.

CHAPTER TWENTY-FOUR

Adam's desperate bid to escape had left him running down the endless hallways careening off people who were too stupid to get out of his way. He could hear the sound of the cop running behind him, but Adam wasn't freezing no matter how many times he kept shouting for him to do so. He also knew that the guy wouldn't take the risk of shooting him because there were too many innocents around him who could get hurt. For a moment, Adam considered taking one hostage, using him or her as a shield as he bargained his way out of there. Instead he ran into the main hall and found himself surrounded by more men armed with guns. They were all pointed at him.

Tweedledum and Tweedledee had obviously called for backup.

He skidded to a halt in the center of the main hall, surrounded by tables crammed with memorabilia. The police tightened their circle around him. He had no escape now.

"Put down your weapon and get down on your knees."

Adam ignored the voice. He looked around at where he had come to rest. Before him was a stand for *The Alchemidens*, and C.J. Hayes's face was looking down on him from multiple items. He'd been so close to making her his. Killing her would have been the ultimate profession of his love for her. He'd have owned her life and she would have been his forever. Adam stared at a poster of Karadine Kourt and smiled.

"Bernett, I said put down your weapon and get down on your knees now."

Adam didn't even turn around to see who was issuing the orders. His eyes never wavered from C.J's face as she looked out at him from the poster. He slowly got down on his knees before her, a supplicant before his goddess.

"Now put down the gun."

Adam smiled up at the poster. He'd touched her life. She would always be his because of that. Just like he was indelibly hers. Always and forever, they'd be burned into each other's memory.

Never taking his eyes from the image of C.J, he shoved the gun firmly into the roof of his mouth. All for the sake of love, he thought, then pulled the trigger.

❖

The race to the nearest hospital from the convention center was a nightmare journey for Cassidy. She hadn't been allowed in the ambulance as the medics worked on keeping Aiden alive. Instead she'd been driven by Chris who'd crammed as many people as he could into his Subaru and floored the gas pedal all the way to the hospital. Once there, they were informed Aiden had lost a great deal of blood and had been taken directly into surgery. The agonizing time spent waiting to hear if Aiden was going to survive was something Cassidy never wanted to experience again.

The police had followed them and exhaustingly taken their statements. Now they were keeping watch over the actors while keeping the press at bay. The news of the shootings had hit the airwaves, and news crews were already lined up outside the hospital to try to get the exclusive.

Cassidy was surrounded by her castmates, all of whom were questioning the nurses as to whether they could donate blood in case it could be used to help Aiden. Cassidy looked down at herself; Aiden's blood was smeared all over her skin and clothing. So much blood, she thought, aghast to find her shirtsleeve was still damp with it. She vaguely heard Mischa calling Joe to get her mother to babysit and then get to the hospital as fast as he could and bring some clean clothes with him.

Am I going into shock? I really don't have time to. Cassidy felt the air in the room start to disappear. It was only Mischa's arm around her shoulder that brought Cassidy back into the room with a gasp. She stared at her. "There's so much blood on me. How can she survive when I'm covered in so much of her blood?"

Mischa hugged Cassidy closer. "The doctors will replace it for her. We just need to get you cleaned up so that when you see her next you look a little less like Carrie."

Cassidy didn't even bite at Mischa's tasteless comment. She couldn't stop looking at all the blood that had seeped into her clothes and was staining through to her flesh. "Oh my God, Mischa. What am I going to do if she dies?"

Mischa gathered her close and held onto her tightly. "She won't leave you, Cass. She fought too damn hard to keep you safe."

Joe arrived not long after, and Cassidy let herself be led into the ladies' bathroom. She stood by to be cleaned up as best as Mischa could manage with just paper towels and a cheap bar of soap. Mischa's sweatshirt hung off Cassidy's smaller frame, but at least it was clean. Cassidy threw her ruined shirt into the trash. She didn't want to ever wear it again.

Detective Whitmeyer finally arrived while Aiden was in her third hour of surgery. Mischa had to literally drag Cassidy off of him. Cassidy slammed her palms into his chest and screamed at him. "That should have been me, you bastard! How did he get close enough to me *this* time?"

It took her a while to calm down enough to finally listen to what Whitmeyer had come to say. He filled them all in on what had gone down in the main hall after Bernett had tried to flee. Then he informed them about Officer Willis who had been tended to by fans who had selflessly stayed in the room trying to keep him alive, despite the danger they put themselves in with Bernett still being there. Willis had them to thank for the fact he would leave the hospital with a story to tell and a scar to brag about. Cassidy felt awful. She'd forgotten all about the officer going down once she'd come face-to-face with Bernett and Aiden had been shot. She was thankful the officer was okay. She just prayed for the same outcome for Aiden.

Whitmeyer had brought something with him from the scene. In an evidence bag was a small box, the one Bernett had tossed at Cassidy after he'd tried to shoot her. Whitmeyer handed it over to her. Cassidy opened it to find a framed photograph. It had been taken on the last day of filming of that first film Cassidy had been cast in. She easily picked herself out of the lineup. She was sitting on the beach smiling as the cast and crew all huddled in for the group shot. Bernett was standing right behind her. For a moment, Cassidy's mind flew back in time and she vaguely remembered turning around after the picture was taken and saying, "We had fun, didn't we?" Cassidy handed Whitmeyer the frame back and wiped her hands off on her trousers, desperate to rid herself of the past that had come back to haunt her in the most devastating of ways.

The cast and writers stayed with Cassidy until the doctors came and delivered the news that Aiden was finally out of danger. Cassidy fell into Mischa's waiting arms and sobbed her heart out. Mischa didn't let go of her either until they could go see Aiden for themselves.

Cassidy had never heard anything sweeter than the sound of the heart machine Aiden was hooked up to. Its steady rhythm called out to Cassidy's own.

❖

The internal injuries Aiden had suffered kept her in the hospital much longer than she cared for. Cassidy spent all her free time at the hospital, going straight from the set to sit at Aiden's bedside until she had to go home for the night. She had taken to reading to Aiden and noticed that Aiden calmed down the minute Cassidy walked in and got her book out. She had learned, during the long evenings where they just talked and shared details about each other, that bedtime stories had never been a part of Aiden's childhood. So the attentiveness she gave Cassidy as she read was more than genuine, and Cassidy made it doubly special employing her talent for mimicry. Cassidy had sworn to herself she would read to Aiden for as long as she needed to. Both of them needed the escape it gave them, taking them far away from the hospital room's antiseptic smell and its confining four walls.

Epilogue

The steady cadence of Cassidy's voice rose and fell as she read aloud from the last Harry Potter book she held in her hands. While she read, she *almost* forgot everything that had happened in the last few weeks. The tale of Harry and his friends wove its magic around her and she lost herself in the story. Coming to the end of the chapter, she paused and reached for her glass of wine.

"I think I like how you do Professor McGonagall best. It's like cuddling up next to Maggie Smith."

Cassidy looked down at her side where Aiden lay propped up beside her on the bed. "And cuddling is as far as you will get with Dame Maggie until you get the all-clear from your doctor." She smiled at Aiden's clearly disgruntled face.

Now that Aiden was finally home. Cassidy was so grateful to have her healthy and healing and *home*. Aiden still sported the sling that kept her left arm supported to ease her shoulder. The bandages that covered Aiden's chest wound were currently hidden from sight by a T-shirt bearing Mischa's face and ample cleavage. Cassidy hadn't forgotten Mischa bringing it into the hospital and presenting it to Aiden with her usual flair.

"Your last *Alchemidens* T-shirt got ruined so I got you a replacement."

"That's not the same shirt Aiden had," Cassidy said, enjoying the smile Aiden had playing on her lips at Mischa's blatant self-promotion.

"Of course not, darling, But let's face it, I am the prettier one *and* the star of the show, don't forget."

Cassidy had snorted with laughter at Mischa's playfully pompous act and they'd continued to tease each other unmercifully to brighten Aiden's day.

She'd all but moved in with Aiden once she'd been released from the hospital. Cassidy wasn't prepared to waste any more time apart from her except for work commitments. Under Aiden's watchful tutelage, she'd learned how to chop vegetables and stir a pot. She could also now make a mean Bolognese even if she did say so herself. They made quite the team in the kitchen and had settled into a very comfortable routine for two people more used to being alone.

They were helping each other to heal by dealing with the trauma and moving on with their lives together. For Cassidy, life without her stalker was like stepping out of the shadows and feeling sunshine on her face for the first time. Aiden's nightmares were less frequent once she was able to get back to her writing. She'd explained to Cassidy that the strength of those imaginary worlds would always be what got her through tough times. They had seen her through her childhood; they would do the same now. That and Cassidy's love and support.

Cassidy put aside her book and shifted so she could see Aiden better. "I got a call from my agent today. The producers of Ellen want us on her show once you're a little better."

Aiden's eyebrow rose in surprise. "You mean you, right?"

"No, it's a package deal." Dramatically, she put her hand to her forehead like a damsel in distress. "Next on the show we have C.J. Hayes, the actress ruthlessly stalked by a madman. And famed lesbian romance writer Aiden Darrow, the woman who loves her so much she saved her by putting herself into harm's way."

Aiden huffed. "Aren't we old news by now? Hasn't some reality bimbo done something scandalous instead?"

"Nope. They want us. I think it's a great opportunity. It gets my show some recognition and your next book will be out by then so you can plug it unashamedly. Also, if they happen to mention you're writing *Guildanan's Quest* while still convalescing, the studio heads will love the free publicity. It's all about putting yourself out there, my darling. That's how you play the game in Hollywood."

"Seems a little weird using what happened to showcase our new endeavors."

"I'd like to do it though. I'd like to sit in the company of Ellen, another lesbian, and boast to her how much I love you and how brave you were facing Bernett down to save me. Even if I do still despair at your selfless crazy act of throwing yourself in front of me like a human shield." Cassidy shivered at the memory of watching Aiden being shot before her, protecting her from Bernett's true intent. "I know you don't see it, but you really are a hero, my love."

"I'll consider it," Aiden said with a sigh. "For you and for no other reason."

Cassidy leaned down and kissed her tenderly on the nose. "We're in the public eye because of our careers. What happened has spun that spotlight down on us a little more brightly at the moment." She ran her hand gently across Aiden's chest. "Just so you know, I'm considering losing this shirt of yours in the wash because having Mischa between us when we kiss is seriously disturbing!" Deliberately, she looked away from the distracting T-shirt print. "While we're talking business...any more news on when you'll start writing for *The Alchemidens*? I know Nicole visited you earlier today while I was on set."

Aiden grinned. "I wondered how long it would take before you brought that up."

Cassidy tried to look suitably affronted. "What? I'm merely inquiring after her health."

Laughing, Aiden gave her an all too knowing look. "Sure you are. For your information, there's a nice little story arc taking place this season that they'll tie up in the season finale. But they'll leave a thread open just enough to introduce a new character for Karadine to interact with."

"And that's where you and your amazing writing skills come in. Blazing the trail for lady lovers everywhere." Cassidy smiled wide. "I am so excited!" She planted a loud kiss on Aiden's lips then pulled back to give Aiden a mischievous look. "Soooo," she drawled the word out nonchalantly. Aiden got a suspicious look on her face. "Love of my life, the one woman who knows me so very well and the show I star in…"

"I know what you want," Aiden said. "I knew Nicole coming here would get your mind working overtime. You want to know if I'll get a say in who they pick for Karadine's lover."

Cassidy nodded. "Well, it's not like you'll want just anyone kissing your girlfriend in scenes you yourself have written."

Aiden pulled her as close as she could without hurting herself. "How about this promise, sweetheart? If I can, and I'm not promising anything, if I *can* get Emma Watson to play the role of your love interest, I'll do my very best to make it happen."

Cassidy couldn't hold back a squeal. "You are the best writer/ girlfriend ever!" She peppered Aiden's face with a series of silly kisses that left Aiden in wreathes of smiles and laughing at her. "Now I have another question."

"I'm not going anywhere so ask away."

"Now that you've gotten your happy ever after with me"— Cassidy shamelessly fluttered her eyelashes at Aiden—"will Hollister ever get the chance to go back to her proper time and be with her wife, Emily?" She watched intently as Aiden considered this for a long, torturous, moment.

"Maybe. One day, perhaps. When she reaches the end of her journeys and can finally rest."

"I've read all your books now, and you know how much I love them, but I have to know something. Is it my imagination that Emily is described physically and facially to look remarkably like me?" The description in the book had given Cassidy pause when she recognized someone curiously like herself being described on the page.

"You've always been my ideal, Cassidy. Let's just say I gave Hollister the woman of my own dreams."

Cassidy leaned down to kiss Aiden with all the love she felt in her heart. "I love you so much and that brilliant imagination you have." She cupped Aiden's face and smiled into her eyes, so thankful to have her where she belonged. "Write us a fantastic future together, my darling."

"With you as my leading lady"—Aiden leaned forward and stole a kiss—"the happy ever after will write itself."

The End.

About the Author

Lesley Davis lives in the West Midlands of England. She is a die-hard science fiction/fantasy fan in all its forms and an extremely passionate gamer. When her Nintendo 3DS is out of her grasp, Lesley is to be found on her laptop writing.

Her book *Dark Wings Descending* was a finalist in the Lambda Literary Awards for Best Lesbian Romance 2013

Visit her online at www.lesleydavisauthor.co.uk

Books Available from Bold Strokes Books

Dyre: By Moon's Light by Rachel E. Bailey. A young werewolf, Des, guards the aging leader of all the Packs: the Dyre. Stable employment—nice work, if you can get it...at least until silver bullets start to fly. (978-1-62639-6-623)

Fragile Wings by Rebecca S. Buck. In Roaring Twenties London, can Evelyn Hopkins find love with Jos Singleton or will the scars of the Great War crush her dreams? (978-1-62639-5-466)

Live and Love Again by Jan Gayle. Jessica Whitney could be Sarah Jarret's second chance at love, but their differences and Sarah's grief continue to come between their budding relationship. (978-1-62639-5-176)

Starstruck by Lesley Davis. Actress Cassidy Hayes and writer Aiden Darrow find out the hard way not all life-threatening drama is confined to the TV screen or the pages of a manuscript. (978-1-62639-5-237)

Stealing Sunshine by Tina Michele. Under the Central Florida sun, two women struggle between fear and love as a dangerous plot of deception and revenge threatens to steal priceless art and lives. (978-1-62639-4-452)

The Fifth Gospel by Michelle Grubb. Hiding a Vatican secret is dangerous—sharing the secret suicidal—can Felicity survive a perilous book tour, and will her PR specialist, Anna, be there when it's all over? (978-1-62639-4-476)

Cold to the Touch by Cari Hunter. A drug addict's murder is the start of a dangerous investigation for Detective Sanne Jensen and Dr. Meg Fielding, as they try to stop a killer with no conscience. (978-1-62639-526-8)

Forsaken by Laydin Michaels. The hunt for a killer teaches one woman that she must overcome her fear in order to love, and another that success is meaningless without happiness. (978-1-62639-481-0)

Infiltration by Jackie D. When a CIA breach is imminent, a Marine instructor must stop the attack while protecting her heart from being disarmed by a recruit. (978-1-62639-521-3)

Midnight at the Orpheus by Alyssa Linn Palmer. Two women desperate to make their way in the world, a man hell-bent on revenge, and a cop risking his career: all in a day's work in Capone's Chicago. (978-1-62639-607-4)

Spirit of the Dance by Mardi Alexander. Major Sorla Reardon's return to her family farm to heal threatens Riley Johnson's safe life when small-town secrets are revealed, and love may not conquer all. (978-1-62639-583-1)

Sweet Hearts by Melissa Brayden, Rachel Spangler, and Karis Walsh. Do you ever wonder *Whatever happened to...*? Find out when you reconnect with your favorite characters from Melissa Brayden's *Heart Block*, Rachel Spangler's *LoveLife*, and Karis Walsh's *Worth the Risk*. (978-1-62639-475-9)

Totally Worth It by Maggie Cummings. Who knew there's an all-lesbian condo community in the NYC suburbs? Join twentysomething BFFs Meg and Lexi at Bay West as they navigate friendships, love, and everything in between. (978-1-62639-512-1)

Illicit Artifacts by Stevie Mikayne. Her foster mother's death cracked open a secret world Jil never wanted to see…and now she has to pick up the stolen pieces. (978-1-62639-472-8)

Pathfinder by Gun Brooke. Heading for their new homeworld, Exodus's chief engineer Adina Vantressa and nurse Briar Lindemay carry game-changing secrets that may well cause them to lose everything when disaster strikes. (978-1-62639-444-5)

Prescription for Love by Radclyffe. Dr. Flannery Rivers finds herself attracted to the new ER chief, city girl Abigail Remy, and the incendiary mix of city and country, fire and ice, tradition and change is combustible. (978-1-62639-570-1)

Ready or Not by Melissa Brayden. Uptight Mallory Spencer finds relinquishing control to bartender Hope Sanders too tall an order in fast-paced New York City. (978-1-62639-443-8)

Summer Passion by MJ Williamz. Women loving women is forbidden in 1946 Hollywood, yet Jean and Maggie strive to keep their love alive and away from prying eyes. (978-1-62639-540-4)

The Princess and the Prix by Nell Stark. "Ugly duckling" Princess Alix of Monaco was resigned to loneliness until she met racecar driver Thalia d'Angelis. (978-1-62639-474-2)

Winter's Harbor by Aurora Rey. Lia Brooks isn't looking for love in Provincetown, but when she discovers chocolate croissants and pastry chef Alex McKinnon, her winter retreat quickly starts heating up. (978-1-62639-498-8)

The Time Before Now by Missouri Vaun. Vivian flees a disastrous affair, embarking on an epic, transformative journey to escape her past, until destiny introduces her to Ida, who helps her rediscover trust, love, and hope. (978-1-62639-446-9)

Twisted Whispers by Sheri Lewis Wohl. Betrayal, lies, and secrets—whispers of a friend lost to darkness. Can a reluctant psychic set things right or will an evil soul destroy those she loves? (978-1-62639-439-1)

The Courage to Try by C.A. Popovich. Finding love is worth getting past the fear of trying. (978-1-62639-528-2)

Break Point by Yolanda Wallace. In a world readying for war, can love find a way? (978-1-62639-568-8)

Countdown by Julie Cannon. Can two strong-willed, powerful women overcome their differences to save the lives of seven others and begin a life they never imagined together? (978-1-62639-471-1)

Keep Hold by Michelle Grubb. Claire knew some things should be left alone and some rules should never be broken, but the most forbidden, well, they are the most tempting. (978-1-62639-502-2)

Deadly Medicine by Jaime Maddox. Dr. Ward Thrasher's life is in turmoil. Her partner Jess left her, and her job puts her in the path of a murderous physician who has Jess in his sights. (978-1-62639-424-7)

New Beginnings by KC Richardson. Can the connection and attraction between Jordan Roberts and Kirsten Murphy be enough for Jordan to trust Kirsten with her heart? (978-1-62639-450-6)

Officer Down by Erin Dutton. Can two women who've made careers out of being there for others in crisis find the strength to need each other? (978-1-62639-423-0)

Reasonable Doubt by Carsen Taite. Just when Sarah and Ellery think they've left dangerous careers behind, a new case sets them—and their hearts—on a collision course. (978-1-62639-442-1)

Tarnished Gold by Ann Aptaker. Cantor Gold must outsmart the Law, outrun New York's dockside gangsters, outplay a shady art dealer, his lover, and a beautiful curator, and stay out of a killer's gun sights. (978-1-62639-426-1)

White Horse in Winter by Franci McMahon. Love between two women collides with the inner poison of a closeted horse trainer in the green hills of Vermont. (978-1-62639-429-2)

Autumn Spring by Shelley Thrasher. Can Bree and Linda, two women in the autumn of their lives, put their hearts first and find the love they've never dared seize? (978-1-62639-365-3)

The Renegade by Amy Dunne. Post-apocalyptic survivors Alex and Evelyn secretly find love while held captive by a deranged cult, but when their relationship is discovered, they must fight for their freedom—or die trying. (978-1-62639-427-8)

Thrall by Barbara Ann Wright. Four women in a warrior society must work together to lift an insidious curse while caught between their own desires, the will of their peoples, and an ancient evil. (978-1-62639-437-7)

The Chameleon's Tale by Andrea Bramhall. Two old friends must work through a web of lies and deceit to find themselves again, but in the search they discover far more than they ever went looking for. (978-1-62639-363-9)

Side Effects by VK Powell. Detective Jordan Bishop and Dr. Neela Sahjani must decide if it's easier to trust someone with your heart or your life as they face threatening protestors, corrupt politicians, and their increasing attraction. (978-1-62639-364-6)

Warm November by Kathleen Knowles. What do you do if the one woman you want is the only one you can't have? (978-1-62639-366-0)

In Every Cloud by Tina Michele. When Bree finally leaves her shattered life behind, is she strong enough to salvage the remaining pieces of her heart and find the place where it truly fits? (978-1-62639-413-1)